C000272012

APPORTION BLAME

ALSO BY LESLEY SEFTON

Addict Child

APPORTION BLAME

Lesley Sefton

Copyright © 2019 Lesley Sefton

All rights reserved. This book or any portion thereof may not
be reproduced or used in any manner whatsoever without
the express written permission of the publisher except for the
use of brief quotations in an article or book review.

This book is a work of fiction. Names, characters, places, and
incidents either are products of the author's imagination or
are used fictitiously. Any resemblance to actual persons,
living or dead, events, or locales is entirely coincidental.

First Printing, 2019

Published by Lesley Sefton
High Peak, Derbyshire

www.lesleysefton.com

CHAPTER 1

Who Did This to You?

THE LIGHTS WERE BRIGHT; the room was immaculate with simple surfaces suitable for hosing. A sensitive newcomer could find the aroma in the room overpowering, but to a professional, usually the only living person in the room, the smell was familiar and hardly noticed at all. Sergeant Wright stood in the viewer's section of the mortuary. He nodded to the mortician, then prepared to take notes.

Amy-Lou's body was cocooned in a white body bag. She rested on a stainless-steel slab with holes in for drainage. The mortician stood over her small body. He wore scrubs and clogs; an ID badge clipped to his trouser pocket. Music played in the background, not quite loud enough to camouflage the sound from the opening teeth of the zipped bag. After the sheath was whipped away, he read the name tag: Amy Louise Walker. This mortician liked to connect to the person he would slice open. 'Hello, Amy Louise. Who did this to you, little Sweet Pea?' He smiled at her before lifting a scalpel off the tray, the stainless steel caught the light from above and sparked a light of its own. He placed the tip of the scalpel onto his subject's chest. The razor-sharp instrument eased into the soft flesh and glided through. He slid the incision from the left collarbone and deviated to the right collarbone to mirror the slice. He pulled the scalpel from the body to re-enter the open wound at the chest, then skated the instrument to the bellybutton. The letter Y had been carved into Amy-Lou's body. *A Y for a why,* he always said. The redundant scalpel was put into the hazardous-waste bin. The mortician peeled off his gloves and went to scrub his hands. He turned the music off to comply with the preference of the pathologist.

CHAPTER 2

No Beers Left

THE CLOCK IN THE HALL began its chime of six. With care, so Daddy would not hear, Amy-Lou opened the back door. She left it unlocked for her return. Outside in the dark rain, she pulled the hood over her head; it buried her. With her chin tucked into her neck, she forged ahead to visit the Red Rose off-licence on Priory Lane to buy sweets.

A buzzer buzzed each time the door to the off-licence opened or closed to herald the arrival or departure of a customer. An unnecessary alarm, because the wooden floorboards creaked when walked on. The shelves in the shop were stacked from floor to ceiling with a variety of goods, from tinned to fresh, from alcohol to confectionary. The service counter was set high with a wooden box on the floor for children to stand on when lured by the display of chocolate and toffee, complete with a penny tray of sweets. An overhead fluorescent light brightened the temptation.

Amy-Lou entered the off-licence. A man was being served at the counter. Amy-Lou pushed her hood back and shook the rain from her fingers. The man looked down at Amy-Lou then turned his attention to the DVDs for rent. 'What do you recommend?' he asked the server.

'This one has a great ending.' She handed him a DVD.

Amy-Lou shifted from one foot to another. She wrapped her fingers around the pound coin in her pocket and turned to leave. The man handed over his money then took the DVD. Amy-Lou stayed. She stepped onto the wooden box.

Mesmerised, she chose sixty pence worth of sweets and held her hand out for the change. 'There you go, missy,' the server said. At seven years of age, Amy-Lou should not have been out alone. 'Where's your Mummy?'

'She's outside,' she lied. She exited the warm shop with a buzz from the alarm and entered the lane with a clatter from the door slamming. She pulled the hood over her head and pocketed the change. After opening the paper bag of sweets she shoved a white chocolate-mouse into her mouth, followed by a coloured caramel. Her little hands sheltered the paper bag from the rain. Her feet swam in the too-big Wellington boots as she struggled to keep a pace.

Had Amy-Lou's daddy looked out of the window, he would not have seen his daughter on the opposite side of Priory lane because parked cars obscured her presence. Whilst her attention was fixed on choosing a sweet, she emerged from between two parked cars and began crossing the road.

Earlier that same evening, at the house opposite Amy-Lou's home, Linda had said goodbye to her son, Richard, and headed out to a waiting car for a weekend away with a friend. As she drove off down Priory Lane, PJ approached the front door.

'Hi, PJ, you're keen,' said Richard, opening the door. 'Come in.' Richard closed the door behind him. 'That's her gone for the weekend. Let the good times commence.'

'Yeah, for sure,' PJ said. 'So, Rich, how've you been?'

What a prick. Richard shook his head. He would be glad when this part of the evening was over. Watching PJ amble into the lounge with his carrier bag rattling he asked, 'What's in the bag, PJ?'

'Beers.'

'Thanks, I'll have one.'

PJ's hand flew into the bag and fished out four beers from a brace of six. Richard could see from the shape of the carrier bag there were at least six more cans of beer. PJ handed him a can. 'Here, take them all.' PJ handed the carrier over. Richard did not hesitate.

They sat on the comfy chairs to drink the high-octane beer. Richard tapped his foot in tune with the music while thoughts of Andrea danced in his head. He looked over to PJ and wondered how the gorgeous Andrea could be related to PJ. PJ sat upright on the edge of the chair, his legs apart, his right hand clutching a beer. He looked over to the framed photo of Richard on the fireplace, a boy dressed in school uniform. 'I like this dance music,' PJ said, filling the void of quiet between them.

'How are things at the shop?' Richard asked.

'The shop?'

'Where you work. It's a shop isn't it?'

'A garage. I'm a qualified mechanic.'

'A garage, you say, well done. And do you enjoy that kind of work?'

'I love it. And we're busy. But my main interest is gaming. Are you into gaming?'

'I spend way too much time on my computer studying. I have no desire to play on it. Anyway, how is that sister of yours?'

'Mm . . . good, I think.'

'Do you know whether she will be out on the town tonight?'

'She always goes out with her mates on a Friday. Why?'

'Just making conversation. Showing interest in you and your family.'

'Oh. How's it going at uni?'

'Good.'

They drank beer after beer while the music swallowed their silence. Richard tipped the last can over his mouth to receive every drop. He squeezed the can tight; it made a popping sound. He scrutinised the can. 'So, your sister, which bar does she frequent?'

'I've no idea. Chuck me a can.'

With a flip of his wrist and not much thought, Richard launched the disfigured can at PJ. The lump of aluminium landed with a crack on the side of his head.

'Ouch . . . why'd you do that?'

Richard shrugged. 'No beers left, mate. I'll check if there's any in the kitchen.'

Richard looked into the fridge at the cold shelves. Two bottles of beer sat upright. He grabbed them with one hand and flicked the lids off with a metal opener. Then he downed one, wiping his mouth with the back of his hand. Returning to the lounge he said, 'Sorry, only one

6

beer left.' He wrapped his lips around the cold neck of the bottle.

PJ produced a portion of compressed marijuana which resembled a piece of stock cube, he smiled. 'Do you want to share a joint?'

'Certainly do.'

PJ pulled a wallet of gold-leaf tobacco, a roach and a packet of RIZLA+ from his pocket. Richard watched as PJ laid out a cigarette paper on his knee. Leaving a space at the end for the roach, he filled the remainder with a line of tobacco, then crumpled the marijuana on top. He licked the edge to seal the roll, and with a flourish twisted the end. PJ lit the thin, packed cigarette. It glowed like an ember from a firework. He handed it to Richard.

Richard inhaled the smoke deep into his lungs. They consumed the joint, passing it back and forth until it was too small to use. The evening was young, and they were all out of beer and cannabis.

Richard jumped out of his seat. He headed to the cloakroom and locked the door. Out of his pocket he took a small plastic bag filled with white powder. With care, he opened the bag and tipped part of the content onto the toilet's cistern. The narcotic fell like refined sugar. Using his credit-card he chopped and herded the cocaine into a straight line. Putting one end of a rolled-up twenty-pound note up his nostril, and using his forefinger to push his other nostril tight, he snorted the cocaine deep into his lungs, deep into his head. He repeated the inhalation up his other nostril. Swiping his finger to collect a smidgen of cocaine, he then rubbed it into his gums. He felt a sultry shiver. He was active again, the cocaine had sobered him, had mopped the clouds of

7

alcohol and weed, leaving him with the certainty he was capable of anything.

When the cocaine hit diminished, Richard needed more alcohol. He grabbed his mother's keys off the hook. 'I'm going to the off-licence. Are you coming?' PJ followed him out of the house to the cobbled lane where Linda's car was parked. It was bitterly cold.

Richard reached up to the car roof and ripped the *Linda's Learner's* sign free, then he threw it onto the boot.

'It's only up the lane; let's walk,' PJ said.

'It's wet. Get in,' commanded Richard as he swayed to the driver's door while PJ slid onto the passenger seat. Richard stabbed the key into the ignition and turned it. The engine sprung to life. The front windscreen wipers were released to flick back and forth. Looking ahead, Richard forced the gearstick into reverse. Gripping the steering wheel with his right hand he released the button on the handbrake. Flinging his left arm around the back of the passenger seat he turned his head in line with his left shoulder. The rear wiper sat idle allowing the rain to obscure his view. With the clutch pedal pressed to the floor, and the gearstick rammed in reverse, Richard pushed his foot on the accelerator to rev the engine. The car's wheels spun faster than they should have. The car shot backwards off the cobbled lane and through a gap between two parked cars.

Richard heard the gruesome thump. He *felt* it. The car stalled. He looked at PJ and saw his shocked expression and knew that something bad had happened. 'What the fuck was that! Get out and have a look.'

PJ whipped out of the car, leaving the passenger door open and dashed to the back of the vehicle. Richard turned on the rear wiper to gain a better view. He prayed he had not damaged his mother's car. PJ dashed back and put his head into the void of the open passenger door. He looked into Richard's waiting eyes. 'Jesus, Richard you've knocked down a kid.'

'Shit!' Richard slammed the gearstick into first. 'Close that door! Get back in the house.' He hit the accelerator hard and swung the car back onto the cobbled lane. He rushed to the back door. Pushing PJ out of the way, he slid the key into the lock of the door. In single file, through the back door they went, through the utility room and into the kitchen.

Through chattering teeth, PJ managed to say, 'You can't leave her there.' Richard ran through the hall to tackle the stairs, three at a time. At his bedroom window he stood back and peered out. He could see the girl lying in the road. He recognised her – the daughter of the neighbour across the road. PJ came into the room and stood next to him. 'Oh, God, she's still there,' PJ whispered.

'For fuck's sake! Get away from the window.'

PJ stared at Richard. 'You've got to do something. We need to go down to her. She can't be dead. Not at the speed you hit her.'

'Whoa! What do you mean, dead? Who said anything about her being dead? She's dazed that's all. She'll get up in a minute. Shit, shit, shit!' Richard paced the dark room. 'I'm not ruining my life for this . . . Jee-zus, man – think!' He lengthened the stride of his pace. 'I have it! We'll go out and walk past her . . . make out we've just seen her. Then we can help. Yes, that's it. Come on. We'll argue the toss if she accuses us of anything.' Richard ran down the stairs, unaware that PJ had not followed him.

PJ continued to stare out of the window, when a car hurtled down the lane, its windscreen wipers flashing back and forth.

Ambulance Please

An hour before, in a house on the estate accessed by Priory Lane, Claire was enjoying a glass of red wine while she sat before a mirror applying makeup.

Her phone began ringing and she dug in her oversized bag to retrieve it. 'Hi Kerry,' she answered. 'What . . . Richard is? You have got to be kidding. No way, he told me he couldn't come over this weekend . . . We'll see about that. I'm going over there now . . . No, you've done right telling me. I'll ring you later. Thanks, Kerry. What? You fancy PJ? Okay, I'll knock on yours first. See you in a bit.'

Claire pulled on her high-heel thigh boots, grabbed her bag and chucked the mobile phone inside. Lifting a bottle of perfume off the dressing-table she sprayed herself. Excess particles of mist fell to the floor. Inhaling the scent, the one she adored, evoked the feel of Richard, a present from him. Taking a final look in the mirror, she sealed her lips together, then headed down the stairs. 'Mum, I'm going out.'

'Hang on.' Jenny scooted to the hall. 'Where are you dashing off to?' You're not going to Richard's, are you?'

'For God's sake!'

'It's you who said you'd have nothing more to do with him.'

'I'm not going to Richard's! Happy now?' Her lie was swept away by the disclosure of a visit to Kerry's house.

Claire left the house through the front door, slamming it behind her. She put up her umbrella before dashing to her car. A light came from the open garage door. As she walked past, she grinned at her dad. He was busy restoring a classic car; he straightened his back and smiled in return. Closing the umbrella Claire opened her car door and slinked into the driver's seat. She threw her bag onto the passenger seat, the umbrella to the footwell. The car stereo sparked to life when she turned the key in the ignition. John watched her reverse off the drive. The boom-boom music from the car's stereo disappeared down the road.

Jenny appeared in the garage doorway. 'You know where she's going?' she said.

'No, but you're going to tell me.'

'She's off to Richard's. After all he's put her through. I tell you I'm sick of it.'

John turned his attention back to the engine. 'How do you know where's she's going?'

'I overheard her on the phone. You know how loud she is.'

'There's nothing you can do to stop her seeing him. Don't get so worked up all the time. I'll have a cup of tea when you're ready.'

'It's all right for you to say that! It's me who has to pick up the pieces. How often is that, eh? Don't get worked up! Seriously?' Jenny stomped to the kitchen to put the kettle on.

Claire drove to the junction which linked the estate to Priory Lane. She flicked the indicator down to make a right turn. Without coming to a complete stop, she looked both ways before pulling out onto the lane.

Driving past the Red Rose off-licence, the heavy rain swamped the windscreen so she turned up the wiper speed and the heater trying to dispel the mist on the window from the wet umbrella. All she could think about was Richard and his deceit. She'd pleaded with him to come home this weekend but he'd said he needed to spend time in the library studying. His words of love and assurance had partly satisfied her, but then she'd just found out that he wasn't studying – he was at his mother's house. The liar, she thought. Her mobile phone interrupted her chaotic thoughts. She glanced at her bag and took her left hand off the steering wheel. Leaning sideways she fumbled in the bag trying to locate her phone. She was almost at Richard's house when she shot forward in her seat. A smack, a deep and haunting thud–thud. She knew she had driven over something. Not just anything – something significant. She slammed the brakes hard and clung to the steering wheel. The ringing from the phone stopped.

Richard hastened to the lane to check on Amy-Lou. Of course, he heard the sickening thuds of the wheels going over the body. The blood drained the colour from his face as he looked to the mangled figure in the red coat. His hand had found its way to his mouth. He looked to the stationary car and met the eyes of Claire in the rear-view mirror.

Claire saw Richard staring at her through the mirror. The mirror that did not reveal the horror waiting for her to discover. Panic hurried her breathing. By automation, she yanked the handbrake on and got out of the car. A patch of ice underfoot caused her heeled boot to skid and she corrected her balance. There was a child in red, a child moulded into the road. Then she screamed.

A lump of sticky toffee oozed out of the child's mouth. Bright red blood flowed past the soggy confectionery into the dark road. Claire fell to her knees by the child's side. A loose stone embedded her knee through the leather of her boot, she did not feel it. Nausea rose from the pit of her stomach. Richard stood over Claire and Amy-Lou. A streetlamp provided a dim halo over the pitiful scene. 'What have you done?' said Richard.

Claire's eyes locked onto the child. Her voice quavered, 'I didn't see her.' Air rushed from her mouth and a smoke of breath drifted to the sky. 'She came out of nowhere. I felt a bump. I thought . . . I thought I . . . oh, God, she's dead, I know she's dead.'

'Looks like it,' Richard said.

Claire sat back on her high heels. Too shocked to cry.

Richard watched PJ approach. 'Claire's knocked down this kid. The girl that lives there.' Richard pointed to the Walkers' house. 'PJ, knock on their door, tell them what's happened to their daughter.' Richard pulled his telephone out of his pocket and punched in three identical numbers.

Claire looked up at Richard. 'Can you ring my dad?' He held up a finger as if to silence her.

'Ambulance, please. There's been an accident, a child's been knocked down. It would appear she's dead.' Richard listened to the instruction on speakerphone from the operator while kneeling by the side of the child. Directed by the operator he played out resuscitation on the child. He compressed the small chest and performed the kiss-of-life. He licked the sweet toffee from his mouth. 'Priory Lane, close to the junction of the roundabout,' he said into the phone.

PJ walked through the open gate of the Walkers' garden and took the too short path to the front door. He paused his finger on the doorbell then pressed it. The handle turned but the door did not open. There was a shuffle of keys before the door opened wide. 'Hello Paul,' Fred said. With his hands shoved in his pockets, PJ looked to the flagstone under his feet.

With his eyes on PJ, Richard disconnected the call of resuscitation and abandoned Amy-Lou. He marched to Fred's gate and shouted, 'I'm afraid to say, but Claire has run over your daughter.'

Fred's eyes narrowed. 'What?' He looked over to see a girl on the road and rushed out to her. His legs buckled and he fell to the hard tarmac.

Claire moved to stand by Richard's side. She brushed a small stone from her leather boot. 'Have you phoned my dad?'

Richard shook his head. Claire took a ragged breath.

Fred did not acknowledge the people gathering. He did not cower from the rain. He looked down on his beautiful daughter and lifted his baby's limp body to cradle her in his arms. The white chocolate mix of toffee leaked from her mouth, her hair was matted with blood, her head smashed. Her green eyes were dull like unpolished gems. Holding her tightly to him he was not able to see his wife walking down the lane on her way home from work.

An umbrella protected Eunice Walker from the horror about to unfold. A man stepped out of a stationary car. Eunice looked to the man, then at the line of stagnant traffic. She held her umbrella upright to get a clear view of the huddle of people stood by the road outside her house. She quickened her pace to see Fred on his knees embracing their beloved girl. 'Please, God! No!' Eunice whimpered. The umbrella fell from her hand and bounced on the pavement.

By Fred's side, Eunice stared at Amy-Lou. The ageing face of Fred turned up to receive his wife. A shared expression of desolation was visible between them. He turned back to Amy-Lou. A tear escaped his eye, fell to his cheek, and tumbled off his chin onto his daughter.

'No! No! No!' Eunice did not form another word. She looked away from her baby, only to be confronted by Amy-Lou's Wellington boot which had separated from her little girl's foot.

'It's okay Eunice,' said Fred. 'She's at rest. Sit here with me. Let's share Amy-Lou while we can.'

Front row mourners stepped forward to hold a canopy of umbrellas over the pitiful family, to shield their loss from the rain.

Richard placed a hand on Claire's shoulder, startling her. 'You need to move your car. The ambulance won't be able to get through.'

'I can't, I can't get in it. Richard, I . . .' She looked at him, expecting comfort, but received none.

'Give me the key,' he said.

'The key? It's still in the ignition. Can you bring my bag? I need to phone my dad.' She began shivering uncontrollably.

Richard left Claire's side and made his way to her car, checking left and right before getting in. He started the engine and moved the car to the side of the road then strode to the bottom of the lane and directed the traffic.

15

The pitch of the ambulance siren climbed. Fred and Eunice did not acknowledge the shrill warning; they were cocooned in a blanket of sorrow. The siren died. A paramedic jumped out of the stationary ambulance and rushed towards them. Illuminated by the ambulance headlights, sharp needles of rain stabbed the road. The driver of the ambulance joined the gathering. He coaxed Fred's grip off Amy-Lou's body. The medic scooped a glob of toffee from the back of Amy-Lou's throat then placed his mouth over hers to blow the kiss of life into her deflated lungs.

'Oh, my baby. My darling baby,' Eunice sang.

Announced by flashing blue lights, a police car screeched to a stop.

A warm coat was wrapped around Claire's shoulder by her friend Kerry who lived at number 18. Claire held the coat tight. 'What's happened?' Kerry asked.

'I drove over that little girl. The one that lives there.' Claire pulled the coat tight, but the garment did not contain her shivers. 'She must have been down on the road. I didn't see her. Maybe she had tripped and fallen down. I thought I had driven over a dog! A dog! Not a child! Can you phone my dad? Tell him to come.'

'I'll nip in the house for my phone.'

'No! Get my bag out of the car. I want to talk to him. I need him to come.' Claire wobbled over to the low wall surrounding the garden of the Walkers' house and sat down. Taking her mobile phone off Kerry, she connected to home. 'Dad it's me. I've knocked down a little girl. She's dead!' She told him where she was and then broke down sobbing. A few minutes later, Claire's parents arrived and rushed over to her. Relief saturated

Claire as she saw them. They would take charge. They would sort this out. They always did.

Eunice rounded on Fred. 'How could you have let this happen! Why was Amy-Lou out in the dark, in the rain? She should have been inside with you. What were you doing? Four hours I was out. Four hours!'

'She was in the kitchen. I had no idea she had gone outside.'

'You assumed she was in the kitchen! You're a disgrace!'

The medics lifted Amy-Lou onto a gurney and wheeled her to the ambulance. Against the advice of the medics, Fred and Eunice clambered into the back of the ambulance with their precious girl. Side by side the childless parents clung to each other, like survivors on a raft.

The ambulance pulled away, its siren now silent.

Onlookers migrated. A police officer asked for witnesses to stay. Richard directed an officer to Claire. As the officer approached, John's arm wrapped around his daughter's shoulders. His face ashen, John said, 'I'm sorry, it was an accident.'

'Were you driving the vehicle, sir?'

'No. My daughter was. It's her car. But, she's a good driver.' John's eyes followed the officer's line of vision as he looked to Claire's high-heel boots.

'Sir, were you a passenger in the car at the time of the incident?'

'No.'

'Is this your daughter?' The officer tilted his head in the direction of Claire.

'Yes, but it was an accident. Claire's adamant the child was already down on the road, she wasn't able to see her.'

'Claire.' The officer jotted down her name. 'And your surname?'

'Jones.'.

'Let's make our way to the police vehicle. Sir, you can accompany your daughter if you wish.'

'Jenny, you go home,' John said. Jenny took the keys off her husband and set off walking holding her hand to her forehead. She suffered migraines.

John took hold of his daughter's hand. They followed the constable to his car. The officer placed his hand on top of Claire's head to avoid injury as he steered her onto the back seat. John let himself in on the opposite side to sit next to his daughter. A screwed tissue on the carpeted floor repelled Claire. She looked to her dad. He returned the look and she read pity in his eyes. He put his hand on top of hers. 'It'll be all right, love.'

The officer took the driver's seat. His uniform creaked as he twisted his body to address Claire. 'At least it's stopped raining. Okay, do you object to a breathalyser, Miss?'

'No, I . . . ' She coughed. 'I had a sip of wine earlier. Does that count?'

'I don't know, Miss. That's what the machine is for.'

John looked up at the scuff marks on the roof liner of the car. He sighed.

PC Smith reached for a small black case and opened it. 'Damn, I haven't any.' From the holder on his left chest, he took out the radio transmitter. The radio crackled to life. '10-8 Priory Lane RTA, mouthpiece for breathalyser.'

The transmitter replied, '10-4 . . . 10-98.'

The officer addressed John: 'Sorry about this.' He looked at Claire. 'I'll be back in a minute.' He exited the car and slammed the door shut.

'Dad, I feel dizzy,' Claire moaned. 'I'm going to be sick.'

'You need fresh air.' John could not open the door, or power down the window. 'Take deep breaths.' Patting his daughter's hand, he said, 'You'll be all right.' She placed her head between her knees, stars zooming in her vision.

PC Smith returned. He had an opaque plastic mouthpiece in his hand. This object reminded Claire of a cigarette holder. She needed a smoke, but her dad didn't know she was a user. PC Smith sat sideways again. 'Okay the machine will estimate your BAC to determine if we need a BT.'

'What are you talking about?' John asked.

'Basically, testing for the alcohol content in Claire's system. If the reading is borderline we will request that Claire takes a preliminary blood test. Do you have any objection, Miss Jones?' Claire shook her head. The officer pushed the mouthpiece onto the machine then switched the kit on. 'We wait for the beep.' The machine beeped. 'Then take a deep breath and blow into this end, nice and slow. Keep blowing until the machine beeps for a second time. Do you understand?' She nodded a yes. Claire took a deep breath and cupped her dry lips around the tube. Blowing into the tube she felt the pressure in her head. Waiting for the result, she fanned her face with her hand and held a deep breath. 'Negative,' the officer said. 'Now we need to carry out a field impairment test.'

'A field what?' John asked.

19

'A drugalyser. To rule out any trace of cannabis or cocaine in the system. These days it's common practice.'

'There'll be no drugs in Claire's system!'

Claire looked to her hands.

PC Smith took a blue tester out of the case. He swabbed Claire's mouth. They waited eight minutes for a reading: negative.

John and Claire squeezed each other's hand. Claire whimpered when Dad compressed her hand tighter. 'You'll be all right,' he said.

'Here you can keep this as a souvenir.' PC Smith handed the detachable breathalyser mouthpiece to Claire. She was surprised by the sheer indifference to this act. The result from the breathalyser and drug test were added to the paperwork along with Claire's name, date of birth and residence of abode. A statement of the event taken from Claire's perspective was written in full. Forced to relive the experience of driving over the child, Claire placed her hand on the back of her neck and stretched her chin upwards. Composing herself she scanned the completed statement. With no desire of correction, and under instruction, she scrawled her signature at the bottom of each page. 'Right, I'll be back in a minute,' the officer said. John and Claire were held prisoner in the car for a second time.

A short way off, Richard was being interviewed by an officer. 'I arrived on the scene after the event,' he said. 'I didn't see what happened. There was just a screech of tyres and then I ran out and saw it.'

PC Smith looked over the shoulder of his colleague who was interviewing Richard and pulled the officer to one side. 'I've recorded the BAC, it's a negative as is the drug test.'

'Do we need the Chief down?'

'I'll radio in. By rights, Chief should attend. But he's tied up with a major incident. He won't appreciate being pulled away. Bob was heading that way when he dropped off the mouthpiece. I'll request the victim support team attend the hospital where the parents are. I regard this a straightforward RTA. The evidence has been gathered. Do you concur?'

'Yeah.' This officer returned to face Richard. 'Thank you for your cooperation, Mr Hamilton. We may need to question you further.'

'Of course. Anything I can do to help. So sad for the parents to lose a child. Thank you, Officer, for the good work you do.' Richard gave a mock salute.

PC Smith unlocked his car. 'Looks like you can go. Take your documents to the police station within—'

'Documents?' Claire had found her voice.

'Driving licence, MOT if applicable, also a valid insurance certificate.'

'Don't you need to take a look at her car?' John asked.

'No. You need to inform your insurance company.' He asked for Claire's email address to send her a crime number. Claire spoke, and Dad listened.

On leaving the scene of the accident, the tyres of the police car flicked fragments of tarmac when it skidded on a small patch of ice.

John and Claire walked to her car. 'Dad, I can't get in.'

'I'll come for it in the morning. I'm not impressed with PC Smith. Not impressed at all.'

'Why? What do you mean?'

'Nothing. He's a bit young that's all.'

'Do you think I'll go to prison?'

'No, darling, well . . . I don't think so. It wasn't your fault.' The frown lines on John's face deepened.

'I had no idea the girl was on the road. She didn't run out in front of me. I would have seen her, but it looks as though I've killed her. How awful! I'll never get over this. That poor girl . . . her family . . .'

'Now, love, you did nothing intentionally.'

'I think I'll go to Richard's.'

'No, you can come home. Mum will want to see you. And we need to ring the insurance, that's if anyone answers at this time of night.' Clutching her dad's arm, they walked home in silence.

A Siren Echoed

On leaving the officer, Richard entered the house. 'You still here PJ? You might as well head on home.' PJ ignored him.

Richard took his bag from the utility room. A red light shone from the washing machine warning the end of a cycle of his clean clothes, but he ignored it and went upstairs. He showered, then admired his reflection as he shaved his face, and in doing so nicked a piece of skin. He slapped a corner of ripped tissue onto the cut to stem the flow of blood. The white tissue turned red. Dressed in designer clothes, Richard pealed the scrap of paper from his chin, the blood flow had stopped. The discarded piece of paper swam in the toilet bowl and turned the water pink. He splashed aftershave on his face, it smarted, enough for him to cry out. Checking his mobile phone he read a text from his mother saying she had arrived safely, which he replied to, and nine missed calls from Claire, which he ignored. He snorted two lines of cocaine up each nostril. He was convinced the cocaine he sourced for delivery to his apartment was of the highest quality because he checked the goods before handing over cash. He would rub his gum with a speck to feel his face go numb. He was not aware that Benzocaine had the same effect, a drug used legitimately in the UK as a dental anaesthetic. Who knew what he was inhaling? From his phone he requested a taxi. Drawn to the window, he pulled the curtain aside and looked out onto the road. His conscience was clear. As far as he was concerned, the girl should not have been out in the dark at that time of night and, anyway, Claire had done the damage, not him.

In the taxicab, Richard instructed the driver to head for town. A siren echoed in the distance. Unbidden, Amy-Lou's lifeless body flashed into his mind. Lowering his eyes he forced the image out.

The town was crawling with young people. Most were dressed for a summer evening, not the temperature of just above freezing. There were two popular nightclubs in town; Richard entered the nearest one. At the bar he ordered a shot and downed the fiery liquid. 'Keep them stacked,' he said to the bartender. Richard leaned on the bar to watch the freestyle dancers. He downed a second shot. His attention magnetised to Andrea, he stared at her body whilst she rocked to the music. Her raven hair shone, in contrast to the blonde girls she danced with. She swayed in tune with the music; her arms sweeping from side to side, she raised them high above her head. She looked delicious. It was evident that she saw Richard watching her and she held his stare. He gave a slight smile which lifted his cheek on one side. Andrea shimmied to an open space where Richard had an unobstructed view of her effortless dancing. He downed another shot. His eyes did not leave hers. He walked over to her, took her hand, and led her to the edge of the dance floor. Lifting her silky hair away from her ear he whispered, 'Come home with me.'

'No, I hardly know you and I'm out with my friends.'

'Ditch them.' His voice was husky and low. He took her ear lobe between his teeth and held it for a few seconds. She closed her eyes and sucked her bottom lip. Richard lifted her face to kiss her ripe lips, a kiss that was long and soft. They were alone in a throng of people. He stopped the kiss. 'So?'

'No! What kind of girl do you think I am?'

'A desirable one. Come home with me.'

'No.'

'Shame . . . I'm going.'

'Still, no.'

'Goodnight until the next time.' He took hold of her hand and turned it over, lifting her soft palm to his lips, he whirled his tongue in the centre of it.

'Don't go. Stay and dance with me.' She encased his arm with both her hands. 'Stay?' She tilted her head and gave a seductive smile. 'I can't go home with you. Not tonight.'

Richard unravelled her hands and kissed her nose before leaving the nightclub.

Out on the busy street in the cold night air, Richard's cotton shirt offered no warmth. His head ached from the climatic difference. He hailed a taxi to take him home. On the lane he paid the driver and added a generous tip. Richard looked over to the Walkers' house; it was swathed in darkness. Shaking his head he turned his back to that misery, then slid his key in the front door and made his way to bed.

The early morning winter sun filtered through a gap in the ink-blue curtain, waking Richard. A moment passed before he realised where he was. He looked up at the ceiling. He sensed a presence and sat up. 'What the fuck are you doing in my room?'

PJ sat in the corner. Last evening's event rushed into Richard's head which ached. His mouth was beyond parched.

PJ stared intently at Richard. 'What are you going to do?'

Richard closed his eyes and sighed. 'What do you mean, do?'

'You can't let Claire take the rap.'

'Behave, man. And what do you think you're doing in my room?' Richard flung the duvet from his body. Wearing stretch cotton boxers, he sprung out of bed then padded to the bathroom to use the toilet. He returned without taking a shower and dressed in a pair of neat fitting light grey joggers and a matching top. 'I need a coffee and a cigarette. You need to piss off home.'

In the kitchen, Richard switched the coffee machine on to percolate. PJ walked in behind to confront him, 'I've not slept. I've been waiting for you to wake up. We should have helped her, the girl, she could still be alive. What're you going to do?'

'What am I going to do? Don't you mean *we*? What are *we* going to do? PJ, you're not an innocent in this, remember that!' Richard reached for a large cup and saucer to pour coffee for one. He lit a cigarette, knowing the smell would dissipate before his mother came home.

'Look, my life, my career, even before it's got started, will be over. Father will be pissed, and as for my mother? Well it would kill her. You don't want to be responsible for that.' Richard moved closer to PJ. 'Who will have their car repaired by a child killer?' He blew an arrow of smoke straight into PJ's face. 'Like you said, I couldn't have killed her at that speed. Claire, the tart, did the damage, not me. As far as I'm concerned, we're not implicated. Understand?' Richard placed his face within kissing distance of PJ's. 'Or maybe I can't remember what happened. Not after those drugs you plied me with. I'm serious – keep your mouth shut. You know, like you did last night when the police asked for any witness to come forward.' PJ examined the floor as Richard continued. 'I'm going for a cooked breakfast. You can run along home, little boy. Forget last night ever happened. Understand?'

After PJ left, Richard went outside and made his way to Linda's car. The learner's sign still rested in the boot. With care he backed the vehicle off the cobbled lane and drove past the scene of last night's horror.

In the fast-food café, Richard placed his order and carried the laden tray to an anchored table then sat on the fixed padded bench. With a mouthful of egg and bacon he checked his mobile phone: missed calls from Claire had climbed to double digits. She answered on the first ring. 'Richard, I've been trying to get hold of you. How dreadful was last night? I can't sleep. The whole disaster is on a loop in my head. I keep seeing the dead girl. The feeling of driving over her . . . I can't cope.' Richard took another bite of his muffin. 'I have to report

26

to the police station with my documents,' she continued. 'Can I come around and see you after I've been?'

Richard swallowed his chewed food and wiped his mouth on a thin paper napkin. 'Okay, but ring first. And Claire, don't worry, you'll get over it.'

Without taking his tray to the self-service station, Richard pushed the heavy glass door to exit the café. Walking towards his mother's car his attention was drawn for the first time to the damage on the car's rear bumper. 'Shit!' He rubbed his hand over the stubble on his face as he examined the dented plastic of the bumper. Convinced the damage was a result of last night's incident, he considered making up a story in which the car was bumped right there outside the café. But no, a quick look confirmed the area was covered by CCTV cameras. He would have to find another place where he could leave the car vulnerable to damage, to apportion the blame.

Richard returned home. He parked the car in its usual place on the cobbles. Taking a deep breath of fresh air he entered the house through the back door. He strode into the living room to look out of the window, to check for activity at the Walkers' house. Their curtains were closed. Richard considered the damage to his mother's car. *Mother knows every inch of that damned car*, he thought. The doorbell shrilled and shocked him out of his reverie. A sergeant in uniform stood before the opened front door. 'Mr Hamilton?'

Richard's heart cranked up a notch. 'Yes sir.'

'I'd like to question you further on the fatal accident that took place outside this house yesterday evening.'

'Of course, come in. As I said, I was a witness after the event. But do step in. Whatever I can do to help. What a

27

tragedy, those poor parents having to face the death of their child.' Richard was aware he was babbling. He could not close his mouth, instead he closed the door after the sergeant had stepped in. 'Would you like tea or coffee?' The sergeant declined. Usually a visitor to the house would be ushered into the lounge, but the debris from yesterday's stint with PJ remained. Richard stood with his back to the lounge entrance and held his arm out to persuade the sergeant to enter the kitchen. They sat opposite each other, a polished glass table between them. The officer introduced himself as Sergeant Wright.

'Can I address you by your Christian name, Mr Hamilton?'

'Please do. I'll just grab a coffee.' Richard stood. His chair clattered to the floor. After reinstating the chair, he ignored the percolating coffee, and filled the kettle to the top. He switched it on to boil, needing time to compose himself.

Sergeant Wright took a notepad out of his top pocket and licked the tip of a pencil. His radio transmitter sprang to life; the code from the machine was not meant for him, so he ignored it. Richard took his seat and cusped his hands around the freshly made mug of instant coffee. The sergeant began: 'So, at approximately 18:20 yesterday, Amy Louise Walker was involved in an RTA which resulted in her death. I see from your statement you did not arrive on the scene . . .' Sergeant Wright paused to confer with his notepad, 'yes, you arrived on the scene from the side of this house. Did you have a purpose to be on the lane? Had something alerted your attention?'

I was on my way to the off-licence, to walk to the off-licence, when I heard, I did not see, Claire's car screech to a halt. I thought she had come to an abrupt stop after seeing me.

'You know Claire Jones?' The sergeant stopped writing and watched Richard's demeanour.

'I do know Claire. She's an ex-girlfriend.'

The sergeant frowned, then wrote on his pad. He took a pressed handkerchief out of his pocket to wipe the tip of his nose then replaced the hanky. 'When did you realise the victim had been hit by a car?' Again, he raised his eyes to Richard.

'I stepped between two parked cars to cross the road when I was confronted by the dreadful sight of that poor child.' Richard released the tension in his shoulders.

'I see. Am I right in saying the off-licence is on this side of the street?'

'Yes, sir, it is.'

'Ah, why then did you step onto the road as if to cross it? You say Miss Jones had stopped to greet you?'

Richard averted eye contact with the sergeant. 'That was a joke. I, um, was aware that she had run over something. My first thought was a dog.'

'Please do not joke, Mr Hamilton, this is a serious investigation.'

Richard drank his coffee in one, in an attempt to hide his flushed face. He placed the empty mug on the table then wrapped his arms around himself, tucking his hands under his armpits. He held steadfast to the account he had given yesterday. Sergeant Wright replaced his notepad in his pocket before leaving the house.

Richard filled his cheeks with air then released the hostage breath. In the living room, he stood away from the window and spied on what he feared: Sergeant Wright was on the lane, close to the cobbles where the damaged car waited. Panic forced Richard's attention to the countryside, to the swathe of trees and hills. Staring at a train cutting through the greenery his mother's voice flooded his mind: *A young girl's been mugged at the station. What a disgrace! In broad daylight.* Linda added her name to the petition for staff to man the station, or at least to have CCTV fitted as a deterrent. *That's it! That's where I'll leave the car.* He swiftly tidied the living room.

Upstairs, Richard grabbed his bag and stuffed in the items he needed. The interview with the sergeant replayed in his mind: *Did I implicate myself?* Richard was glad to leave his mother's house and return to the safety of the university campus. He crept to the window; the sergeant had gone.

With care, Richard wrote a note – *Andrea, I want you.* Then he added his phone number. This note was folded with precision and pocketed. He took his mother's keys, then unclipped her car key. He scribbled another note on a scrap of paper: *Gone back – need books – car at train station – key on driver's wheel.* He left this note on the glass table then placed the house keys under the outside dustbin. Then he left the house.

Richard drove the short distance to Andrea's house. He got out of the car, headed to the front door, and posted a note. When Richard left, PJ went downstairs to retrieve the note. The message was addressed to Andrea. After reading the contents, he screwed the note into a ball and dumped it in the waste bin.

Social Media Crackled

Sunday, and social media crackled with messages to join the support of sorrow at the loss of Amy-Louise Walker. A declaration was posted by one mourner that anyone who wanted to be united in grief should place a lit candle in their window. Twinkling lights shone far and wide. The Walkers' gate was a modern-day memorial to grief. A hypnotic scent from the wretched display swelled the air. Attached to the gate were teddy-bears, flowers and heartfelt notes of pity. One card described Amy-Lou as a star soaring to the sky; Eunice should treasure this one.

On returning from the spa weekend, Carol parked her car near to Linda's house. 'Wonder what's happened there?' She pointed to the colourful blooms.

Linda reached for her bag from the back seat before vacating the car. 'I won't invite you in Carol. I need to see Richard. But thanks for a lovely weekend.'

Carol had parallel-parked the car under the daunting eye of her friend the driving instructor and now she had been dismissed. 'Why do you worry so much about Richard? At his age, he's more than capable of looking after himself.'

'I knew you wouldn't understand; you don't have children.' Linda closed the car door with care.

'Let me know what happened there.' Carol pointed to the adorned gate.

Linda placed her right fist on the centre of her chest as the flowers drew her attention. She knocked on her own front door. She knocked a second and a third time. She raced to the back door and knocked on that. She popped her head out of the side gate; her car was not parked on the cobbles. She heaved a sigh. She unclipped the fastener on her shoulder bag and took out the telephone from its purpose-pocket. She chose Richard's number and listened for the beep of his voicemail. 'Richard it's me, Mother, where are you? I'm home and locked out.' With no winter coat, Linda rubbed her arms in an attempt to get warm. She returned to the lane and observed the Walkers' gate. Beyond the gate she saw their curtains were closed. She did not knock on their door. The telephone clutched in her hand chirped a message: *Back at the apartment – key under the dustbin.*

Kerry Langford stepped out of her front door and Linda beckoned her. 'Do you know what's happened there?' Both were mesmerised by the morbid display.

'Their little girl was killed on Friday. She was knocked down.'

'Outside their house? That's dreadful! Poor Eunice and Fred. What a horrendous thing to happen. Who's responsible? Do they know?'

'Claire ran over her. You know, Richard's girlfriend? She says she didn't see Amy-Lou. She reckons the kid must have already been lying on the road. Either that, or she ran out between parked cars, that's what I think. The only other person on the lane, and he didn't see it happen, was Richard.'

'Really?' Linda shivered, then excused herself. With arms folded, she marched to the dustbin to pick up her keys. In the kitchen she found the note left by her son and read it. Then she put the note in the kitchen drawer which held all the other notes written by him.

Linda changed her heels for flat shoes before setting out to the train station to collect her car. Richard had parked the car back-to-back with another car. When Linda arrived, her car's front grill faced her, its redundant headlights welcomed her. She could not know her son had purposefully parked the car in this direction. She could not see the damage to the car's rear bumper.

CHAPTER 3

See the Rain?

MONDAY MORNING and Claire and her dad were preparing to visit the police station. Rain fell, pin-rod straight. 'Have you got the documents?' John asked. 'I don't want to make another journey.'

'Yes, Dad.' Claire took her bag off her shoulder to check the contents for the sixth time. John witnessed the tremor in his daughter's hand and looked away. He stepped into the garage and turned the handle of the up-and-over garage door with unexpected force. He drove his van off the drive, parked it on the road, then got in the family car and waited for Claire to join him.

'Put your seatbelt on, love,' he said as she got in the car.' John continued to roll the car out of the garage. The rain pounded the windscreen.

'Dad, please, I've got to get out. Seriously, Dad, I'm going to be sick. See the rain? What if you can't see? It's going to happen again! You can't see them in the rain.' Sweat prickled her back, she wiped her forehead. Instinct pushed her head between her knees.

'Pull yourself together. We have to go to the police station.' John put the handbrake on.

'I know Dad! Please, I feel really ill.' Claire pressed the electric button to slide the window down. She gulped for air as the rain re-styled her hair. Feeling the benefit of her action, she said, 'I can't go, not in the car, not in the rain.'

'Then we'll walk, but you need to get a grip on this. You don't want to be a prisoner of the rain.' He reversed the car back into the garage.

On foot they set off to the police station. John wore a rain-jacket, its hood covering his head. Claire held an umbrella. On approaching the station, Claire remarked, 'It doesn't look like a police station.' The old building, on a side street, had been made new with a grey exterior and a blue door.

'This must be the entrance.' John pushed the button on the wall by the side of the door. The intercom sprang to life.

'Hello,' the box said.

John levelled his mouth with the transmitter. 'Yes, hello, we've brought documents. My daughter was involved—' A beep interrupted and a click from the locked door invited them to enter. Claire collapsed her umbrella and shook the rain free. A civilian officer stood behind the enquiry-desk. Opposite this officer was a man and woman describing a dispute they had had with a neighbour. John and Claire occupied the vacant seats opposite the desk and watched the sketch play out. John leant his body to his daughter. 'It's not very private,' he whispered. Claire's eyes widened at the thought of an audience.

An internal door was pushed open by a scruffy, undernourished lad. He walked with shoulders pushed back and a prominent swagger. The civilian officer raised her eyes as the lad strutted past, he made a fist at her and lifted his middle finger then pressed the automatic door button to be released.

The man and his vocal wife finished their spat. She said she was disgusted with the police for refusing to get involved. A civilian matter, they were told.

John approached the desk. Claire rustled in her bag for the documents. After the receptionist rang for assistance, Sergeant Wright entered the foyer with a folder tucked under his arm. After pleasantries, the sergeant showed John and Claire to a vacant interview room. 'I was detailed to visit you today, Claire, you've saved me a journey.' Sergeant Wright waited until dad and daughter were seated, then he sat on the chair facing them.

'What happens now?' John asked. He took the documents from Claire's tight fist and handed them over. A sour smell of sweat lingered in the room, left, presumably, by the cocky lad.

'We wait on the coroner's report.' Sergeant Wright plonked the file on the table. The file's cover displayed a bold number and the abbreviation URN. The sergeant saw Claire look at the file. 'Unique reference number to your case,' he said.

Exposed by the open file, John saw a sketched plan of the scene. He laid his hand on his daughter's hand and squeezed it. The paper was marked TC01 – fatal injury. Deceased: Amy Louise Walker. Accused: Claire May Jones. The sergeant spoke: 'Have you informed your insurance company of the incident?' He looked to Claire for an answer, but John replied.

'Yes.'

Sergeant Wright took hold of a bunch of papers from the file and tapped them on the table to align them. 'There will be a post-mortem. A substance was present in the child's mouth, maybe in her throat.' He looked at John. 'It may be the deceased choked before the accident, making the RTA circumstantial. The coroner will consider all the evidence.' The sergeant pulled the top of his pen and placed it on the other end. A decision will be reached by the coroner whether the case should go to trial.'

'Like I keep saying, she was already down on the road. She must have choked to death!' Claire said. Both her dad and the sergeant gave her a weak smile.

'Doesn't Claire need a solicitor here?'

'If she requests one; if she thinks that necessary.'

'No, Dad, I don't.'

'Could the coroner find Claire guilty, or . . .' John began.

'No! The coroner's job is not to apportion blame. His job is to determine whether the child's death could have been avoided given the evidence. If he is in any doubt he will – actually it might be a lady coroner at this court – anyway, a hearing will be ordered.' The sergeant paused to readjust the position of the pen top to keep it in line with the logo. 'The coroner will consider all the elements of the accident, and whether Claire's driving was a factor in the fatality. If this is the case, a court hearing will be ordered to determine whether Claire's driving was deemed dangerous or careless. The latter carries less of a penalty, probably non-custodial.'

'Oh!' John said.

Claire's eyes filled with tears. 'I keep saying, and no-one listens, that girl was already lying in the road. She must have been.'

'That will be part of your defence. You should enlist a solicitor to prepare your case.' The sergeant looked up from his pen and smiled at Claire. She did not register his gesture of kindness. 'At this stage we are preparing documentation. You will be contacted when this is complete and notified whether there is to be a hearing. If a hearing is necessary, you will be informed of the date.' He took the lid off the pen and meticulously replaced it over the thin nib.

The door to the police station closed with a click after expelling dad and daughter onto the dry street. 'A solicitor? That sounds expensive,' John said. Claire pulled her bottom lip between her teeth and held it there. She tucked the damp umbrella under her arm. 'Bloody hell, girl! How often have I told you not to charge around in that car with your music blaring? You're an idiot, a bloody idiot!'

Claire had expected this response sooner. They remained silent, walking alone among the masses of people, a dad and his daughter whose perspective on life had changed in an instant.

Approaching home, John said, 'I'm sorry. I didn't' mean to lose my temper.'

'I know, Dad.'

'I've been thinking, I'm going to get some leaflets printed. See whether anyone witnessed the girl on the road like you say she was when you ran over her.'

'Thanks, Dad.'

Jenny ran out of the house to greet her husband and daughter. She flung her arms around her baby.

Too Much to Bear

The memorial of grief attached to the gate of the Walkers' house had expanded to such an extent that offers of condolence were piled on the pavement. Word had spread the way bad news does. Devotees of misery appeared in droves to stamp their identity on the wretched display; desiring a share of the heartache. The curtains at the Walkers' house remained closed.

Tuesday morning, and Linda peered out of her window at the fluorescent pink balloon tied to a lamppost. The air-filled piece of rubber bobbed about, eager to break free and escape to the sky. A trio of candles sat on the pavement waiting for the return of pilgrims to light them. But a new day beckoned, so Linda finished her cup of tea before checking her watch. The mirror welcomed her face as she tousled her hair. A driving lesson was booked for nine am, so she grabbed her keys and left the house.

Linda waited in her car outside a block of flats. She checked her diary for the name of this new client passed on to her by a colleague. Eight minutes tiptoed by when a door opened on the ground floor of the flats and a man came out. He had greasy hair, neatly parted to one side, and he wore a light-weight cream jacket, zipped to the neck. His trousers stopped at the ankle, allowing his white socks to make a statement. Striding to the car he opened the passenger door and sat next to Linda.

'Hi, I'm Linda.'

'Hello, yes, I know. Linda, what a lovely name, which originates from the German meaning of soft and tender.'

'Really?' Linda pulled her skirt past her knees.

A blank card sat on today's page of the open diary, waiting for this client's details. Linda clicked the top of her silver pen and poised the implement to write. Her habit of writing was to hold the pen near the nib, forcing her head forward to see what she penned. 'Can I see your provisional licence?' She asked, looking across at him. The man stretched his leg to gain access to his trouser pocket. He took out his licence and handed it to her. As Linda wrote the details on the card, she calculated the man's age from the jumble of numbers – forty-five-year-old. 'Have you driven a car before?'

'No, Linda, not me.'

'Okay, I'll drive you to a quiet road to show you the basics.' On the way to the location, Linda tried to engage her client in conversation, but his responses were monosyllabic. At the housing estate of winding roads, she pulled the car to a stop. 'Can you get out and come around to the driver's side.' Linda slid over to the vacant warm passenger seat, sitting sideways to face her client. 'Okay, you have three pedals at your feet.' She explained the procedure of clutch control, accelerating and braking. She asked him to put the gearstick into first. He orchestrated his feet on the pedals, set the car in motion, and without instruction carried out each gear change with a flourish.

'Pleasant day,' he said. Turning his face towards Linda.

'Keep your eyes on the road, please. Yes, it's a pleasant day. Can you pull the car to a stop by the second lamppost on the right?' They swapped seats. 'As you're a beginner, I'll drive you home.'

Relaxed in the passenger seat, the man said, 'I like you. You remind me of my support worker. She gives me her time, like you do.'

'Okay.' Linda increased the speed of the car and headed back to the block of flats. She parked the vehicle. The man requested another appointment. Out of the car, he handed Linda her fee. His eyes met hers, and she looked away. Linda reached over to close the passenger door then bent her head over her diary. Her hair fell to create a curtain as she pencilled in the booking. A knock on the window startled her. The man stooped and put his face to the window.

'Do you know your bumper's damaged?'

'No, that's okay, thank you.'

He watched Linda, with her damaged bumper, drive away to her next appointment.

'Hi Tracey, are you well?' Linda slid over to the passenger seat to allow Tracey to take the driver's seat.

'Did you have a good weekend at the spa?' Tracey asked.

'Lovely thanks.' Linda checked the notes on Tracey's progress. 'Okay, we'll drive to the test centre. The route I have in mind will give you practice on roundabouts.'

'The test-centre! Am I ready for that?'

'To familiarise you with the area. Not take your test, relax.' Tracey drove the car without instruction. 'Take the first exit at the roundabout.'

Tracey signalled a left turn and moved the car into the left lane to join the traffic. When it came to her turn to leave the roundabout she saw a gap in the traffic and proceeded to leave. A lorry rounded the roundabout at speed on the right. Tracey stomped the brakes. 'If in doubt, both feet out,' she said. The taxi driver behind them was looking to the right at the roundabout. He smashed his taxi into the back of Linda's car.

'What the!' Linda said.

'Oh, my neck!' Tracey wrapped both hands around the back of her neck.

'When I get out, you slide over and get out on my side, away from the traffic. Sheesh! This is all I need. I have a test booked in two hours.' They stood on the embankment watching the taxi driver march over to them. Other drivers, mesmerised by this calamity, risked another collision.

'I've seen it all!' The taxi driver shouted. 'A woman driver taught by another woman!'

'Excuse me!' Linda said. 'You're the one who slammed into my car.'

'Slammed into you? You, stupid woman, you stopped in front of me. These learner drivers shouldn't be on the road if they can't drive. I'm supposed to be at the airport in ten minutes.' He raised his hands in the air.

'You should have waited for my pupil to leave the roundabout. Surely you saw the brake lights. And you're going to the airport? You were in the wrong lane.'

'My neck's aching; will I get compensation?' Tracey asked.

'In the wrong fucking lane! Don't cite the highway code to me! Bloody women. I can't hang about here.' Insurance details were swapped without further conflict.

'Tracey, I'll drive you home. You've had quite a shock.'

'I don't have to pay for this lesson, do I?'

'No, Tracey, you don't.'

Linda yanked the handbrake on outside Tracey's house. 'How do I get compensation?' Tracey asked.

'Compensation?'

'For my neck injury.'

'Oh! Through my insurance. I'll sort it. I have your details.' Linda ran a hand round the back of her neck.

At home, Linda cancelled the driving test booked for that afternoon. The car was no longer roadworthy, the bumper was damaged and a brake light had been smashed. She rescheduled lessons. She rang a male colleague to offload the man from the block of flats, adding, 'I didn't feel comfortable with this pupil. If he tells you he's a novice, well, he isn't.'

Later that day, Linda stood at the open door of the repair garage, where PJ worked. She grimaced at the banging and clanging. Looking into the male environment for someone to assist her she noticed a calendar hung on the wall, opened on the page of February, displaying a naked female, except for a fur hat and boots. The model stood provocatively and proud. Dan came out of the office cubicle.

'Dan, hi,' Linda shouted. Dan sauntered over to her. 'Can I book my car in for repair?'

'Sure, Mrs H. I'll just get the diary.'

Linda could see the top of PJ's head, his body under a car. He slid out on a flatbed with castors. Linda beckoned him. He paused, sickened by the sight of her car. The wrench in his hand found its way to the floor as he ambled over to Linda. Wiping his greasy hands on his oil-stained grey overalls he kept his head down.

'Did you see what happened on Friday, when Amy-Lou was run over?' Linda asked.

'No,' PJ muttered.

'But I was told Richard did?'

'I . . . don't know.'

'Well, you were with Richard on Friday evening.'

Dan strode over with the diary in his hand. Without answering, PJ walked back to the car he was working on. 'I can squeeze you in and make a start this afternoon, but I don't have a courtesy car.' He surveyed the car. 'Rear-ended? It's going to need a new bumper at the very least.'

'That's fine. So, annoying!' She separated the car-key in the way Richard had then headed for home on foot.

Dan drove Linda's car to the body repair shop, accessed through the backyard of the garage. He told PJ to strip the bumper off the blue Fiesta. Surveying Linda's car, PJ felt the bile rise in his gut. The image of Amy-Lou, dead on the road, haunted him. He swallowed several times to compose himself. Then he unscrewed the fasteners off the bumper to detach it from the car. A button, red and shiny fell to the floor. PJ looked around, made sure no one saw him, then picked the button up. He rolled the shiny red object between his thumb and forefinger, transfixed in thought. He reconnected to his situation and put the red button in his overall pocket.

On her way home from the garage, Linda entered the Red Rose off-licence to buy flowers for Eunice. The door buzzed her entry. From a bucket of water, Linda chose a bunch of lemon roses.

'I've sold lots of flowers recently. Terrible what happened on Friday – that poor child and her family. You know, the little girl was in here before it happened. I thought it was odd. Usually she comes in here with her mummy; she said her mummy was outside. Ah, well, makes your heart bleed.'

44

'Yes, dreadful. These flowers are for her mum.' The door buzzed Linda's departure. Near to home, she looked over to the Walkers' house, the curtains still closed. She took a deep breath, followed by a sigh, and crossed the road between two parked cars. Linda heaved the laden gate open, careful not to disturb the floral display. At the front door she reached for the brass knocker and gave three raps. A shuffle of keys preceded the opening.

'Hello.' Fred said.

'I'm so sorry for your loss. I've brought flowers for Eunice, and you, of course.'

'Yes, thank you. Come in. Please come in and see Eunice.' Fred held the door wide. Linda followed his silent footsteps to where Eunice sat at the kitchen table; a cup of cold tea in front of her.

'I'm so sorry.' Linda grimaced on seeing the pallor of Eunice's skin. Grief had robbed this mummy of her last trace of youth.

Fred took the cold cup of tea from his wife's vision. 'I'll make fresh tea.' All three listened to the kettle reach boiling point. Fred stirred the tea then tapped each china cup twice with a spoon. He placed a steaming cup in front of his wife. 'Here, Linda, sit here.' Fred pulled a heavy oak chair away from the table then placed a matching cup with saucer before Linda. Then left the kitchen to bury his sorry in the garden. Evidently, earth was what he was familiar with, not digging into his wife's mind. Linda sat in the chair provided, opposite Eunice.

'Just like that!' Eunice said. Clicking her middle finger and thumb together. 'She's gone. I can't comprehend it.'

'I know. Every mother's worst nightmare, to lose a child. Do you know what happened? Or would you rather not talk about it?'

'Apparently, Amy-Lou stepped out in front of a car. The driver didn't see her. It's not like Amy-Lou to do that . . . I mean, it wasn't like her. I drummed into her the importance of road safety. But she was never allowed out on her own. To be honest, I still can't get my head around how she managed to leave the house. Fred says he wasn't aware she'd gone out. That wouldn't have happened on my watch!'

Linda looked around the kitchen.

'You know, Linda, I couldn't connect with Amy-Lou when she was born. I rejected her. Can you believe that? This is my punishment for feeling that way.'

'No, you mustn't think like that.'

'You see, I suffered from postnatal depression, it started when Amy-Lou was four weeks old. It came on quickly, a black shroud over me, every thought, every emotion. As though I had been pushed into a corner, and I didn't want to come out. I was so lonely, yet I craved to be alone. It was a dreadful time.'

'I'm so sorry, I didn't know. You should have come to me, I was only across the road.' Linda took a sip of tea. Her eyes were drawn to the pile of dirty crockery in the sink.

'I mean, I wanted her. I was thrilled to be pregnant. Fred and I had tried to conceive for so long. It was summer when I started to show.' Eunice wrapped one hand around the warm cup of tea, the other hand she placed around her middle-aged tummy. 'I bought these cute maternity dresses. I was so proud to be with child.' She smiled for the first time since her loss. 'Fred was

46

thrilled. He took to Amy-Lou straight away, and he stayed that way.'

'Some say it's easier for men. They don't have the imbalance of hormones to deal with after the birth of a baby.' Linda placed her cup on the saucer, chinking the china together.

'I couldn't bond with her, my baby. They, the health workers, recommended I retain eye contact with my baby. This was supposed to help. But I could barely look at her. I believed her to be the reason for the crippling change in me. She was the one who'd robbed my health, my state of mind. Anyway, now I'm wretched because I can't hold my baby, because I can't look into her eyes. Those gorgeous green eyes. How ironic is that?'

'Terrible. How did you turn that situation around? How did you connect with her, Amy-Lou? Because clearly you had.'

'A combination of things; time, support. Fred was excellent, I loved him for that. I felt guilty because Fred's passion is to teach. I took him away from that for a while.' Eunice took a sip of tea. 'And medication did the trick, I'm sure of that.'

'Whatever works.'

'Yes, I'm an advocate for medication.' Eunice placed her elbow on the table to support her chin. She fixed her gaze on the toy dog.

Linda tipped the remnant of tea into her mouth and swallowed. She shifted her sitting position.

Eunice scraped back her chair. She scooped the toy dog into her arms and stroked its fur. 'There's to be a post-mortem. The thought of a stranger slicing my baby open is too much to bear.' Eunice sang a lullaby into the ear of the cradled dog. Linda spilt a tear to clear her vision and left without a goodbye.

CHAPTER 4

Spoonful of Sugar

AFTER THE MORTICIAN sliced open Amy Louise Walker, Sergeant Wright blew his nose. He refolded his handkerchief then checked the preliminary notes he had made.

Ten minutes behind schedule, the pathologist entered the room. He nodded to the mortician then checked the gallery to register the sergeant. Placing a helmet on his head he slid the visor over his face. To highlight his subject, he reached for the spotlight hanging from a jointed fixture above. He cleared his throat and switched the dictaphone on to record his credentials, the date, the time, the deceased's name. 'The body is that of a female child, average height and weight for a . . .' He checked the docket. 'For a seven-year-old. The eyes are partially open, the iris is green. A haematosis, one-point-five centimetres by three centimetres is present on the left temporal scalp. A circular wound, one-and-three-quarter centimetres by one-and-a-half centimetres is present on the skull. The hair is encrusted with what appears to be blood – send sample for analysis. Trace elements of goo are in the posterior oral cavity – appearance would suggest confectionary – send sample for analysis. There is no obstruction to the airway.' He continued with the dissection, taking out and weighing Amy-Lou's organs which he sliced for tissue samples. He put the organs in a plastic bag then placed the bag in the open cavity of Amy-Lou's body, at the request of the parents; organ donation had been refused.

At the stainless-steel sink, the pathologist peeled off his latex gloves and threw them in the disposal. He scrubbed his hands and nails and nodded to the mortician for a second time. He looked up to the gallery – it was empty. Sergeant Wright's daughter was a similar age as the victim. He had dabbed his eyes with the square of his handkerchief while leaving the gallery. The pathologist walked out of the room, abandoning Amy-Lou; it was not his job to fix her, move her, or clean away her presence.

Music brought the room to life, as the mortician tapped his foot to the beat of the Bee Gees. He stitched Amy-Lou back together, taking more care than usual; his way, when dealing with young ones. He zipped the child in the airless bag, then slid her onto a slab in the cold store where she would wait for the undertaker. After prepping the room for the next body, he turned the music off. The transcript of the autopsy was e-mailed to the coroner. The unique reference number would link all paperwork. The coroner's secretary collected the relevant information, and to the preference of this coroner, printed it off and placed the paperwork in the coroner's tray.

Sitting at her leather-topped desk, the coroner read the report of Amy Louise Walker. Making a headband with her spectacles, she leant back in her sprung back chair while deciding an inquest was necessary. She issued an interim death certificate to allow the grieving parents to lay their child to rest.

A family of six arrived at Billy Booker's Funeral Parlour. They paid no attention to the splendour of the mahogany walls, the plush purple carpet, or the gold-legged furniture. They sat down in the receiving room, which bore a sign saying *Peace*, and waited for Billy to tend to their needs.

The operational division of the funeral parlour was located below stairs in a restricted area. In deference to the deceased these doors wore nameplates too. In a room marked *Sacrament*, Amy-Lou waited for service. Billy Booker no longer prepared bodies – his son would take care of her.

Willy Booker entered the Sacrament room and wiped his hands on his rubber apron, then dabbed menthol under his nose and donned a pair of latex gloves. Making neat incisions into Amy-Lou's arteries Willy pushed plastic drains into the forged slits. Amy-Lou's bodily fluids trickled out down the sink hole, and left her limp, like the deflated pink balloon outside her house on the lamppost. Into the incisions and via the drains, Willy fed embalming fluid to resurrect her appearance; to stop the flesh from deteriorating further. The units which held the stock for his job ran along one wall. These units were shiny-white, similar to a modern kitchen. His rubber boots caught the floor with each step as Willy walked to a cupboard. He pulled the handle of a slim, wide drawer and chose two eye caps, their surface rough to keep the eyelids shut. He pushed the drawer with his knee, and a magnetic seal ushered the drawer back in place. Willy hummed a tune as he returned to the side of Amy-Lou. With his forefinger and thumb he eased her eyelid apart and popped in a cap repeating this process to the adjacent eye before taking hold of the pretty dress her parents had sent, then he dressed Amy-Lou, putting the white lace-trimmed ankle socks onto her delicate feet. With care, he brushed her hair, then glued strands of her auburn locks over the damaged skull. He turned her head, just slightly, to disguise the disfigured skull. With the tube of glue still in his hand, he smeared a thin line onto her lips and sealed them together. To finish, he brushed a healthy glow of powder onto her cheeks.

Amy-Lou now rested in a small coffin on a bed of pink silk. She waited for her mummy and daddy to visit.

Eunice had gathered what little strength she had to witness her baby laid out in a coffin. On entering Billy Booker's Funeral Parlour, Eunice dissolved and could walk no further. Led to a room marked *Angels,* Eunice sat with a glass of water in her shaking hand. She could not advance into the depths of the funeral home.

Chaperoned by a woman wearing a neat black skirt suit, Fred approached his child's coffin. He looked down on his beautiful daughter, his love, his friend, his life. He took hold of her cold hand. He tried to rearrange her hair to its usual style, he could not. He kissed his daughter's sealed lips; the lack of warmth ushered his tears. He sobbed over her small frame. 'Daddy's here, I will never leave you, darling.' He held a fist to the left side of his chest. 'You remain here. I will carry you always in my heart. Goodnight my baby. God Bless your soul.'

Directed to the room marked *Angels,* Fred sat down next to Eunice. He took her clasped hand in his. Billy Booker entered the room to address them. 'Are there any items you wish to place in the coffin for Amy Louise?'

'Topsy, the toy dog, the one she loves . . . loved.' Fred said.

'No! Not Topsy, he stays with me. It's all I have. Take one of her teddy bears . . . the pink rabbit.' A colony of soft toys waited on the bed at home for Amy-Lou.

The day of Amy-Lou's funeral arrived. A black hearse glided down the lane. A black limousine was a pace behind. Fred watched out of the window for the arrival of his beloved dead daughter. Upstairs, Eunice sat on the edge of the marital bed. Fred shouted up to her, 'She's here, love. Come down.' Eunice pulled at the crumpled tissue in her hand. Fred opened the front door to a funeral director, neither Billy nor Willy, but a stranger. A tall, slim man with grey hair, who declined the offer to enter the house. He stayed outside with a colleague; their hands clasped in front of their bodies. They were dressed in black with not a speck of dust or a fleck of hair on their perfectly pressed suits. Fred climbed the stairs to collect his wife. Taking her hand he pulled her into a standing position. Placing his arm around her waist to hold her steady, they ambled down the stairs and shuffled outside to the car that waited for them. Eunice refused Fred's suggestion to look at the flowers arranged in her daughter's name. Nor did she look at the coffin which sat on a brass plate shielded by polished glass.

Black cars, black coats, black earth and grey clouds mingled with the myriad of dark emotions. Linda, the single representative from the lane, attended the funeral of Amy-Lou. Pallbearers employed by the funeral home carried the deceased child into the church to the tune of 'A Spoonful of Sugar' from *Mary Poppins*. If anyone realised the irony of the tune playing and its theme for a sweet tooth, they did not acknowledge it. Mourners followed the huddled bereft parents at a respectful distance. The church filled with colleagues and onlookers. The aroma of lilies perfumed the musty, sacred atmosphere. Outside, strangers waited to receive the grief that did not belong to them. When the service came to an end, Fred and Eunice were ushered by a funeral director to stand by the exit of the church. Like waxen figures of sorrow, they received and thanked the mourners. Many tears flowed, many tears were wiped away. Mourners not connected to the deceased departed, in wait for someone else's heartache to come their way.

With its doors open, the black limousine lingered, an embodiment of doom, like a raven in a nursery rhyme. Fred ushered Eunice into the car. She banged her head on the car's roofline but did not wince. The limousine left the church grounds and crept to the cemetery; neither parent looked out of the window. Fresh earth had been dug and artificial grass covered the disruption at the side of a small grave. Wailing started, low and rhythmic as the coffin was lowered into the ground. Eunice grabbed a fistful of soil offered to her by the funeral staff from a tray. She dropped to her knees. Fred lifted his wife to her feet and wrapped his arms around her. She sobbed onto his chest while the handful of soil fell from her fingers.

There was a wake, planned and paid for to celebrate the life of Amy Louise Walker. Fred and Eunice did not attend. They went home to grieve some more.

What a Tragedy

Harry Richard Hamilton lodged near the university in an apartment his father had gifted to him. Richard thought back to his childhood when he visited the house in which he now had an apartment. It had been his grandmother's large Edwardian home. When she died, Richard's father had grieved; his mother had not. His father was the sole inheritor of this house. Richard reminisced further to when he had stood outside this house with his small hand cupped in his father's hand. So acute was this memory that he could feel the skin of his father's calloused hand and replay the conversation of that day. 'Son, this used to be a prestigious area, but not anymore. The house, I'm afraid, has devalued.' Richard absorbed his father's disappointment and tried to squeeze love into the manly hand he held. He had been fascinated by the hubbub of the street they stood on; the neon lights that flashed the sale of food, the litter whipped by the wind, teenagers huddled on street corners like skeletons wrapped in grey skin.

Mr Hamilton Senior was a pragmatist; he supplied the area with the house it required. As the house was near a university it would be ideal for student accommodation, and so he reconstructed the property into separate apartments to let to students. This was his first venture into property development, which inspired him to continue and purchase properties to convert.

As a child, Richard had lived with both parents, a family unit with a fissure about to split. Linda adored her son to distraction but failed to attend her marriage. When Richard reached the age of ten, his father left home. This event was a huge blow to Richard who was unaware of his parents' lack of commitment to each other. An event he never really got over. He decided at an early age never to have faith in relationships again. His childhood had been the happiest of times. On leaving the family, Mr Hamilton Senior settled the mortgage on the family home and gifted the house to Linda. He issued a declaration on the divorce petition that he would provide funding for private education and university fees for his son, and in return, he would no longer support his ex-wife. As an adolescent, Richard lived with his mother on weekdays, convenient for grammar school. Weekends and holidays were spent at this father's house. Whichever home he stayed at, he missed the unity of the other parent.

Hamilton Builders Limited was commissioned to convert a closed-down factory into luxury apartments. The owner of the property was a wealthy and attractive heiress. Before long, Mr Hamilton and the heiress were talking about more than just building matters. Love bloomed, marriage happened, and Mr Hamilton found himself wealthier than ever before. Though Richard was happy with the financial benefits of his father's new marriage he felt deeply for what he perceived to be his mother's loss. He thought her weak for allowing their family to fall apart. Richard was adamant he would never love a woman then leave her in the way his father had left his mother. Rather than creating loyalty within Richard's remit, this ideal had the complete opposite effect and he vowed never to be vulnerable to another.

A bright and articulate individual, Richard studied the legalities of corporate law. Before committing to this choice, he had researched the best way to make money. He read – *If you want to make big money, then corporate law is for you.* He was smitten; insane hours, working under pressure, all appealed to him. He could work for his father's firm with the option to freelance in corporate law. No doors would be closed to him. At twenty-one years of age, Richard was a third-year student on a four-year degree programme.

In the house of apartments, Richard lay on a bed. He looked at the ceiling then turned on his side to admire the tan of the girl who slept beside him. He took a strand of her blonde hair and twisted the honey tones around his finger. She stirred. 'Mm . . . hi, handsome.'

'Sleepyhead. Thanks for last night.'

'Enjoyed being of service. Any plans for the day?' She turned her head to look into his eyes.

'Study. I'll have to love and leave you.' Richard got out of bed. He dressed in the clothes he had discarded in the early hours of that morning. 'You have it nice in here; my father would be impressed.' Richard returned to his penthouse suite. He showered, drank coffee and though he never drank alcohol during the week, he snorted a small amount of cocaine. His conscience was spiked by the chemicals he inhaled. The memory of the thud of the car knocking over the girl caused him to shudder. He inhaled a little more cocaine.

Richard strode up the steps of the university's main entrance. He pulled the handle of the heavy door, individual panes of leaded glass caught the light at different angles, allowing the glass to shimmer. Majestic was the term to describe this building, and privileged were the students who studied there. Inside, Richard climbed the stairs to the top floor. Here the steps were made of stone; smooth indentations from years of use had formed a half-moon edge on each step. He knocked on the door of the principal's turret. 'Come in.' In the small room Richard took the only free seat. He was not content with the mark awarded on his last essay: B plus. 'I'll be with you in a minute,' the principal said. Books and papers littered the room in an organised way. The view from the small window did not do justice to the sweeping grounds. Richard looked away from the catalogued chaos and tried to engage the principal. 'Now, what can I do for you, Richard?'

'Sir, I would like to resubmit this paper.' Richard held out his essay. 'I'm not satisfied with the mark awarded. Though I do agree this essay is only worthy of a B-plus.'

The principal pyramided his fingertips. 'It's a decent mark, Richard. Admittedly, it falls below your usual standard. But a mark is a mark, and yours is a B-plus.'

'I have mitigating circumstances. Sir, I witnessed a fatality . . . no, not the accident, but the aftermath . . . outside my mother's house. A child was killed, run over by a car. The experience has taken its toll on me.'

'I'm sorry to hear that. What a tragedy. It must have been hellish for you. Not something I normally accept – jigging about with results, but under the circumstance, I'll grant you a two-week extension for a resubmission. Is that all?'

'It is, sir, thank you.'

The principal swivelled his chair to face the desk. 'By the way, thank your father for his generous donation. You may want to look at the presentation of your findings. Leave the rest of the essay as it is.'

'Thank you, sir.' Richard closed the door, smiling. On his way to the cafeteria, a group of students, intent on discussing the benefit of space exploration and its positive effect on the world of technology, bumped into Richard. His essay fell to the floor, the papers scattered and exposed a red ring with B-plus at the centre. Jeers from the students infuriated Richard. He was annoyed with himself for allowing his attention to slip, depriving him of a higher grade.

CHAPTER 5

Painkillers

TWO WEEKS HAD PASSED since Amy-Lou's funeral. Eunice had confined herself to bed and this Friday morning was no exception. A gap in the closed bedroom curtain allowed a fleck of daylight into the room. Fresh air in the bedroom had depleted and the smell of a sick person lingered. Fred opened the bedroom door and saw his wife was asleep. For the first time since their trauma, he drew the curtains wide and cracked open a window. Eunice stirred. 'Come on, love,' he said, 'Try to make an effort. We could go for a stroll. It's a beautiful crisp day.'

'I don't want to.' The quilt moved with Eunice as she rolled over to turn away.

Fred went to the kitchen and filled a glass with cold water, which he took back to Eunice, insisting she drank it. 'I think we need the doctor to come and visit you.' He felt her brow as she sipped the water.

'Yes, I think we do.'

Two hours later, the doctor arrived. Fred opened the door wide and guided the doctor to the kitchen. 'She's lost all interest. She won't eat, I have to force her to drink.'

'Understandable, she's grieving.' The doctor kept hold of his bag. He refused the offer of a seat.

'I appreciate that. But my wife has suffered depression in the past. I fear it has returned. It was horrendous the last time when postnatal depression took hold of her. She was incapacitated for months.'

'And, how are you? I can prescribe something for stress.'

Fred sighed. 'No, thank-you I'm fine. I need to be on top of my game for Eunice.' The doctor followed Fred up the stairs to the bedroom.

Seeing Eunice, the doctor asked, 'What's the problem?' She complained of severe back pain. Fred pulled his chin back toward his neck, his eyes grew wide with surprise. The doctor continued, 'I see. Can you sit up for me?'

'No, too painful.'

'Can you lie flat, so I can examine you?'

'No. I need strong painkillers. I need Tramadol.'

'I see.' The doctor was on his way home for lunch, he wrote the prescription of choice, tore it off the pad, and handed it to Fred.

Downstairs in the hall, Fred said, 'I wasn't aware she had back pain, but I am worried about her mental health. Like I said, she has been very ill with depression in the past.'

'Time,' the doctor said. 'The passing of time will heal her.'

The doctor hurried away. Fred stood at his open front door and stared at the prescription in his hand, and said to no-one, 'Right then, I'll go to the chemist.' On his way home from the pharmacy, Fred entered the Red Rose to buy a bunch of flowers to liven the bedroom. The assistant looked at him without comment. Fred chose yellow roses and added a box of chocolates. Back home in the kitchen, Fred prepared a cup of tea and stirred sugar in. He placed the flowers, now in a vase, on a tray, along with the chocolates and the pills, and took them to the bedroom.

Eunice was alert when he entered. She used her elbow to push herself into a sitting position. 'Have you got the painkillers?'

'Yes, dear.'

'Can you bring me a cup of cocoa? I haven't the stomach for more tea . . . and bring a spoon.'

'A spoon? Of course, dear.' He returned with a steaming mug of frothy cocoa.'

'The spoon?'

'Spoon?'

'For God's sake, man, how am I supposed to stir it without a spoon?'

'I stirred it. Why do you . . .' Fred held his breath. Back in front of Eunice, he held the spoon out, like a shield. He sat on the bed.

'You don't need to sit here and watch me drink cocoa. Go back to the garden.'

'I thought you might like some company, but I guess not.' He kissed her forehead before he left the room.

Eunice placed her feet on the floor and looked around the room before standing. She ignored the pretty fresh flowers and focussed attention on a framed picture of Amy-Lou. Topsy, the toy dog, now resided in the marital bedroom. Eunice moved to the dog and said, 'Why did she leave us, Topsy?' She scooped the dog in her arms and put it in bed, its head resting on the pillow. Looking out of the window she saw Fred rounded over a patch of soil. Back at the bed, she pulled the quilt to nestle the dog and sat next to the inanimate object. For a while, Eunice sat with her elbows resting on her parted knees, her head in her hands. With a sigh, she drank several mouthfuls of cocoa to make room for the poison of her choice. She opened the bottle of pills. The child safety lock caused her little difficulty in releasing the gateway to drugs. She tipped the capsules out of their container, then took a capsule from the dip of her nightgown and used her thumbs and forefingers to pull the edible plastic apart to tip the contents over the mug of cocoa. The powder cascaded onto the bed of frothy chocolate. She repeated the process until all the capsules were empty. The jewel-coloured shells tumbled to the floor. She took the spoon and stirred the mound of toxic powder into the cloudy drink. Pinching her nose, she swallowed the lot. With the toy dog in her arms, she lay down, and pulled the quilt over her shoulder. 'Mummy's coming, darling, mummy's coming.' A breeze wafted the lemon curtain when her soul had risen.

Parched Blooms

Richard had pulled his fist by his side and spat out a *yes* when he heard his mother's car had been rear-ended, obliterating the damage he had caused. He wondered why he had not heard from Andrea. Time for him to return to his mother's house. He rang her: 'Hi, can you collect me from the station at five o'clock on Friday?'

'Of course, darling. Or I can block my appointments and drive down to pick you up?'

'No, the station's fine. I've a paper to work on so I can use the time spent on the train.' Richard terminated the call.

Linda's car had been repaired to a high standard. The garage deserved its good reputation. Friday afternoon, a cancelled lesson gave Linda time for leisure, so she took a bucket of hot soapy water to the cobbled lane to sponge the grime of her car. She unreeled the hosepipe to spray the suds away. After drying the car with a chamois leather, she finished the job with a polish. The lid of the polish tin slipped out of her hand and rolled down the cobbles onto the lane, where a gutter stopped its journey. Linda chased after the lid, but before she bent to retrieve it, she saw Fred standing outside his gate. 'Hi,' she shouted over to him.

'Hello, Linda.'

She crossed the road to speak with him. 'How's Eunice?'

'Not good. She's taken to her bed, and to top it all she has a bad back apparently. Says she can't cope with people's sympathy and all that.' He swept his hand in the direction of the decaying floral display. The parched blooms hung their heads in sorrow. 'Actually, I'm quite worried about her. Linda, let me ask you, do you think it improper to dismantle all this? But then again, I don't have the stomach to clear it. I was going to sift through the gifts, read tributes, organise and file things but . . .'

'Richard will be here in an hour. If you like, I'll ask him to get rid of, er, clear it away.'

'Would he? That would be marvellous.'

Linda screwed the lid onto the tin of polish. 'Consider it done.' She returned to the cobbled lane to tidy away the cleaning apparatus, then changed into her smart casual clothes before making her way to the train station.

Richard stepped out of the train's first-class compartment. He walked to the exit of the station. His shoulder pulled to one side from the weight of his bag. 'Hello, Mother.'

'Hi, darling. It's so lovely to see you.' On the car journey home, they chatted until Linda drove onto the lane. 'Oh, yes, can you nip across the road and get rid of all that?' She extended her arm to the withered display.

'Me! Why should I clear it?'

'Because it's a caring thing to do for a neighbour, and I said you would. I can't do it. I'm at the dentist in half an hour, and it'll be dark when I get back. I'll walk to the dentist. You use the car for the tip run.' She parked the car on the cobbles then looked at Richard. 'Please Richard, those poor parents have to witness that every day.'

'You offered. You clear it. You're too community-spirited.'

In the kitchen, Linda opened a cupboard; a can of air freshener fell to the floor. She picked it up and out of habit sprayed the room. Reaching back into the cupboard she pulled out a roll of black bin liners and handed them to Richard. 'Please, Richard, do it for me.'

After finishing hoeing the soil and as Fred could not tempt his wife to take a walk on this crisp Friday, he collected the skeleton leaves from the lawn and carried a pile of them to the compost heap, where several would find their way back to the lawn. He had told Eunice that when the ground softened, he would plant new shrubs and flowers and they could watch them grow. He straightened his back and grimaced. Held his waist with the palm of his hand. He looked up to their bedroom window. 'I'll have one of your painkillers later, dear,' he said to the fluttering lemon curtain. He filled his lungs with air and held it for a moment. At the back door, he took his muddy rubber shoes off and entered the kitchen in his stocking-feet. He lumbered to the stack of dirty pots in the sink then switched on the tap for hot water to flow. Fred finished pot washing, wiped the table, and hung the pot towel over the handle of the Aga. He put his fist into the small of his back as if to test if the pain was still present. 'A soak in the bath is what I need.' He was getting accustomed to talking to himself.

The doctor had diagnosed Claire as suffering from post-traumatic stress and prescribed medication to calm her nerves. Claire rounded the bend at the bottom of the lane, taking the walk her mum had insisted on. It was the first time she had chosen courage from her mangled emotions to walk past the scene of the accident. She could not avoid the area, not when Richard was in residence. She saw him and inhaled fresh air deep into her lungs increasing her heartbeat. She took a pill out of her pocket and popped it into her dry mouth creating saliva to swallow the drug. Increasing her gait she greeted Richard. 'Hi,' she said, to his back as he stretched to collect items off the gate. She stared at the band of his underwear.

At the start of their now troubled relationship, Richard had lavished time, gifts and money on Claire.

He had taken her to the best hotels for weekend stays. He had been attentive, almost to the point of smothering. Claire always believed she could reignite his appetite for her.

'How are you?' he asked.

Claire knew better than to unburden her true state of emotion. 'I do feel better, but I'm still off work. I keep experiencing . . . keep expecting something awful to happen. I've avoided this area, but today . . . and you're here. Why haven't you returned my calls?'

Richard clicked his tongue. 'I thought it best to give you space. You've had a lot to deal with.' A car drove past and skidded to a stop. Claire froze. Wide-eyed she looked in the direction of the screeching tyres. 'Easy Girl, you're way too tense.' Richard placed his hand on her arm. She covered his hand with hers and felt the warmth of his skin, he pulled his hand away. Claire stared at the soft toys, the ones that waited to be loved.

'I didn't see her, the dead girl. She must have been flat on the road. I'm sure of it. Dad's having leaflets printed to hand out; to ask if anyone saw the child lying on the road.'

'Leaflets! It was raining hard, that's why you didn't see the kid. Have you considered that?'

'Maybe, but I don't think so. It looks as though I'll lose my licence; dangerous or careless driving. Anyway, I don't care. I never want to drive again.'

'Tell your dad not to waste his money on leaflets. It's pointless. I need to get on and finish this.' He looked in the direction of the decaying mess.

'I can help.'

'Please do. Grab a sack.'

'Richard, can I come around tonight?' She scooped some cards off the ground and shoved them into a limp sack.

'I'm busy.'

'Please, Richard.'

'Maybe . . . I'll text you.' He wrinkled his nose. 'Go home and take a bath. You look as though you could use a rest.'

Claire walked home with a slight bounce to her step.

Richard ripped the remainder of dead flowers off the gate, leaving the fasteners in situ. Slime from an early floral offering trailed on his hand. Its rotten smell reminded him of the breath of a woman he had paid good money to visit. He cursed his mother and wiped his hand on a teddy bear. He gathered the soft toys and rammed them into a black sack. The stagnant flowers greeted the fluffy toys of comfort. The sack split and the contents fell out. *Shit! Why did I agree to this?* He tore the fifth bag off the roll. The trio of hollow candles chased the cuddly toys into the new sack.

Richard reversed Linda's car off the cobbled lane and parked it by the side of the Walkers' gate. The learner sign stayed on top of the car as the boot space was needed for the harvested black sacks. He yanked the deflated balloon free from the lamppost and shoved it on top of the bags now loaded in the boot. He drove to the refuse tip, with no consideration of saving mementoes – nobody had asked him to.

Filling the bathtub with hot water caused steam to thicken the atmosphere. Fred threw in some bath salts then eased himself into the welcoming heat of the water.

Tepid water woke Fred. He slid upwards, slopping water over the edge of the bath. Wrapped in a fluffy white towel, he wandered to the bedroom to gather his loungewear. He opened the bedroom door carefully, noticing his wife's motionless body under the quilt, he crept out of the bedroom, leaving the door ajar. He redressed in his gardening clothes and retrieved his much-needed glasses. Downstairs, he switched on the television and turned the volume to low, then settled into his comfy chair where he soon drifted off to sleep.

When he woke again it was evening and the only light was the glow from the television. The enormity of the loss of his daughter and the state of his wife had taken its toll. 'I think I'll retire to bed,' he whispered as he switched off the television. In the dark bedroom he closed the window against the cold and drew the curtains against the night. Without switching on his bedside lamp, he kissed Eunice on her cold cheek, whispered good night, then fell into a deep sleep.

Richard took time to work on his paper for resubmission after carrying out this neighbourly duty of liberating the gate of grief. Then with no intention of inviting Claire to come over, he splashed Erudite aftershave onto his face, and in case he got lucky, he ladled more of the erotic scent into his pubic hair. At the front door he shouted to his mother, 'I'm going out. Don't wait up.'

Linda dropped the knitting from her knee and scrambled to the hall. 'You're going out? I thought you were going to the Red Rose for wine. I've made your favourite dinner.'

'Tomorrow night. I promise.' Richard offered his cheek and Linda kissed it. The taxi waited in the middle of the road, covering the spot where Amy-Lou had died. Linda peered through the curtain to watch her son be driven away. The aroma from his aftershave lingered.

Richard expected Andrea to be out on the town. He entered the same club as the last time they had connected. Approaching the bar to order a shot, he said to the barman, 'Line up six.'

A woman Richard had coupled with in the past sashayed up to him 'Hey, big boy, how's my royal highness?'

'Push off.' Richard turned his back to her smile.

She took her handbag off the bar and walked round to put her face in line with his. 'Piss off! Who in the hell do you think you are?' She stormed to the ladies-room. Richard slugged his last shot.

Outside, Richard scanned the crowd for Andrea. He recognised the crew she had danced with when he kissed her. Someone grabbed his arm. With a clenched fist he yanked his arm free and turned to face his assailant. 'Sorry I didn't mean to alarm you,' Andrea said.

'Hell girl, you've got one hell of a grip.'

A giggle ignited her eyes. 'Have you just got here?' She collected her hair in one hand and swished the lock over her shoulder then tilted her head in line with the mane of hair. Richard looked over her head to feign interest in the crowd. 'Come for a drink with me at the club?' She asked.

He stared into her eyes. 'No, you come with me for a bite to eat.'

'Okay, sure. I'll just let my friends know.'

Richard and Andrea entered the Italian ristorante. 'Mr Ricardo, this way please, our best table for you and your lady.' Richard and Andrea sat opposite each other. Piped Baroque music floated in the background. She surveyed the room and exuded indifference to the rich dark wood, the eclectic art, and the huge vintage crystal chandelier. She paid attention to the single red rose, ready to bloom, in the slim vase to the side of the table.

'So, how've you been?' she asked.

'Good.' He took hold of her hand and turned it over to stroke her palm. With his free hand he clicked his fingers to alert the waiter. 'Il menu per favore,' Richard said.

Andrea took her hand from his hold. A half-smile lighted her eyes. She chose a delicate pasta, free from garlic.

'Per due, con uno bottiglia di Burin.' Richard added a bottle of wine to the duplicated order. His eyes did not leave Andrea's.

'When did you learn to speak Italian?'

'Father has a villa at Lake Como. I've been going for years. I'll take you. It's beautiful, like you.'

They ate their meal through chit-chat. Andrea ordered two scoops of ice-cream. Richard ordered a shot of sambuca. The small glass of liquor arrived with a coffee bean on top: tradition has the liquor set alight, but Richard held his hand out to indicate no; he did not want the alcohol content to evaporate. He asked, 'So tell me, what do you do? Are you a student?' He wiped a smudge of ice-cream off her lower lip, then edged his thumb into her mouth before easing his thumb away.

Her cheeks were on fire. 'I'm a legal secretary.'

'That's a coincidence, I'm a law student.'

'I know.'

Richard beckoned the waiter. 'Il conti per favore.' He paid the bill, adding a generous tip.

Andrea mouthed, 'I'm nipping to the loo.'

The capo cameriere thanked Richard for his custom. 'Prego,' Richard replied. He too went to the restroom to use the toilet cistern, to chop, line and inhale cocaine. He inhaled deeply consuming every speck before stepping out into the cold night air. Beads of sweat pearled his forehead. He knew of a shaded place to take Andrea, behind the ristorante.

In the restroom, Andrea looked into the gilded mirror to reapply her lipstick. 'Get a grip,' she told her reflection. After putting the lipstick back in her bag, she snapped the clasp shut. Richard had not waited for her so she left the ristorante. She saw him, his back lent against a wall, his feet apart to leave room for her to stand between. She wandered over to him, one high-heeled foot in front of the other.

'Come here,' he whispered. He pulled her close to kiss her and tasted her lipstick. She responded to his open mouth with her tongue. He took hold of her hand and led her to the shadows where he caressed her lips with his. The buzz from the street, the whisper of distant music, the clatter of bottles chucked in the recycle bin, did not appear to penetrate their world. She returned his kiss, then pulled away. With his arm around the small of her back, Richard held her in place. He moved his head forward to counteract the distance she had put between them. He continued to devour her responsive mouth. He lifted her miniskirt, and his smooth fingers stroked the flesh between her thighs. He sensed it was too much for her – this rush of lust she was experiencing.

'No!' She pushed him away.

'Why?' he moaned.

'It's too soon.'

'Shame, what a perfect moment.' He readjusted the crotch of his trousers.

Andrea's face flushed from Richard's already light stubble. She looked to his mouth, wet with their connection. 'It's too soon,' she repeated. A catch in her voice. Walking away from temptation, she made her way to the street, to the safety of onlookers. Richard took care of his desire and settled his penis back to its natural position. He joined her on the street. 'Can we go dancing?' Andrea asked. The blush of passion radiated her cheeks making her even more beautiful.

'No. You go ahead. Catch up with your friends.'

'Where are you going?'

'Home.' He took his telephone out of his pocket and asked for her number. With a smile on her face, she recited the digits. He kissed the top of her head inhaling coconut oil. He watched Andrea melt into the crowd. He looked at the screen of his telephone and scrolled the contact list. He placed a request. Then strode over to the taxi rank to jump into a waiting a cab.

You're the Best

While Richard had been clearing the debris from the memorial gate at the Walkers', PJ had walked down the lane, with Kerry Langford six steps behind him, decreasing to four. Spurred on by her colleagues, she had shot out of the salon when PJ left the garage. Almost overtaking him, Kerry called his name, 'PJ, wait up.' He turned his head and slowed his pace, thinking she had a message for Andrea. 'Hi. I've been meaning to catch you. Terrible what happened the other Friday. Did you see where the girl came from? Claire is convinced that the kid was already flat on the road.'

'No, I . . .'

'Never mind. Do you fancy going for a drink tonight, with me?'

'Me! Mm.' PJ intended to spend the evening and most of the night gaming. Shocked at the invite he replied, 'Yeah, sure.' A smile spread over his face and reached his eyes, they sparked to life. PJ, in common with his sister, had the bluest of turquoise eyes, a family gene, and Kerry smiled at them.

'Cool. I'll meet you outside the new cocktail bar in town – Melange. Say eight?'

'Okay. Where's that?'

'Opposite the town hall! I would say come with me, but I'll be in town earlier with the girls from work.'

'Oh, I'll see you there.'

PJ entered his house and made a coffee then went to his room to clear his head with a game of Lore. PJ was a gaming addict. He mostly played Lore and he was a pro. Eager to reach level six he switched the computer on. Climbing the heights of Lore quicker than anticipated caused excitement to ride in his belly. If he reached level ten before the end of the month he would be invited to participate in the tournament. Listening to the whir of the computer's hard drive, he waited for the internet to connect. The novelty of being asked out by Kerry robbed him of concentration on the game. Wondering what to wear he paused at the lopsided door of the wardrobe. The door hung open and emitted a blaze of colour into the room – purple, gold and red, not from

74

the clothes, but from the posters stuck to all available sides of the closet. The posters displayed King Kreep, the nemesis of Lore, at his finest. PJ looked into the hollow at the absence of coat hangers, he stared at the heap of grey and denim. After checking the time on his prestige watch he ordered a taxi to take him into town.

At a high-end clothing shop, an assistant helped PJ choose some new attire. A pair of fine-wool trousers in navy-blue were presented to him, with a pale-blue striped shirt. The assistant suggested tan brogues and a tan belt. In front of the ornate full-length mirror, PJ smiled at his transformation. The assistant had recommended against buying a jacket, though it cost her commission. She told him, 'Nobody wears a jacket on a night out in this town.' He paid for the ensemble. Rarely did he spend money on anything other than gaming. Then nipped into the chemist to buy aftershave, an expensive one, popular with the ladies, the pharmacist told him. The thought of buying condoms did not enter his head. After getting fixed up quicker than expected, he had time enough to walk home; another taxi would be an extravagance too far. On the lane he averted his eyes from the Walkers' residence. Carrying his fancy carrier bags, he dragged his burden of unease up the lane.

PJ dumped the bags in his room. He showered, then dressed in his new clothes. Checking the watch he never took off, and with time to spare, he logged onto the computer. The screen mirrored the hue of the colours from his wardrobe. He typed his name and added his character to the game. Seconds ticked by before other contestants joined him. PJ's fingers marched over the keyboard at a terrific speed. His attention was gripped by the black and white images. He zipped through the forest of dead trees, skidding over and swerving past fallen logs and broken branches. Having accomplished this area, he found himself at the water's edge. He paused, rotated the view on the screen, and determined there was no other way than to plunge into the murky water and swim down. Beneath the layer of scum, the water was clear. He zoomed his character to the bed of the reservoir and crept up behind his assailant. PJ sat forward in his chair and clicked to advance his character – boom! He had captured and destroyed a key opponent. *Victory* flashed across the screen. The sound of magnified claps with cheers filled his small room. He checked his watch to calculate if there was time to fit in another level, another achievement. He now regretted his date with Kerry as he wished to stay home and charge ahead in the rankings. He was on fire today.

PJ ripped the cellophane off the aftershave. A virgin aftershave user, he was taken aback by the tingle on his skin. He pounded down the stairs. A waft of the exquisite scent slinked under Andrea's bedroom door. The aroma whipped up her nose. She ran down the stairs after her brother. 'Hang on, where are you going?'

'Out.'

'I can see that. What aftershave are you wearing?'

'Erudite.' PJ had studied the label.

'Oh, okay. Have a good time.' He knew that, in her own way, Andrea loved him.

PJ intended to arrive at the cocktail bar before Kerry. Outside Melange he checked his back-pocket to make sure his wallet sat there. In his new clothes he fitted in perfectly with the revellers around him. Kerry headed his way, a perfect modern girl with her hair fashioned in the latest style. A beam from a united smile connected the pair. 'Hi, you,' she said, linking her arm through his. They melted into the crowd and headed inside the bar.

The ceiling in the Melange cocktail bar was littered with sunken spotlights shining a cool blue. Techno tunes competed with the chatter of party people. Jostled together by the congregation, PJ, at Kerry's request, ordered two mojitos – one of which was a mocktail. PJ was bemused to see leaves of green in the cool liquid. 'Mint,' Kerry informed him. She giggled at his expression. 'Taste it, it's delicious.' She sucked on the straw of her virgin drink. PJ discarded the straw and swallowed the liquor, a mint leaf stuck to his tooth. Kerry placed her tongue to her tooth then pointed at him. 'You've got mint on your tooth.'

He remembered a line from one of Andrea's magazines. 'It'll be in your mouth in a minute.' He pulled at his shirt collar as his ears turned pink.

'Cheeky!'

Using his tongue to dislodge the piece of mint, PJ chewed it. A couple who shared a seat stood to leave the crowded bar. Kerry grabbed PJ's hand and pulled him to the white leather settee. She caught the waiter's attention to order a chocolate Martini for PJ and a virgin mudslide for herself. 'How come you don't drink alcohol?' PJ asked.

'Because, I mm . . . don't like the taste.' They chatted and giggled. 'Can we go to La Vita? You okay with that?'

'Sure. What's La Vita?'

Through laughter, Kerry sprayed a mouthful of drink. 'It's a nightclub; everyone knows that.'

'Oh yeah, that La Vita.' PJ took another swig of his drink in an attempt to disguise his ignorance. Leaving the cocktail bar Kerry shivered, and buoyed by alcohol, PJ put his arm around her. She snuggled into him. Inside the club, they made their way to the bar. PJ ordered a bottle of beer and a sparkling water. The latest dance tunes boomed into their space. With the music pulsating, Kerry tried to coax PJ onto the dancefloor. He refused. Tired of shouting over the music, Kerry led PJ outside. Hand in hand they sauntered home. At her front door she pulled him close to kiss him. With instinct he responded to her long and searching kiss. She took a step back and said, 'You look so handsome and smell divine.'

'Do I? Thanks. You too . . . not handsome, I mean.'

'I know. Do you want to go out again? With me.'

'Yeah. When, tomorrow? We could meet—'

'No, come here to my house. Say after lunch?'

'Right then.' He looked up and down the street. 'Can't wait for tomorrow,' he added.

'It's been lovely.'

'Me too!' PJ waited for Kerry to enter her house before he turned to go. Despite his resolution, he stole a glance at the Walkers' house to see remnants of fasteners clinging to the gate. Guilt came to ride with him again, but he was experienced in burying unwanted emotions.

He hurried up the lane to his house. With the key poised in his hand, PJ's attention was drawn by the hammering of high-heeled shoes from the pavement on the opposite side of the lane. The clatter of heels belonged to Claire as she marched down Priory Lane. She wore a low-cut see-through blouse and her short skirt exposed her lace topped stockings. PJ entered his house and went upstairs. He was not in the frame of mind to smoke a joint, nor after drinking alcohol, did he wish to switch his computer on. He went to bed.

After leaving Andrea in town Richard got out of a taxi at the bottom of Priory Lane. He walked the remaining distance, turned up the cobbled lane, past his mother's car, and through the gate. He followed the path to the back garden then climbed five steps to the garden's summer house where Claire waited. Feasting his eyes on her, he said, 'Hi, doll.' He opened the door of the summer house for them to enter.

Richard pulled Claire to the rattan settee in the dimly lit hut. He sat; Claire knew to remain standing. Richard lifted her skirt. He shuddered, making her aware of his desire on seeing her lack of underwear. He nibbled at her breasts through the gauze fabric in the way he was familiar with. A wave, first small and elusive rolled and crashed through his whole being. An orgasm flooded and rode through him. With a final thrust Richard lent back. 'Claire, you're the best.' She nestled into him and kissed his neck. When passion floated away, Richard told her to go home.

The house was dark and silent when Claire returned home. She closed the front door with care and tiptoed to her room carrying her shoes by the heel. She stripped off the clothes she wore to allure Richard and hid them in a drawer. Naked, she slid between the cotton sheets of her bed and luxuriated in her recollection of the night. How Richard had chased away her anxiety, whispering his love for her, told her what an amazing body she had. She blanked out his question: 'Are you up to date with contraception?' She had lied to him, said she was, and prayed she would fall pregnant to have a hold on him forever. Uninvited, an image of the poor dead girl popped into her head. Claire reached over to the bedside cabinet and released one too many anxiety pills, then swallowed them without liquid.

Andrea returned home from her night of dining with Richard. The streetlighting threw pockets of warmth over the lane. In the house Andrea filled a glass with water then went upstairs. She undressed then looked into the full-length mirror, she smiled at her reflection. She murmured Richard's name then linked his surname to her, 'Andrea Hamilton'. She felt on the brink of change.

CHAPTER 6

The Red Button

DAYLIGHT ARRIVED and lit the lemon curtains, inviting a pleasant hue into the bedroom. Rested, Fred reached his arm over to his wife's body. He patted the mound her hip had made. 'Morning,' he said. He took his glasses from the bedside cabinet and put them on to stare at the ceiling. He took a deep breath before throwing back the duvet then slipped his feet into the waiting slippers. He walked to the window and pulled the curtains wide allowing light to flood the room. 'Eunice, it's weekend, time for you to leave your bed. Come on now, wakey-wakey. Bad back or not, at least come downstairs and watch television.'

He sauntered over to her side of the bed then stopped abruptly at the sight of the capsule shells scattered on the floor. The empty medicine bottle on its side. The fallen empty mug. 'What the . . .' He dragged the duvet off his wife's body. 'Eunice! What have you done?' He grabbed her by the shoulders to pull her up, the toy dog trapped under her arm, then he shook her. 'Eunice,

Eunice, don't do this . . . Eunice!' He released his hold on her, she fell like a corpse. He slapped his forehead. 'That bastard girl, that fucking Claire. She'll pay for this, taking our baby from us.' He paced the room. 'I told the doctor you were ill. Would he listen? No, he's the expert! Well not about you he isn't. I'm that expert!' He shook Eunice, he kissed her cold, porcelain skin. He took the toy dog from her side and flung the object across the room. The dog hit the wall and fell to the floor; a smile still planted on its face.

At the same time, PJ was the only resident in his house out of bed. He stepped into a pair of clean overalls, contorting his body to pull them on. The red button fell out of the overall pocket. He took hold of the shiny object and frowned. After experiencing a turn in the washing machine, the button from Amy-Lou's coat was unharmed. Out of respect, and as a penance for his guilt, PJ placed the red button by the side of his computer. The sight of this tiny red object sunk his heart and robbed him of his growing confidence, but he reckoned he deserved to feel this way and left the button as a reminder before leaving the house to serve the morning at the garage.

Richard awoke to the aroma of bacon. He yawned, ruffled his hair and remembered the nightmare he had slept through: Screaming children clawed at his body before the rain came and washed the entangled children down a stream, all the while he was glued to the middle of the road.

With a feeling of unease, Richard went to the bathroom. He returned to his room and dressed then

82

wandered into the kitchen where his mother greeted him. 'Morning, darling, did you have a good night?' She shook the frying pan to allow the bacon to sizzle.

'Nothing special. I should have stayed home with you.'

'Well, you're staying in tonight.' She tipped the bacon onto a warmed plate. 'Did you meet anyone special?' She opened the window allowing the smell of fried meat to escape. After winking at her, he took hold of a piece of bacon and bit into the flesh, then pulled the meat off the rind with his teeth. Linda buttered muffins.

While Kerry waited for PJ to finish his morning's shift, she sprang out of bed to take a shower washing her hair to restyle it. The purple streaks had faded amongst her auburn locks; she would try pale-blue next week. In the kitchen she sat opposite to her mum, and said, 'I'm not coming shopping.'

'Kerry, you promised. It's the first Saturday we've had off together in ages.'

'Don't look so worried. I've got a date.'

'Who with?'

'PJ, you know the guy who lives up the lane. Andrea's brother? He works at the garage facing Cutz.'

'When did you get with him?'

'Last night. At La Vita, the club I go dancing with the girls.' Disclosure of going to a cocktail bar would have been reason for concern.

'Was Claire out?'

'No, she hasn't been out since the accident, and anyway she doesn't get on with Andrea.'

'Oh dear. So, what sort of name is PJ?'

'His name. Don't start finding fault.'

'As if . . . have you told him? You know you'll have to if it gets serious.'

'Mum! I'm not discussing that.'

Claire usually liked to have a lie-in on Saturday mornings but since the accident, she always woke early. Slinging her long legs over the side of her bed she sat up. She looked down on her nakedness and smiled at her voluptuous, pert breasts, which on her slim frame magnified in size. She revelled in the delight of Richard, and what she had received from him last night. She inspected her body for bite marks, her smile grew wider when she found two. She slipped on her dressing gown and out of a growing habit popped two of her anxiety pills in her mouth. She examined the blister pack of pills and frowned. *Would the doctor give me more?* She sauntered down the stairs. 'Morning,' she said.

'Someone sounds a little perkier,' Jenny said.

'Do you know, I do feel better, but I'll be glad when the hearing is out of the way.'

'That's the spirit,' John added.

'Time,' she paraphrased between a mouthful of crunch, 'is a healer.'

'I'm glad to see you're more settled,' Jenny said.

John pushed his empty bowl away. 'We're going for the leaflets I've had printed. You never know, someone's memory might be jogged. When we have them, we'll go and distribute them. Are you coming, to help?'

'I think you're wasting time and money. I can't see the point.'

'The point is, *young lady*, you're convinced the girl was already down on the road. If that's true and someone can verify this, your culpability could be minimised.' John shook his head.

'Leave it, Dad. Just accept I'll lose my licence.'

'Claire! It could be a lot more serious than that.' John turned to his wife. 'It might help her court case to have a witness.'

Claire put her spoon down. 'See! I feel sick now.'

'Leave her, John.'

'She should fight for her licence. She should fight for her future.' John took his mug of tea to the garage.

After leaving Claire at home, John drove down the lane, with Jenny by his side. They listened to radio chit-chat. Jenny looked out of the window as they passed the Walkers' house. She could see a ribbon, collapsed on the lamppost, the knot from a balloon held there. John flicked the indicator down for a left turn. Jenny's eyes followed the road. At the junction, John waited for a break in the traffic. Back on the road, he flicked for a right turn and drove onto the unmade road of the industrial estate. Most of the units on the estate were closed, their steel shutters pulled down for the weekend.

John parked the car. Jenny stepped out, straightening her skirt. They could hear the clatter of a printing press; they inhaled the airborne fumes. 'These leaflets had better be ready,' Jenny said. They entered the premises through a side door, left open to let heat escape from the press. A desk, littered with papers, was pushed against a wall. They waited in the cluttered room. Jenny popped her head into the mouth of the production room, where a light bulb cast a shadow. 'Hello!' She shouted. A brass bell was prominent on the littered desk. Jenny marched over and bounced her palm on the plunger; this action alerted no-one. 'This is ridiculous,' she said, rubbing the indent on her palm. From her canvas bag, chosen to match an outfit she no longer wore, she freed her mobile phone from its compartment and selected *Printing Press*. John startled when the shrill ring from the desk's telephone pierced the room. A woman with indigo fingers appeared through the door's hollow. Jenny slid her thumb over the phone's screen to disconnect the call.

'Too late,' the lady printer said. 'Ah, the leaflets, I'll just get them.' She disappeared into the room of clatter. On returning she carried a box with a leaflet taped on top: a picture of Priory Lane, taken on an ordinary day, to show the scene of the fateful accident. The cardboard box was slapped onto the counter. John handed over a cheque then took hold of the box. 'Hang on,' the woman said. 'Tara said something about this. Tara!' A teenage girl came to the doorway, wearing dungarees. She had a ring pierced through her nose and a tattoo on her neck. John and Jenny shared a look. 'Tara, didn't you say something about this?' The lady pointed to the box tucked under John's arm.

'Oh yeah, about the girl. Jeff at the paper said he would be interested in doing a feature.'

John stepped into the conversation. 'I'd be willing to speak with him. Jeff, you say?'

'His number's right there.' Tara pointed to a copy of the local paper. 'Ask for Jeff Winslow.'

'Can I take that copy?'

'Sure.' The lady with indigo fingers cleared some letters off the newspaper. 'Here.' She shoved the folded newspaper under John's arm, on top of the box.

Back home, Jenny made a pot of tea. She changed her shoes, comfortable ones for walking. Waiting for John to finish his drink, she wandered into the hall. Through the frosted glass of the front door a mass of red was evident as the postman headed up the drive. The letterbox creaked and the correspondence was trapped in the flap. Jenny freed the letter addressed to her daughter. After scrutinising the postmark, she flipped the envelope over to read the return address: Crown Prosecution Service. 'John! It's a letter for Claire from the court.' She held the letter out to him. He ripped the seal open and took out the letter then flicked the letter from its three-fold. 'Read it out,' Jenny said. She sat on the bottom stair, to steady her legs.

John scanned the typewritten letter: 'Prosecutors pursuant . . . causing death dangerous slash careless driving. Contrary to Section 2B of the Road Traffic Act 1988.' His sight fell on the bold lettering of his daughter's name. He lowered the letter. 'Claire's attending court in four weeks.' Jenny's complexion lost the shine it once had. 'We'd better employ a solicitor. Where's Claire?' He asked.

'Leave her be. She's gone back to bed. She's not sleeping well. I heard her up and about last night. I might have been dreaming, but I'm sure she went out for a walk.'

'Well, there's not a lot we can do about this letter on a Saturday. May as well crash on, bloody hell! Move on and deliver the leaflets. Are you still coming?'

'Yes, I want to help.' She took their coats off the hook.

With lust coursing through Richard's loins, he pushed his face flat against the cream bedroom wall to direct his vision to Andrea's house. But his attention was caught by the green and yellow emblazoned vehicle parked across the road. Linda shouted up the stairs, 'Richard, what are you doing? Come and have a cup of tea.' Richard heard her ascend the stairs.

Linda sidled up to her son. She slung her arm around his waist. She looked down on the roof of the quick response vehicle.

'Wonder what's happened there?' she said.

'What?' He no longer referred to the Walkers' by name.

'Eunice . . . she's not at all well.' Linda tilted her head back to look at her son. She tapped the side of her head and pulled her lips in a tight sorrowful line.

Richard doubled his mother's appraisal. He pointed a finger to his temple and made a circular movement. 'Cuckoo.'

'Richard! That's too unkind.'

'Sorry Mother. Disrespectful, I know. I'll have coffee.'

Kerry dressed in boyfriend jeans, a tangerine jumper and sneakers. She applied mascara to her lashes and nude lipstick to her lips. Looking out of the window, she saw the emergency response vehicle parked across the road. She peered up the lane but there was no sign of PJ returning from work. She opened a drawer and took out a file to perfect the shape of her nails.

PJ returned home from the garage earlier than expected. Before going to Kerry's house as arranged, he switched on his computer. All morning at work, he had played the game in his head to perfect the moves he would make. Online, he connected to the other gamers who shared his passion. He shouted through the microphone attached to his headset. His father and Andrea no longer paid attention to the occasional cries of excitement coming from his room. PJ searched for his adversary amongst the quivering and bright purple moonscape, enticing the villain out from behind the spacecraft then pouncing on his prey, wiping the enemy out with a strike. PJ worked the keyboard like a magician in a crowd. He sat forward in his chair. 'Come on! What's next?' He heard, before he saw, an army marching, their leader Dom at the helm. 'Come on you fucker! I'll have you.' PJ fired a single missile and Dom was brought to his knees. Edging further on his seat. Bleep . . . bleep: his watch declared it was time for him to meet Kerry. 'Shit!' *What to do? What to do?* His attention was compromised by the red button off Amy-Lou's raincoat. Taking the button in his hand he made a fist around it. With his eyes closed, his conscience screamed – *Inform the police.* But then the doubts kicked in. *What good would that do? It wouldn't bring the kid back to life. And Claire had driven over her.* His mind sprinted to the accident, to when he should have looked after the girl. He took a deep breath and placed the button back. Logging off from the game, he changed his clothes, splashed on some aftershave, and left the house. In the lane he stared at the blaze of green and yellow from the paramedic's vehicle parked outside the Walkers' house. Air rushed to his lungs, he forced it out before heading to Kerry's house.

'PJ,' Richard shouted, as PJ passed the cobbled lane. 'I want a word.'

PJ halted, and through habit, looked away from Richard, but courage cruised his veins, and he looked Richard in the eye. 'What?'

'Are we cool?'

'With what?'

'Don't be smart, the business over the road?'

'What business?'

'Exactly! I like your style.' Richard smiled, a smile of relief. He went to pat PJ on the arm, but PJ rolled his shoulder back.

As Kerry popped her head out of the door, she saw PJ in conversation with Richard. PJ approached her. 'What did he want?' she said.

'Nothing.'

'Has that arsehole upset you? You seem a bit, well, shaken.'

'No, it's just, he was asking about—'

'I know, he was asking after Andrea, and you're not happy about it. He's a player. You should warn your sister.'

'Yeah, that's it. What's she doing with him?'

'All the girls fancy Richard; not me though.' Kerry turned to walk down the hall to the kitchen. Her ponytail swished with each step. Taking two cans of Pepsi out of the fridge she handed him one.

'Thanks.' He pulled the ring-tab and guzzled the fizzy liquid.

'So?' She asked, 'what do you want to do?'

'I don't know.'

'Go to the park?'

'Sounds good to me.'

She took hold of her coat. 'Come on, before my mum gets home.'

Richard watched PJ and Kerry walk down the lane, arm in arm. He took his hand out of his jogger pocket and, without smartening his appearance, he crossed the road by the paramedic vehicle and headed up the lane to visit Andrea.

He knocked on her door and a short while later the door opened. 'Hi,' said Andrea. She took hold of her hair from the back of her neck and placed the silk locks around her left shoulder.

'Hi, Gorgeous.' Richard gave a slow, measured wink.

Andrea's dad shouted from the kitchen, 'Is it Bill?'

'No Dad, it's for me.' She lowered her voice. 'Bill is Dad's drinking buddy.'

'Sorry, is this a bad time?'

'No, it's just . . .' She pulled the door behind her, leaving it ajar.

'Fancy hooking up tonight?'

'I can't. It's my friend's eighteenth. But you can come with me?'

'No thanks. How about next week?'

'Yes, definitely. Friday?'

'Sure, Friday it is.' He leant to kiss her, to whisper 'sexy' in her ear. But Andrea leant back and the door crashed open.

'Is that Bill?'

'No Dad!' Andrea's cheeks flushed as she said goodbye to Richard. With his hand held high to signify his departure, Richard strode down the lane.

Linda stepped out of the back door to check on the garden's summer house. She was startled by her son. 'You made me jump. I thought you were in your room.'

'I nipped out for air. The paramedic is still across the road.'

'Oh dear, that poor family. I can't begin to imagine.'

Richard put his arm around his mother. 'Well, you don't have to. I'm going to catch the three o'clock train. I need to study.'

'You said you were staying 'till Sunday! I thought we were spending this evening together?' She picked at a piece of skin to the side of her thumbnail.

'If you are going to put pressure on me, I'll stop coming altogether. I've not been to Father's in ages.'

'You're right. I'm sorry . . . you're a young man, you don't want your mother nagging you.'

With his bag over his shoulder, Richard asked, 'Can you take me to the station?'

'What, now?'

'I fancy a coffee and a newspaper.' He collected Linda's keys to speed her along. Linda backed the car onto the lane. With her son sat by her side, she slid the gearstick into first and aimed the car down Priory lane.

Hand in hand, PJ and Kerry strolled through the open wrought-iron gates into the park. Saturday afternoon, and the park lacked playing children, the cold weather a possible reason. On the pond to the right, a brace of ducks quacked their presence. 'PJ, they're laughing at you,' Kerry said.

'Why are they laughing at me?'

'It's a joke.'

'Oh, sure. Look at those two ducks, they're huge.'

'They're not ducks, they're Canadian geese. You do make me laugh.'

'Yeah, yeah, I thought they were geese.'

Kerry told him of her desire to own her own salon. She asked him about car mechanics and declared her attraction for a man in overalls.

'Seriously?'

'Definitely . . . well, you in them anyway.'

He lifted her hand to his lips and kissed the back of it.

'Why thank you, kind sir,' she said.

They sauntered along the path that wove through the grounds of the park. Distributed by the wind, several leaves fluttered and fell. There was a dampness to the air, and the ancient trees sheltered the dank earth. The birds that had stayed home for winter produced a cacophony of sweet music.

'I didn't know birds were so noisy,' PJ said. He had not been to a park, or anywhere for that matter, in a long time. He listened to the tumble of the natural waterfall. He sighted the molehills that interrupted the cultured landscape. Kerry ran forward and jumped on a small mine of quarried soil. PJ copied her, jumping on a second mound. Kerry squashed a third. They counted the molehills they had flattened; Kerry won by two. Laughter interrupted their quickened breath. Their hands found each other again, like magnets.

The paramedic had informed the police of the death of Eunice Walker. The police had informed the undertaker.

Understated, stylish and black, the van with privacy glass drove down Priory Lane. The paramedic told Fred, 'Your wife died several hours ago.'

'Jesus Christ! You're saying I got into bed with her last night, and she was dead?'

'You'll know more after the autopsy. But yes, I'm afraid it would seem so. I'm so sorry.'

'That bastard girl!'

'Sir?'

'Nothing.'

The undertakers entered Fred's house and made their way upstairs, directed by a policeman. These strangers entered the marital bedroom, a room that used to be sacred, an intimate space when in the early hours of each morning Amy-Lou would jump on the bed and wriggle between her mummy and daddy. Now this room was host to the authorities, and Fred was the outsider.

The undertaker unzipped a black body bag and Fred left the bedroom. At the oak table, Fred sat down and buried his head into his arms.

Priory lane was empty when Eunice, a macabre caterpillar, slid into the back of the waiting black van.

At the park the low winter sun shined on PJ and Kerry. Patches of frost clung to the shielded grass. A cluster of snowdrops pushed their heads out of the ground in search of winter sun. Kerry sat on a swing by the side of PJ and matched her sway to his. 'I've fancied you for ages,' she ventured.

'Really?' He turned his head to look at her.

'Don't look so surprised! You're very attractive.'

'Am I?' He pushed his shoulders back, then forced his swing to climb higher. 'That's great . . . I mean, that you find me attractive.'

'So, what about me?' Kerry whipped her head round to witness his response, but his momentum of swinging had fallen out of tune with hers. She could no longer match his gaze.

'What about you?'

She laughed. 'Do you fancy me?'

'Who wouldn't?'

'How long have you fancied me?'

'Since last night.'

'PJ!'

'What? I never thought of fancying anyone.' High in the air he jumped off the swing and took up position behind her. He grabbed the chains of her swing to still her and kissed the top of her head inhaling the sweet smell of her.

Sliding off her swing she said, 'Sit down so I can sit on your knee. The swing creaked under their double weight and rocked with kinetic energy when they shared a kiss.

In flat boots, a warm coat and a hat with fur pom-pom on top, Claire headed to the park. She scurried past the ducks and took the path to the swings. 'Oh, look at you two love birds,' she said. PJ's face was aflame.

'Hi, Claire.' Kerry wiped her mouth with the back of her hand as she got off PJ's knee. He zipped his jacket and folded his arms over his lap. Two dogs ran at each other. A woman holding an empty lead shouted her dog's name. All watched until the fracas stopped. 'Where are you going?' Kerry asked of Claire.

'Just a stroll to clear my head. Apparently, exercise is good for clearing the mind, good for stress.' PJ looked to the ground. He stared at a patch of worn rubber under the swing. His ears a perfect shade of rose. 'Well, I'll carry on and head on home.' Claire had planned the route to pass by Linda's house to maybe catch a glimpse of Richard.

'I'll ring you later,' Kerry said. She hugged her friend, then watched her walk away.

PJ stood away from the swing. Harbouring unwanted emotions and wanting to expel thoughts of Claire's connection to the death of Amy-Lou, he said, 'I saw Claire last night, after I left you.'

'Did you? You sure? She said she wasn't coming out last night.'

'She was all dressed up, kind of sexy. If you like that sort of thing.' The hue of rose of PJ's ears travelled up the chart to crimson.

'Sexy hey? I bet she was on her way to see Richard.'

'No, Richard's seeing my sister.'

'PJ! That wouldn't stop Richard. I've told you, he's a player. You need to have a word with your sister. I can't, I'm friends with both girls . . . it's awkward.'

CHAPTER 7

Hard-Earned Money

MONDAY MORNING and the Jones' house was quiet; being too early for the noise of routine. Lack of sleep forced John out of bed. He dressed in his discarded clothes; he would not be comfortable in the dressing-gown and slippers bought for him many Christmas's ago. He headed down the stairs. By the telephone, he placed a notepad, pen, and Jeff Winslow's phone number. He sat by the telephone and strummed his fingers on the notepad. Running a hand over his chin he remembered, 'Bloody hell! The holiday.' He jotted a reminder to cancel their vacation for next month. He continued to strum his fingers on the pad.

Jenny came to his side. Her careworn dressing gown tied at the waist. 'Have you had breakfast?'

'No, I've no appetite.'

The radio playing in the kitchen told John nine am had arrived. He stretched his arms, took a deep breath, then placed the call. 'Can I speak with Jeff Winslow in

Features?' John passed on his name and the reason for his call.

'Hi, is that Jeff Winslow?'

'It is, indeed, Mr Jones. I believe you wish to discuss the accident on Priory Lane, to run an editorial? We published a paragraph on the fatality, but nothing in-depth.'

'My daughter is accused of killing the girl.'

'I see.'

'Claire, my daughter, is convinced the child was already down on the road. I was hoping a piece in the newspaper might bring forward a witness.'

'It's worth a shot, and it is of public interest, just a sec.' The sound of flicking pages travelled through the phone. 'Can you do eleven this morning?' John provided the address with postcode. Then wandered into the kitchen and slapped Jenny on the backside.

'I'll have tea and toast,' he said. 'Tell Claire to get out of bed. She should be involved with this interview for the newspaper.'

Jenny sighed. 'Leave her be. She doesn't want the publicity.'

'Oh! And we do?'

At eleven-fifty, a car door slammed, and Jeff Winslow strode up the path to the front door. John extended his hand to Jeff, who offered no excuse for being late. 'Would you like a brew?'

'No, thanks.' He clasped John's hand with a firm shake. 'You have to keep an eye on the toilet stops in this game, being out and about.' Jeff used his gregarious nature to advantage: befriend the interviewee, let them into your world to learn about theirs. Sitting at the kitchen table, Jeff took out his smartphone, and set it to

98

record. 'Okay with you if I record our conversation?' John nodded and pushed his notepad to one side. Details of the accident, from John's perspective, were swallowed by the recorder. 'Could we go to the scene of the accident? Are you okay with that? I could go on my own?'

'No, it's fine. I pass there most days. I'll get you that leaflet I've had printed.'

Outside the Walkers' house, Jeff clicked away on his smartphone, taking pictures of an ordinary lane on an ordinary day. 'The story should run . . . what day are we on? Ah, Monday. The article will run in Wednesday's release.' Both men looked to the Walkers' house. The calm exterior belied the recent tragedy; time had dipped and glossed over the horror.

Pressure from customers had started to build, and it was time for John to return to work. Wednesday morning arrived. John drove to the newsagent at six that morning. He could see the newspaper on the counter. The article had made the front page. John handed over the exact money then began to read the headline. Without lifting his head, he moved to one side to let the paperboy enter the shop. John's eyes searched from left to right absorbing each detail. 'Yep, yep,' he said. And there it was, the question he had asked to be printed: *Claire Jones is adamant the child lay on the road.* John continued to read: *Think back readers, were you on or near Priory Lane on the evening stated? Anything, however trivial, you may recall, could help the investigation. If so, please contact the police or this newspaper.* John folded the paper and shoved it under his arm, then started his working day.

John wove from lane to lane on the motorway in the heavy traffic. A horn blasted. 'You too!' John gestured.

He sat forward in his seat and hit the accelerator hard. The ring from his telephone halted the radio. 'Jones Joiners,' he replied.

'Dad it's me.'

'What's up?'

'The solicitor rang. He's had a cancellation and can fit me in this afternoon.'

'Can't Mum go with you? I've loads of work I need to catch up on.'

'She's got a headache.'

'Again! Right. What's the time of the appointment? Claire, I need to work to pay for all this, it's getting out of hand!'

'I know Dad, sorry. Two o'clock.'

John disconnected the call without a goodbye.

Champions Solicitors was a prominent feature on the high street. The sandblasted building was adorned by the company's name, whose letters were fashioned out of stainless steel. John arrived before Claire and waited outside. She headed toward him. Holding out his wrist he tapped his watch. 'It's five-past!'

'I know, Dad. I had to walk.'

He pushed the door open. 'And who's fault is that?'

'Dad, please!'

At the curved reception, John pulled his work jacket straight and smoothed his hair. 'We've got an appointment with Mr Sinclair. Sorry we're late.' The young receptionist came from around the desk. John ushered his daughter to walk before him and they followed the receptionist down the corridor, where the walls were painted duck-egg blue. John marvelled at the mahogany doors. His hard-earned money would soon be helping to fund this extravagance. The receptionist stopped outside one of these splendid doors. She peered through the glass porthole and entered a code into the keypad, then stepped inside holding the door open for Claire and John. Mr Sinclair, dressed in suit and tie, stood to greet them. John shook the hand that held out before him. Claire copied the gesture. The receptionist left the room, the door clicking behind her.

'Please, take a seat.' Mr Sinclair offered two leather chairs. He waited for his client to be seated before taking his own, then introduced the conversation.

Claire looked to the bookcase, filled with leather-bound books, some maroon, some dark blue. The order of this library was spoilt by littered papers, neatly wrapped and secured with pink ribbon. Claire focussed her attention on the back of Mr Sinclair's laptop and read the logo. She made a low clacking sound with her mouth. It was dry, too dry to swallow a pill.

'Claire! Are you listening?' John asked.

'Sorry, can I have a glass of water?'

'Of course, would you prefer tea or coffee? Would you care for a beverage John?'

'No, thanks.' A glass, filled with ice and lemon, and a bottle of water was set in front of Claire. She rummaged in her bag for her pills, her tiny allies. John's eyes rolled.

'Okay.' Mr Sinclair checked his watch. Claire took another sip of water and swallowed a pill. She waited for calm to rush over her. 'Right, the coroner has requested a hearing, the purpose of which is to decide if the accident could have been prevented. We need to put forward and oppose this assertion to the Crown of Prosecution.'

'Prosecution?' John asked.

'Indeed. The defendant, in this case, the deceased's father, is entitled to representation.'

John looked to his daughter and saw her eyes widen.

'I shall read the statement you made to the police,' Mr Sinclair said. 'I want you to tell me, Claire, if there are any discrepancies?'

Dad and daughter listened. John chirped in: 'Correct, correct.'

Mr Sinclair lifted his eyes to look directly at Claire. 'As your representative, I urge you to speak for yourself. In court, the magistrate will take notes of everything you say. For you to remain silent, may suggest an air of guilt. Do you understand?' Claire's eyes filled with frequent tears. 'Don't get upset, dear. Lorna Webb is our expert at putting clients at ease. She will run through mock questions, make you familiar with the format.' He slid a box of tissues in Claire's direction.

Claire regained her composure and asked, 'Can my Dad come to court with me?'

'Of course, but he will not be with you in the witness-box. You will have to speak up.'

John reached over and patted Claire's hand. 'You'll be all right, love.'

'The hearing date has been set. The next time we meet will be at the coroner's court.' Mr Sinclair glanced at Claire, then turned his attention to John. 'I think we have covered everything.'

'You mentioned some practice questions?' John asked.

'Yes, you can make an appointment at reception.' Mr Sinclair stood and offered his hand for a farewell shake.

Walking down the elegant corridor, Claire asked, 'Dad, do you think I'll go to prison?'

'No! Surely not. Prison? Come on let's make that appointment. I'll give you a lift home.'

Yellow

When Fred lost his baby girl he had managed to contain his grief; his main priority had been to support the grieving process of his wife. Now, Eunice lay on a slab in the morgue, the gates of his grief and rage were released. 'Claire Jones, that tart from the estate, sat in my class years ago wearing a mini-skirt. The cocky bitch. That bastard girl.' To infuriate him further, the police had visited that day to ask him when he realised his wife had died and to enquire whether he had any life assurance policies in his wife's name. 'Outrageous, I'm a suspect now!' He chucked an empty mug into the sink to hear it chip. He marched to the hall cupboard in search of the ancient copy of the Yellow Pages directory. He flicked through the thin paper. 'Sa . . . se . . . sol.' A bold advert leapt from the page: *Champion Solicitors*. Fred folded the sheet, took hold of the telephone, and punched in the required number. 'Oh, right,' he said, on hearing they could not take his case: A conflict of interest as they were representing Claire May Jones. 'Bastard girl!' He shouted to the disconnected line. Underneath the Champions' advert was a name and telephone number in small print. Fred recited the number out loud as he dialled. He made an appointment to see Mr Fen, then flung the Yellow Pages back in the cupboard. A bottle of whisky was shaken by the book. Fred reached for the bottle to stop it from falling. A click from the seal allowed the whisky to breathe. Fred took a swig from the bottle.

In front of the idle television, Fred downed the bottle of smooth alcohol and rubbed his stomach as the heat chased right down to his belly. He fell asleep in the chair and stayed there until morning. The next day was spent in a similar fashion, except he took a bottle of whisky to bed. Another morning stormed in. In the kitchen, he opened a cupboard to search for painkillers. 'Typical! My wife's dead with a pharmacy of pills inside her, and I can't find one bleeding Aspirin.' He drank black coffee, then took a shower. The water pummelling his body.

Fen, Buckley and Amish Solicitors: Fred read the name from the board above the window. Inside, the décor was off white and in need of paint. He approached the desk where a woman, long past the age of retirement, spoke into a telephone. She did not look up to acknowledge Fred. He went to look out of the window. A family of three walked past in the street, happiness shared between them. He heaved a sob. Aware the telephone conversation at the reception had ended, he took a deep breath and presented himself at the desk for a second time. 'Yes?' The receptionist asked.

'I have an appointment with Mr Fen at three.' The clock on the wall showed the time as two-forty-five.

'Take a seat.' The chairs in the waiting room were made of the same moulded grey plastic as the ones at the doctor's surgery where Eunice had worked. He sighed. A gardening magazine offered no distraction, and he plonked it back on the table. A single ring came from the telephone on the desk. 'Mr Walker, you can go up now. First door on the left.' Even in his soft-soled shoes he could be heard climbing the wooden slatted stairs. The door was open. The room was sparse; an interview-room. Mr Fen sat behind a desk, two unoccupied chairs facing him. Fred took the seat nearest to the door.

'Mr Walker, nice to meet you. Before we start, I need to make you aware that you are entitled to be represented by the CPS, at no cost to yourself.'

'I am aware of that. But I prefer to choose my own counsel.'

'As you wish. I gather from the information I have that you wish to prosecute a lady driver?'

'She's no lady! My daughter was killed by this dangerous driver. Out of desperation, my wife has since taken her own life; I link the two. I need some sort of justice.' Fred released a tissue from the box in front of him and pinched his nose.

'Mr Walker . . . Fred, it must be difficult for you, but if you could inform me of the facts, so I can decide if we have a case to pursue.' Mr Fen's pen glided over a yellow legal pad while Fred gave the details.

'I'm beginning to see a theme with yellow,' said Fred as he reached the end of his story.

'Sorry?'

'Your yellow pad. Yellow pages, lemon curtains, yellow flowers. I didn't realise, until today, that I hate yellow. No matter. Carry on.'

'I see.' Mr Fen coughed from the back of his throat, a habit of his. 'From what I have gathered, you do have a case. But I should point out that we cannot determine, at this stage, whether the perpetrator's driving would be classed as dangerous or careless. There is a difference in the punishment handed down. In respect of your wife, we can use this tragedy to lead the accused, but there is not a court in the land that would apportion blame for the taking of one's own life. I will liaise with the police and the coroner for a wider perspective.' Mr Fen opened his diary. 'Are you free to meet on the same day, at the same time next week? By then I would have studied all relevant information.'

'I've nothing else pressing.'

Fred descended the stairs. He ignored the receptionist. Out on the busy street, he waited to cross the road to make his way to the off-licence, Booze 'n' Basics, for whisky and crisps.

You Should Tell

Kerry finished styling the hair of her last client. At home a beef casserole simmered in the oven, the delicious aroma seeping into the hall. 'Mum, I'm home.'

'I'm on the phone.'

Kerry took off her coat. Catching the end of her mum's conversation, she listened. 'I know, at last. She seems keen. Anyway, she's home. I'll ring you tomorrow.'

'Who's keen?' Kerry asked.

'Just telling Vi that you're courting.'

'Courting?'

'Seeing someone.'

'Mum keep your nose out of my business. Jeez, telling everyone.'

'Aunty Vi isn't everyone. She's pleased for you . . . after all that other business.'

'I wish you'd let that go.'

'I still think you should tell DJ.'

'PJ! If it makes you any happier, call him Paul.'

'The longer you leave telling him, the bigger the deceit.'

'Are you working tonight?'

'Twelve-hour shift, I'm on at eight.'

With tension in the air, the beef stew was shared between two warmed bowls. After eating, Kerry cleared the table and stacked the dishwasher. She climbed the stairs to her room to text PJ and invite him to come over. Her mum knocked on the bedroom door. 'Can I come in?'

'You will anyway.'

'Enough. I want a chat.' Mum looked professional in her nurse's uniform; someone you should listen to. She sat on Kerry's bed and checked her fob-watch. 'Look, we've been settled here for almost four years. You need to absorb the past and bring it out in the open. If you're going to share your life with someone, you have to share your past. Someone always has a tale to tell; you tell it first.'

'I know, but what if he doesn't accept it?'

'Then he's not the lad for you.'

Kerry examined her nails. 'I will tell him, but not yet.'

'Don't leave it too long, or there will be tears. Give your mum a kiss.' Unexpectedly she received a hug too. 'I'm going downstairs. I've just enough time to watch my programme.'

Kerry stepped out of the shower, then dressed in a new outfit, a cropped fluffy jumper, and short kilt. She cleared the teddy bears off her bed and shoved them into the wardrobe then covered the bed with a faux fur throw and set the dimmer switch to low. The doorbell rang. She ran down the stairs to open the front door. 'Hi.' She stood to one side to allow PJ to enter. His body brushed past hers when he turned to kiss her offered cheek and she inhaled his aftershave.

'Something smells tasty,' he said.

'Me?'

'No, food.'

'We had beef stew.' She closed the door.

'Who's that?' Mum shouted.

Kerry rolled her eyes. 'Best come and meet my mum.' PJ shifted his stance. He coughed to clear his drying throat and tugged at his fringe. 'Don't look so worried, Mum's cool.' He followed Kerry into the living-room. 'Mum, this is PJ . . . Paul.'

'Hi,' Mum and PJ said together.

'PJ, relax,' Kerry said. She led him upstairs, his eyes level with her pert bottom. They sat on the bed and chatted; they canoodled. PJ fidgeted as he tried to disguise the movement at his crotch. 'Take your jeans off,' Kerry said.

'What? No! Your mum's downstairs.' Kerry sat upright and undid his belt. She unbuttoned the waistband of his jeans and unzipped his fly. She pulled her jumper over her head to expose her push-up bra forcing her breasts to overflow the cups, her nipples were barely covered. PJ stood and kicked off his jeans. 'What if your mum comes in?'

'She won't.'

He deliberated whether to take his worn boxers off, when his penis sprung to view. Kerry got off the bed and eased him to the floor. She straddled him then pulled her panties to one side and slid herself onto him. He groaned, long and low. She moved with precision. With a straight back, she pulled her bra cups down, bathing in his admiration and the expression of sheer lust on his face. PJ was done. She eased off him and reached for her jumper. They relaxed in each other's arms as he played with her hair. The front door slammed. Mum was on her way to the hospital. 'Do you want to share a joint?' PJ asked.

'No thanks. Not for me.'

'Sorry. Have I upset you?'

'No. But, I don't do drugs.'

'I don't do drugs . . . well, not really. Just a bit of weed, now and then. I can take it or leave it.'

'I'd prefer you left it.' They dozed to the sound of the central heating pump.

Chased by Bubbles

Richard palmed the soft keys of his Mac Air. He hit the full stop and leant back in his chair. He had finished this paper. His next assignment could wait. Allowing his mind to wander he directed his thoughts to Andrea. He would not prat about in town on Friday trailing Andrea like a hound. Neither did he want the added complication of bumping into Claire. He stroked the screen of his mobile phone and chose Andrea's number. 'Hi, sexy,' he said.

'Hi.'

'There's a hotel I'd like to take you. What do you say to this weekend?' Silence. 'Well?'

'In the same room?'

'I can book separate rooms,' he lied.

'Okay.'

'Catch the two o'clock train on Friday. I'll meet you at London Paddington.'

'Okay. My friend's eighteenth was brilliant. You should have come.'

'What are you wearing?'

'I wore—'

'No. What are you wearing now?'

'A dressing-gown.'

'A dressing-gown! Who are you? My mother?'

'It's a short silk one.'

'What's underneath?'

She spat out a laugh.

'Tell me.' Richard unzipped his fly with his free hand.

'Lingerie,' she lied.

His voice lowered. 'Describe your lingerie.'

'It's a teddy.' She flicked the page on her magazine and found the teddy in the photoshoot. 'It's black with thin straps tied at the shoulder.'

'I would undo those straps with my teeth.'

'Oh, with lace covering the bust.'

'Say tits. Say swelling tits with hard nipples.'

'Richard! Dark, huge nipples.' She laughed, a nervous laugh.

'That's my girl. That is my girl. Touch your tits and tweak those fantastic nipples.' He groaned.

'Yes . . . yes . . . I am,' she lied.

'Sexy Andrea. You are the best.' He shot his seed into his hand, took a deep breath, then shuddered. 'I'll see you Friday. Bring the teddy.' He disconnected the call.

Andrea looked at the phone in her hand. She scrutinised the glossy photo of the black teddy.

The next day after work Andrea caught the bus into town. She entered a lingerie boutique and focussed her eyes on the floor. The walls were adorned by graduated hangers displaying the tantalising pieces of upmarket underwear. At the back of the shop, Andrea selected a black lace teddy with solid straps. The assistant wrapped the garment in red tissue paper and popped it into a boxed carrier bag, then sprinkled a handful of sparkly hearts onto the purchase. Without uttering a word, Andrea left the shop. At a haberdashery stall on the market, she paid cash for a length of slim back ribbon, a needle and cotton. Back home, she replaced the elastic straps with ribbons.

Friday arrived. The train Andrea travelled on was smoother than the local trains; her body swayed to its rhythm. Destination reached, she stepped off the train into the hubbub of station life. Alone, she scanned the crowded platform searching for Richard's face, his body, his way of walking. She rang his mobile: straight to voicemail. Parched for a refreshment she wandered into a coffee shop and ordered a cappuccino. Looking around the café she saw Richard bent over his laptop and headed toward him. 'Remember me?'

Richard snapped the lid of the laptop closed. He checked his watch. 'Sorry, I had no idea of the time.' He weighed her up. He did not like her long skirt but admired her biker boots – edgy and different to what he was used to. He collected his belongings. They headed for the exit. By Richard's side, Andrea negotiated the bustle of travellers.

A bellboy took Andrea's overnight bag from her hand. He led them to their room and opened the door with a plastic card. A queen-sized bed with an organised display of pillows and cushions greeted their arrival. Andrea side-glanced the bed. She looked out of the window at the cathedral. 'Sorry,' Richard said. He winked at the bellboy, then handed him a tip. 'There weren't any single rooms available.'

Andrea turned from the window to face Richard. 'Obviously not!'

The bellboy departed.

Without taking off his shoes, Richard flung himself backwards onto the bed. 'Take your boots and that skirt off.'

She hesitated and looked at Richard before unbuttoning her coat. She placed it on the chaise-lounge. She flicked her hair over one shoulder. Looking Richard in the eye, she acknowledged with a smile the desire which seeped from his expression. She unzipped her skirt and let the garment fall to the floor. She bent to retrieve the skirt, unwittingly displaying her perfect bottom, enhanced by lace topped stockings. She peeled off her sweater. Richard unleashed his penis. 'On second thoughts, leave the boots on. Get on here.' He stroked himself. She obeyed.

The music boomed, and the drinks flowed at the nightclub of Richard's choice. 'Just nipping to the loo,' Andrea said. Even though Andrea had complied to his sexual wants he needed her to be more liberated, in short, he had experienced better. He watched her disappear through the door marked *Ladies*. From his pocket he took two pills. He chased one down with a slug of liquor. The remaining pill, he dropped into Andrea's untouched cocktail. The pill floated to the bottom of the glass chased by bubbles which disappeared without trace. Richard smiled.

Back at the swanky hotel, Andrea got off the toilet and lay on the cold floor trying but failing to cry for help. Pressing the side of her face onto the marble tiled floor, she lay there, anchored to the floor and swam into an unconscious state.

Richard lay on the bed longing for Andrea. Waiting for the wild time he hoped the secret drug would bring.

The sexy black teddy with the ribbons undone anticipated a life form. The Egyptian cotton sheets caressed Richard's body. A feather pillow cradled his head. His desire for Andrea would not let him rest. His penis was on full alert and needed relief. 'Andrea come here.' Getting off the bed naked and protruding to his full extent, he headed to the bathroom to reintroduce her to how large he was. He opened the bathroom door. 'What the . . . Andrea, get up.' He prodded his foot into her ribs but gained no response. 'For fuck's sake!' His thoughts jumped to the pill he had dissolved in her drink. 'Jeez-us. Not more drama!' He took her by the shoulder to roll her over.

'Don't,' she moaned. 'I'm going to be—' Projectile vomit fountained from her mouth.

Richard leapt out of the way. 'For fuck's sake!'

Andrea scrambled to the toilet bowl. She knelt over the white ceramic, wrenching her guts into the water. She muttered, 'I feel terrible.' She wretched again, but there was nothing left inside.

'Get in bed,' Richard demanded. Andrea tried to stand but collapsed on the floor. Her hair swathed in the vomit.

'For fuck's sake!' Richard took her arm and held it around his neck then hoisted her up.

'I feel so ill. What's happening to me?'

'Too much to drink. I didn't know you couldn't handle your liquor.' He dragged her to the bed and flipped her onto the bouncy mattress. The black teddy received a splash of vomit. Richard returned to the bathroom, nauseated by the smell, he grabbed a towel from the rack and flung it over the vomit. Then washed his hands. Searching the tray of toiletries until he found a shower cap, he stuffed her vile hair into it. Lost in fitful sleep, she whimpered at the intrusion. He washed his hands again. With a flaccid penis, he got into bed and pulled the sheets over himself.

Andrea woke. She hoisted herself up to look at the time on the bedside illuminated clock – a bright green 08:30. She rolled over to Richard, his back to her. She pulled at the duvet to cover her shoulder and plunged back to sleep.

The brocade drapes did not allow any light into the hotel bedroom. The maid knocked on the door of the bedroom and waited. She swiped the master key in the lock and opened the door. Before she entered she shouted, 'Housekeeping.' Stepping into the room, she apologised to the body forms under the cover. 'Sorry, sorry.' She left the room and closed the door.

Richard sat up. Andrea stirred. He checked his accurate watch: Eleven forty-five. 'Better get cracking. I'm not paying for an extended stay.' He got out of bed, placed his hands on his waist and paraded his erection. He looked to Andrea, the shower cap still in place. He went to the bathroom to take care of himself. When he stepped over the dirty towel and inhaled the rancid smell, his mind was changed for personal sex and he took a shower.

Andrea sat up. A belch came from her stomach, she placed her hand over her mouth and held it there. She stood. 'I'll take a shower, after you.'

'Be quick. We should have vacated this room by eleven.'

'Sorry about last night. I've no idea what happened. I've never felt so ill, must be sickening for something.'

'Clean this vomit in the bathroom, I don't want charges put on my account.'

Andrea heaved several times, as she cleaned away her sour deposit. After taking a shower she dressed. Water dripped down her back; her hair now a mane of curls.

'You need to keep a check on the amount of alcohol you drink. Not a pretty sight, a woman legless.' He combed his hair in the mirror.

After another apology from Andrea, they stepped out onto the bustling street. She took deep breaths. 'Where're we going?'

'I could do with getting back to uni.' He steered her away from the oncoming crowd.

'Oh, I see. Okay.'

A man, smartly dressed in an expensive suit, passed by. He side-glanced Andrea, the way men did. Richard noticed. He took a look at her pale face, her drying hair – *still lovely* – *my, was she gorgeous.* 'Didn't know you had curly hair,' he said.

She ran her fingers through the curls. 'Don't. I hate it like this.'

'You, foxy little minx.' He winked at her. 'But you do need to reign in the drinking.'

'Is there a chemist? I have a horrendous headache.'

'There's one at the train station.'

'I'm sorry, I can't understand it – I've drunk way more in the past. I've never had a reaction like that.'

'Maybe it's because you're getting older?'

Andrea's eyebrows raised. Richard hailed a taxi. The driver pulled his cab to the kerb. Richard hurried forward to open the cab door. 'Train station,' he instructed. Andrea slid onto the back seat. 'I'll ring you.' He slammed the cab door shut then walked away.

Whistles blew. Trains pulled out of the station. Metal on metal drummed a rhythmic passing. People rushed through farewells, welcomed greetings. The echo from the service announcement reverberated in the hustling space. Andrea was swallowed by the crowd. She found the chemist, bought paracetamol with a bottle of water. Then waited for the train to take her home.

CHAPTER 8

Whisky

FROM THE KITCHEN WINDOW, Fred surveyed his neglected garden. He took another slug from the bottle of whisky. Daughter, gone. Wife, gone. Parents, gone. Sister . . . long lost. He checked the clock on the wall on hearing the time he realised there was an hour to go before his appointment with Mr Fen. Taking two Aspirin out of the packet he dissolved them in half a glass of whisky, then downed the concoction and shivered. With his jacket unbuttoned, Fred left the house. Making progress on foot for half an hour, he looked down at his feet and saw he was still in his slippers. 'Well, at least they're moccasins,' he said. 'And anyway, why should I care?' He arrived at the solicitors at the precise time of his appointment. After being instructed to take a seat, he did not this time look out of the window.

Fred sat opposite Mr Fen, and listened, taking off his glasses he polished them with the hem of his jumper. 'I have most of the documentation at my disposal,' Mr Fen said. 'I am waiting for a subpoena to allow me to trace the activity of Miss Jones' mobile telephone.' He paused and took the telephone off its cradle. 'Betty, has the subpoena for Jones arrived?' He replaced the handset. 'Not as yet.'

'Why do you need that? My name won't be on that list. I can assure you!'

'Good Lord, no! That thought had not crossed my mind, that you had contacted Miss Jones. No. The telephone company can pinpoint the time and whereabouts of Miss Jones through her phone usage. If she used the phone at the time of the accident, we have cast-iron evidence of dangerous driving. We can pinpoint the time by collaborating with the emergency . . . are you all right, Mr Walker . . . Fred?'

'I feel a bit . . .'

The aroma of alcohol too rich for the liver to process seeped out of Fred's pores. Mr Fin had no choice but to inhale the stale fumes. He did not comment, having dealt with many sad cases. 'There is no need to detain you further. I will take your case, pending the coroner's hearing.'

'What you talking about?'

'If the coroner states no blame, there is no case to answer. Can I get you a glass of water?'

'States no blame! What are you saying?'

'If the coroner finds Miss Jones not guilty due to the circumstances presented. Don't worry, this is not the only course of action. You could make a civil case against the accused. We can discuss what that entails if and when. If you wish to proceed, please stop at reception and pay a retainer. We accept five hundred pounds at this stage. Naturally, if the case does not go to court you will be reimbursed, less charges so far.'

Fred scraped back the chair he was sitting on. He lumbered down the stairs to hand his credit card to the ignorant woman behind the counter. The transaction machine sprung to life and coughed out a receipt.

Outside, in the fresh air, Fred headed for Booze 'n' Basics. He did not purchase crisps. He took home two bottles of whisky disguised in a brown paper bag.

Once home, Fred balled his jacket into a pillow and lay down on the settee.

Too Late

The telephone rang to the empty Jones' house. The caller waited for a response, with John's leaflet in his hand. With no answer he replaced the handset, his laboured breathing returned to its natural rhythm. On the evening of the accident this caller had driven past the bottom of Priory Lane, returning from an illicit visit with his current crush. He had looked up the lane and seen a heap of red, but the bouncing rain had obscured his vision. He had practised what he would say: 'Thought I saw something . . . not sure what it was.' He was aware of the precise time he witnessed this, due to being late for meeting his wife to watch their child's recital. He screwed the leaflet into a ball and threw it in the bin.

Coming into the house Jenny had grabbed the telephone. 'Too late.' The line was dead. She tapped in the code to retrieve the number, but the caller had withheld. She had promised to stay home should anyone ring in response to the leaflet but had snuck out for half an hour to buy cigarettes which no-one knew she smoked. In her eagerness to answer the phone, she had stepped over the mail on the mat. Closing the front door, she retrieved the handful of letters. With the efficiency of a croupier she shuffled the envelopes: an invitation to a sale, a gas bill, an advertisement flyer and a letter addressed to Miss CM Jones; Champions Solicitors logo was embossed on the back of the envelope. Jenny's hand ran to her mouth. She placed the letter addressed to her daughter on the coffee table, the rest of the mail she took to the kitchen. Keeping the gas bill she binned the rest. Back at the coffee table she examined the letter addressed to Claire; the quality paper did not allow her to peek at the content.

Jenny took a fresh cigarette out of the packet and opened the back door. Outside she lit the nicotine stick placed between her lips. She inhaled and smoke fell from her nose eventually she stamped the stub on the ground and brushed away flakes of ash with the side of her hand from her jumper. She sprayed air freshener outside, and over her clothes. Extra sprays were flirted inside the kitchen as she closed the door. In the garage, Jenny took off her shoes but forgot to put her slippers on. She unwittingly filled the kettle to overflowing, then nipped to the loo.

Picking up the envelope addressed to her daughter, Jenny went to the kitchen and set the kettle to boil for a second time. She held the envelope's seal over the billowing steam, boiling water spouted out causing her to drop the letter in the puddle of water. The envelope was damaged and easy to pull apart. She scanned the damp letter in her hand: *We have today been informed that Fen, Buckley and Hamish Solicitors . . . Mr Frederick Walker . . . prosecution . . . dangerous driving . . . pursuing manslaughter.* Jenny did not go on to read: *This letter is of courteous intent – we could apply for a hearing extension, but this would be counterproductive. The coroner is investigating the same issue as the prosecution. If you agree, no further action by you is required at this stage.* She put the letter on the radiator to dry.

Claire entered the hall to her home and was taken aback by the sudden appearance of her mum. Jenny tried to kiss her daughter but was offered a cold cheek. 'Are you okay?' Jenny asked.

'Yes. Stop fussing all the time.'

'I . . . you see . . . I had an accident with a letter addressed to you. I dropped it in the sink and it got wet. Anyway, seeing as it was spoiled, I read it. I was trying to save you any upset by what it might say.' Jenny handed the crinkled paper to her daughter.

Claire read each word. 'Great! Anyway, it makes no difference. I'm going to be found guilty.'

'Oh, Claire, don't say that!'

'I'm going to bed. Wake me at five.' Claire closed her bedroom door. She listened in case her mum had followed, then pulled off her boots, opened her bag, and took out her phone. Scrolling the contact list, she rested on Richard, and pressed the screen hoping he would answer but yet again was delivered straight to voicemail. She left another message. With her head on the pillow, her coat still on, Claire fell asleep.

CHAPTER 9

Peace and Prosperity

COLD SUNSHINE greeted the day of Claire's court hearing. Jenny dressed for attendance, fiddling with the buttons of her blouse. In her agitation she dropped a mug of tea and it shattered into large chunks. She kneeled to collect the shards. 'Ouch!' She sucked the fresh blood from her finger.

John came to her rescue. 'Move out of the way. You're going to have to get a grip. Get to the doctor before you have a breakdown. I've enough on my plate, without you going under.'

'I'm fine.'

'It would be better if you stayed home. I've got Claire to look after. I don't need the extra burden of you.'

With a sigh, Jenny went upstairs to change into her comfy clothes. With her husband and daughter out of the way, she could smoke cigarettes to her heart's content.

The coroner's court was small. John sat on a fixed chair in the courtroom with Claire. He looked around.

Mr Fen sat alone. Fred was not in attendance at court, losing him the opportunity of gaining pastoral care.

Mr Sinclair sat next to John. 'Remember,' the solicitor said, 'this hearing is to dissect the event with the aim of preventing similar deaths occurring. It is not a trial and therefore does not apportion blame.'

Time approached for the coroner's presence. The coroner's assistant and Sergeant Wright were present. The court was open to the public, though no reporters or other parties were present. Claire looked around the room searching for Richard, he was not there. She looked past the microphone placed on the high bleached wood desk where the coroner would take seat, then refocused her attention to read the inscription on the polished shield fixed to the centre of the wall behind the desk. She could not decipher the Latin words, but at the base of the shield, she read: *Peace and Prosperity*. Stretching her arms, she readjusted her seating position, then checked in her bag to make sure her phone was switched to silent. She took a deep breath. John put his hand over hers and gave it a gentle squeeze. They swapped smiles. She sensed a presence and turned. It was Richard. Claire wished she had not come with her dad.

A middle-aged, plump woman, dressed in black with a pearl necklace her only softener, entered the court from a side door – the coroner had arrived. Her hair was coiffured, she wore thin-rimmed glasses. She took her seat behind the desk with the microphone.

The assistant's voice was loud and clear. 'Calling Sergeant Wright to the witness box.' Sergeant Wright cleared his throat, then flipped open his notebook. He answered questions and recited facts. He took a pressed handkerchief out of his pocket and flicked the linen to unfold the creases then blew his nose; a microphone amplified the sound. Unaware of why people snickered, he refolded the handkerchief and placed it back in his pocket. He stood down.

The second person to be interrogated was Claire. She told how she was convinced that the deceased child was already on the road. 'Must have been.' Her voice wavered, tears leaked from her eyes. She pulled a tissue set in front of her and wiped her nose, making sure her cleansing could not be heard. She took hold of a stack of plastic cups and pulled one off. In doing so, she sent the stack flying. 'Sorry,' she said. A clerk rescued the scattered cups, she took the one out of Claire's hand and filled it with water. John watched his daughter being cared for.

'Miss Jones, are you sufficiently composed to continue?'

'Yes mm . . .' She couldn't remember how to address the coroner.

'Was your concentration, whilst driving at the time in question, impaired in any way prior to the accident?'

'No.' She remembered the serious nature of not being truthful. 'My phone rang, but I didn't answer it.'

'I see,' the coroner said. She wrote on her pad, then directed her stare to her assistant. 'Why have I not received a copy of Miss Jones' phone activity?'

The assistant shrugged, even though she was responsible for the oversight. John shifted in his seat. 'You may step down.' Unsure of what was expected of her, Claire remained in the box. 'Return to your seat.' Claire looked at Richard. He smiled, then lowered his eyes. Claire took her seat and Dad patted her hand.

Richard took the vacated witness box. 'State for the record your relation to the event.'

'I did not witness the child being killed. I appeared on the scene after the event. But, it is safe to assume that she, the child, ran out between the parked cars into Claire . . . Miss Jones' path.'

'Mr Hamilton, it is not safe to assume anything in my court.'

'Sorry, Your Honour . . . Ma'am. I meant in all probability.' Richard swept his hand to the back of his neck. He decided not to offer any additional comments. He chastised himself, he knew better. Beads of sweat appeared on his forehead.

'I will adjourn to read and absorb the supporting documentation, including phone records, to allow me to prepare written findings. This court will reconvene next Tuesday at ten.' The coroner pushed back her chair, straightened her jacket, and left through the door she had entered.

Mr Sinclair addressed Claire. 'You were champion. See you here next week at ten.' Claire turned her head to catch Richard's attention, but he had left the courtroom.

Back home in her room, Claire continued to pop pills. She reclined on her bed and listened to the music she and Richard had shared. She checked her phone for absent messages. Without taking a meal she undressed and tried to fall into what would be a restless sleep.

A week later, Claire and her father claimed ownership of the same seats at the coroner's court. Richard sat at the front of the court. He did not look round to acknowledge Claire, much to her disappointment. Mr

Sinclair arrived with two minutes to spare. The coroner entered the court, took her seat, and spoke into the microphone. 'It is my intention to order a trial, as there is sufficient doubt to warrant a full investigation.' She switched the microphone off and left the room.

'So be it.' Mr Sinclair said. A slight smile appeared on his face.

'I'm going to trial?' Claire asked.

'Yes, dear. I'm afraid so.'

John heaved a breath. 'Claire, let's go home.'

Mr Sinclair followed his client outside. 'I see no immediate need for contact with you; we have all the evidence we require. You can make an appointment to see me if you have any concerns. I trust my secretary sent you a list of the fee structure?'

'Yes, we have that,' John said. 'Trust me, we have that.'

Claire felt a jab in the small of her back. 'Hi sexy,' Richard whispered in her ear. 'Hello, Mr Jones. Are you well?' He said.

'Fine, thank you. Come on Claire.'

'Wait, Dad.' She turned to Richard. They wandered several paces out of earshot.

'How are you?' Richard asked.

'Good.' She lied. 'The tablets I have help, but I'm running low on them. I told the doctor I had lost them, so he prescribed more, but I'm worried I still won't have enough.'

'Leave it with me. I'll get you something of use, diazepam, but it will be expensive. Do you want to pop round tonight, say eight? Usual place.'

Claire's face radiated a smile. 'Yes, I'll come with you now. I'll tell Dad.'

'No! Don't piss him off. And bring a hundred for the meds.'

'What did he want?' John asked when Claire returned.

'Nothing. Just asked how I'm coping.'

'Let's get back and see how Mum is. Any thoughts on the coroner's decision?'

'Going to court will be the same as today, won't it?'

'I expect so.'

King Kreep

Visits to Kerry's bedroom had become a regular occurrence for PJ. She had reassured her mum that she would tell PJ her history when she was ready; when their relationship was ready.

Snuggled together on Kerry's bed, they listened to their favourite tracks. PJ twirled a strand of her hair. He loved every inch, every second of being with her. With her head on his chest, she moved slightly to the rise and fall of his breathing. The music came to an end. 'PJ?'

'What?'

'Should I start calling you Paul?'

'If you want.' PJ was used to his nickname, brought about because his mum had found hilarity in saying, 'Go and get your PJs, PJ.' If asked by his dad whether he missed his mum, he would say, 'Sometimes.' Mum had abandoned the family when PJ was seven and Andrea was five. She had traded her children for her line manager who offered a life of fun. When the affair was no longer illicit, the magic turned black and strangled the sport out of the pair. She did not return to her husband or to the house where her children lived – a neglected Victorian terrace that disgraced the lane.

'Paul,' she giggled, 'why don't we go to your house?'

An image of his house jumped into his head; it did not sit right with him. 'It's nice here. And I'd be distracted, I'd want to crack on with my gaming challenge having my computer there.'

'I know. But we don't want to get bored. I want to learn more about you. Meet your dad. See how you live.'

This was not her first request, and he knew it would not be her last. 'Okay, come tomorrow.'

'Really? I'll come over at seven.' She kissed his cheek and he smiled.

'I think I'll shoot off home.'

'Have you gone in a mood?'

'No, I want you to come. I'll go and tidy my room. And I want to crack on with my progress of the gaming challenge.'

'Crazy boy.'

He pulled on his trainers then kissed her on the lips before saying goodbye.

Entering his house, he shouted, 'Dad, are you still up?'

'Yep. What'd you want?'

PJ followed the voice to the living-room. 'There's a girl coming tomorrow night.'

'What girl?'

'A mate.'

'Oh, a mate . . . a mating mate?' He winked at his son. 'Don't worry, I'll put my best bib and tucker on.'

'No Dad. Just stay out of the way.'

'Ay, lad, I'll do that.'

PJ went to his room to scoop an armful of clothes off the floor and jam them into the wardrobe. With the side of his foot, he shoved the other stuff under his bed. He switched his computer on. 'Universe of Lore, your master awaits,' he said to the screen. 'Come on King Kreep bring it on.'

The following evening, PJ's dad left the house before seven o'clock. Andrea was at night-school. The house belonged to PJ. Kerry knocked on the front door and he guided her to his room. A male presence, not unpleasant, but not sweet either lingered in the room. She looked around at the barrage of dark colours that came from the gaming posters stuck on the wall. Her gaze wandered to the ceiling where the largest poster was mounted, the same design as the others, though they were different in detail to a knowing eye: a sword here, a dagger there. 'It's a wonder you don't have nightmares with all this gloom plastered to your walls.'

'Nightmares! This is the stuff of dreams. This, my girl is The World of Lore.' He drew back his leg and positioned his arm in a striking pose.

'Law?'

'Lore! Lore, it's the Universe of King Kreep.' PJ regained his posture.

'Ah, that's where Richard should live.' She laughed. Sitting down on the edge of his bed she ran her hand over the thin quilt.

Sitting on his chair with his back to the computer, silence filled the room. He turned to face the computer. 'Here, I'll show you.'

Kerry stood behind him. She put her arms around his shoulders and kissed the top of his head before resting her cheek next to his. They viewed the screen together. Logged on to the internet, PJ received messages from fellow players, all of whom highlighted his prowess. 'Hey, you're good at this,' Kerry said. He played a few tactical moves before being faced with the decision of which avenue to take. He could not concentrate when Kerry was playing with his hair. Nor did he want to spoil the illusion of perfection, so he logged off.

Kerry sashayed around the room. She picked up a bright yellow stuffed toy. 'Wouldn't have put you down for cuddly toys.'

'Wash your mouth out! Cuddly toys! That's Pac-Man.'

'Pac-Man?' She laughed.

'A gaming icon from the eighties.'

'Get you . . . and what the hell is that?' She pointed to an antiquated computer enjoying pride of place on the shelf.

'Same era. It's the 48k ZX Sinclair Spectrum. An important invention for gamers because it made it possible to code your own games.'

'Listen to yourself, you sound like a documentary.'

He laughed. 'I bought that ZX from a car boot. I couldn't believe my luck, it's in perfect working order and only cost me a tenner.'

She surveyed his cluttered desk. 'You should tidy this. I'll do it. Where's your bin?'

PJ pulled an overflowing bin out from under the desk. His face reddened when a screwed-up dirty tissue landed at her feel. He picked the tissue up and rammed it deep into the rubbish. 'I'll go and empty it.' He took the bin outside to the dustbin.

With her middle finger and thumb, Kerry lifted the shiny red button off the desk. She turned it over, then put it back. PJ returned with the empty bin and he held it out. Kerry showed each item from the cluttered desk for his approval before chucking it in the bin. She came to the red button watching for his reaction.

'Keep,' he said.

'A keeper. Why?'

'No reason.'

'There must be a reason.'

'I found it.'

'Where?'

'I can't remember.'

'If it means enough for you to keep, you must remember.'

'It, I . . .' He scratched the back of his head. An honest boy by nature, he had been bullied into keeping Richard's secret.

'You're lying to me. Aren't you? She's the reason you didn't want me to come around here.'

'She? Who's *she*?' Sweat prickled his back.

'Your ex, that's who *she* is!'

'Ex? There's no ex.'

'Oh, now you're telling me you're still with her?'

'Wow! You're way ahead of me. There's no ex. You're my first girlfriend.' For the second time that evening his face coloured.

'Am I? Aw, I'm your girlfriend.' She nestled close to him and rubbed her nose against his. 'You are cute. So, what's the story with the button?'

He moved away from her to draw breath. 'You really don't want to know.'

'Okay,' she said, 'I have a secret to share. Then you can tell me yours.'

She pushed PJ onto the bed and fed her hand up the inside of his thigh . . . then the front door slammed and moments later the sound of Andrea's footsteps pounded up the stairs. PJ pushed Kerry to one side and sat up. 'I can't. Not when someone's in the house.' He wiped his mouth.

'No! But you can in my house, with my mum downstairs.'

He got off the bed and sat in front of the computer. 'I'm not used to it, that's all. Not here.'

'It! Not used to it? And I am? Cheers.'

He turned to face Kerry. 'You know what I mean.'

'You're a funny one.' Kerry smiled at him and ruffled his hair. 'This hair needs styling.' She smoothed the strands of hair back in place. 'I'll cut it for you tomorrow when you come over.' PJ was glad that the opportunity to share their truth had passed. 'Did you tell Andrea I was coming here?'

'No. Why would I?'

'I think I'll go and chat with her. Which is her room?'

'The one with Andrea's name stuck on it.'

'Smarty-pants. Is it okay with you if I go?'

'Sure.' Time was running out to compete for the tournament, so he switched the computer on.

Kerry knocked on the door with the black and white letters arranged in Andrea's name.

Andrea got off her bed to open the door. 'How did you get in? Did I leave the front door open?'

'I was in your brother's room.'

'Really?' Andrea opened the door wide to allow Kerry to enter. Kerry looked around the room. Necklaces hung from hooks on the wall. A pair of pink ballerina shoes, tied by their ribbon, dangled from the ceiling light. Cushions, plain and simple, each a different colour, layered the wall by the bed. An open bookcase housed an assortment of hats. A wooden chair, turned upside down, was fixed to a wall, the rungs metamorphosed into rails where scarfs were hung. Everything had a place, and everything was in place. Andrea lit a long stick which was suspended over a slim dish. The stick smouldered and released a swaying column of fragrant smoke. She waved the extra-sized match to quell the flame. This was a first, a visitor to her room. 'So, you and my brother, is it getting serious?'

'Yes, he's a slow burner, but lovely. I really like him.'

Andrea's smile reached her eyes. 'Yes, he's quiet, but with a good heart. Don't tell him I said that.'

Kerry sat on the small settee that was jammed into the window recess. 'What's the story with you and Richard? I asked PJ to have a word with you about him. He said it was none of his business.'

'No. My brother wouldn't interfere. There is no story.'

'Good. Don't get involved with him. He's an arsehole. I know you don't get on with Claire, but he's been awful with her. I heard you went away for the weekend. Anyone interesting?'

'My, how quickly news travels. It was a disaster. I won't be going again.'

'Spill. What happened?' Kerry pushed her back into the settee before folding her arms.

'It started off really well, but then, I don't know, I suppose I had too much to drink. I felt so ill.'

'That's not like you. I've never seen you drunk.'

'I know. I don't know what happened. I drank less than usual.'

'Maybe someone spiked your drink?'

'Do you think? Must have been while we were on the dance floor. Oh, that's shocking! Why would anyone do such a thing?'

'It takes all sorts, that's what my mum says.' Kerry, on mentioning her mum, quickly changed the route of conversation. 'Who did you go with?'

'I didn't. I met someone there.' Andrea diverted her eyes away from Kerry.

'You went to meet a stranger?'

'No! I went on my own to meet someone I know.'

'Don't be so secretive – it was Richard, wasn't it? You went to meet him.' Andrea closed her eyes before nodding a yes. 'Richard! You have to be joking. You're way too good for him. Look at you, you're gorgeous. He's had more girls than—'

'Yes, all right. He won't be having me again.'

'Again? So, he's had you then. That's him gone. He'll have lost interest.'

'Actually, he keeps ringing and texting. But I'm ignoring him.'

'Please do. He's forever picking up and dropping Claire. She's obsessed with him. It's been going on for years.'

'No, he doesn't see her anymore.'

'Yes, he does. It's current, honestly.'

'I didn't know that.'

'You say your brother has a good heart; Richard has a dark heart. Stay away from him.' Their conversation ran dry. Kerry left the room, closing the door behind her. She popped her head around PJ's door. She saw his fingers trip over the keyboard like a concert pianist. 'I'll be off then,' she said.

'Damn!' He raised his hands to his head; her interruption had cost him. 'I can't leave the game at this stage.'

'It's okay.' She stepped into his room and kissed the top of his head. 'I'll see myself out. Come over tomorrow night. I'll cut your hair.'

PJ travelled back to fantasy and blasted his way to victory.

CHAPTER 10

The Sooner the Better

TIME FOR CLAIRE to visit her boss. Her intention to return to work had not been fulfilled. She carried a further sick-note in her bag.

'Hello, Claire. Are we to have you back?' He took the certificate from her hand. 'No. I see not. I do understand your predicament, but you must be aware that your contract states two weeks sick leave at any one time. Under the circumstances, I've allowed you to exceed this period. But business is business and we cannot prolong it further.'

'Oh, I didn't realise.'

'Look,' he said, handing back the sick-note, 'send this to the government work and pensions department. Claim statutory sick pay.'

With a quiver in her voice, Claire asked, 'Does this mean that I've lost my job?'

'Not at all. You're a valuable member of the team. Where are you up to with proceedings?' Claire's eyes lowered, and her countenance fell. 'Your court-case? The accident.'

'I thought you meant proceedings about my job. I'm waiting on a date.' She could see from his reaction he wanted more. 'For a court hearing,' she added.

'Let me know how you get on. Please feel free to call by any time.' He ushered her to the door. Claire contemplated visiting her work colleagues but decided against doing so. She headed for home.

Claire held her head down, her hands thrust in her pockets as she walked up Priory Lane on her return to home. Andrea was watching Claire out of her bedroom window when her phone rang so she took her eyes off Claire to look at the screen: *REPLY!* The sender was Richard. Andrea deleted the message then put the phone back in her pocket.

When Andrea did not respond to his text, Richard placed his phone onto a library book. This was a new experience for him, to text a woman, for her not to respond. His desire for Andrea had reawakened. His phone vibrated, he picked up the handset with enthusiasm: Claire. He cancelled the vibration then chose the book from the top of the pile to read what he needed to.

Disappointed that Richard had yet again refused her call, Claire threw her phone back into her shoulder-bag. She rang the doorbell to her home, but her mum did not respond. Claire searched her bag but could not locate her house key. She slipped down on her haunches to tip the contents of her bag onto the doorstep. She separated the items. There was no key. She had gotten out of the habit of carrying keys as she no longer drove a car. She shoved the tipped contents back in her bag, then lifted the letterbox. 'Mum!' Not gaining a response, she walked to the side gate and pulled the bolt free. Marching down the path to the back door, she discovered it was locked. Desperate for the toilet, she returned to the front of the house, closing the gate behind her.

Jenny headed down the close. 'Mum, where've you been?'

'What, love?'

'I've no key!'

'Sorry. I went for a stroll.' Jenny pushed the packet of cigarettes further down in her pocket. Cigarette shopping was now a daily event.

'Hurry up. Open the door.' Uncrossing her legs Claire barged past her mum. She trod on a letter addressed to herself as she raced to the toilet.

Jenny retrieved the letter, making her way to the kitchen, she hung her coat on the hook. Claire thundered down the stairs. 'I'll have coffee,' she said to the simmering kettle.

'There's another letter for you.' Jenny pointed to the offending article.

'It'll be the court date. Claire ripped open the envelope. She scanned the content until her eyes rested on the date. She folded the letter to its original state and placed it back in the envelope. 'Three weeks' time.'

'The sooner the better, eh?'

'The sooner the better? What if I'm sent to prison? Is that the sooner the better!' She stormed out of the kitchen, leaving her coffee untouched.

Guess What?

PJ faced his computer and checked the time on the screen. Almost there. He tapped the third finger of his left hand on the X key, then he stabbed the key again. With a flourish he pressed the Return key with his right index finger. He pushed his chair back. 'Wow! Amazing! I've only gone and done it. I've only gone and won a place on the tournament. King Kreep, here I come!' He smiled at the images that danced before him. The recognition he deserved played out on the screen. The spectacle stopped, and two empty boxes appeared on the screen: username and password. PJ pulled open the drawer to his desk. Screwed paper mushroomed out. He rifled through the loose leaves of his purple book. Anxiety claimed him. 'Where in the hell is the password?' He laced his hands behind his neck and looked up to the ceiling. The image of King Kreep stared back, its eyes glowing with fury. PJ stood on the chair to pull a corner of the poster away from the ceiling. Username: Pyjama, password: myworld19. He punched these details into his computer. From the screen, King Kreep's finger beckoned then pointed to an image. PJ clicked on the icon where an entry form was displayed. Without hesitation, PJ filled in the form and pressed Enter. His e-mail clicked an incoming message: a VIP ticket to King Kreep's tournament to compete in the final. He selected the print icon, and the printer sprung to life.

PJ would need to take a week off work. He knew this would not be a problem; he had not used any of his holiday entitlement. He Googled the train schedule and paid for a ticket, then he booked a place to stay. Leaving his computer live, he grabbed his jacket and headed outside.

He thrummed his fingers on the frosted glass of Kerry's back door which Kerry opened. 'You're early,' she said, kissing his cheek.

'You'll never guess what?'

'Won the lottery?'

'Better than that! You can't buy this. I've won a place on the King Kreep live tournament.'

'Good for you. When's that, then?'

'In three weeks. The gig runs for a week, so I've booked a place to stay.'

'A place to stay? Can I come?'

'Oh, I never thought . . . would you want to come?'

'Yeah.'

'I'll nip back home and book another ticket.'

'No use my laptop. Come upstairs.' A naughty glint sparkled in her eye.

The next day and the home-made cheese-and-onion pie enhanced by a grated cooking apple was delicious. Kerry helped herself to a second slice. She held her knife and fork to the side of her plate. She looked at the pie. 'Mum, I'm going away for a week.'

'Lovely, is Claire going?'

'I'm going with Paul. He's won a place in a tournament.'

'Are you sure that's a good idea?'

'I knew you'd be like this. I could have lied to you.'

Mum pulled her mouth tight. She shook her head in little disappointing sweeps. 'Have you told this lad your story yet? Because obviously you're getting serious with him.'

'I'll tell him when I'm ready. I just want to have some fun.'

'And your idea of having fun is what landed you in trouble.'

'Give it a rest. I'm doing well. Give me some credit! Whether you like it or not I'm going.' Kerry slammed the knife and fork onto the table and stormed out of the kitchen.

PJ decided he would take Kerry to the venue location on the Friday so they could enjoy the weekend before the tournament began on Monday. He booked a taxi to take him and Kerry to the train station. He held the cab door open for her and she slid across the back seat to make room for him. Her mum did not wave them off, nor did she wish her daughter happiness.

The train station hustled with the throng of people. A loudspeaker echoed accurate times. PJ looked up at the departure screen and saw their train was to about to leave platform three. Kerry grabbed the handle of her pull-along. PJ hitched the shoulder strap of his backpack. They ran to platform three as a whistle blew. The doors to the train were open. These inexperienced travellers jumped in. Kerry put her bag on the crowded luggage rack. They were forced to sit apart from each other. After several stops, a double seat became available and PJ grabbed it. Kerry leant her head on his shoulder.

The train lulled its passengers. PJ stroked Kerry's hand which she had woven through his arm. She fell asleep. Two hours of countryside flashed by when she stirred. She rubbed her neck. 'Are we nearly there?'

'I think we must be.' He shuffled his position, glad to have her weight lifted from him. Kerry unzipped her handbag and produced two packets of crisps. They munched on the snack.

A message was broadcast: 'Next stop, Euston.' Kerry crumpled the crisp packets and then made her way to the bin by the side of the sliding doors while PJ lifted her bag off the rack. They faced the doors, waiting for them to open. The station was bigger and noisier than the one they had left. People flowed, organised in their hurry, juggling past one another, not connecting with anyone, eager to be somewhere else. Trains arrived and departed to the screech of durum-de-drum. The sounds obliterated the squeak from the loose wheel on Kerry's case. PJ and Kerry walked the length of the platform and through the turnstile.

'Let's grab a coffee,' Kerry said.

Nodding in the direction of the bar on the corner of the upper level of the station hub, he said, 'Or a beer?'

'Hell, to the yes. I'll have a vodka on the rocks . . . a double.' The buzz of the station had beckoned. She hoisted her bag on to the escalator, in clear breach of the sign saying not to. The bar was open to the front, allowing travellers to hear the announcements of trains arriving and leaving. PJ and Kerry sat at a small, round table. Kerry's face glowed. PJ grinned with excitement. He had never witnessed such hustle and bustle. He loved it. Kerry downed her drink. In the early stages of her drinking career, she had been a happy drinker. She asked for another double then downed that drink faster than the first one. PJ did not mention her past comment of not liking the taste of alcohol. He finished the last dregs of his pint. 'I want another. Paul . . . I lurve you.' It was amusing to PJ to see how animated she had become. He had no concept of the danger which might lay ahead.

PJ took Kerry's case from her. He grabbed her hand to take her to the tube station. Knowing he would be unfamiliar with the layout he had read maps before arriving here. He scanned the coloured lines of different routes. With Kerry's hand still gripped, they stood on the steep escalator. Now at the tube station which would take them to the bed and breakfast, PJ was mesmerised with the speed of the tube; so fast, he thought it would pass them by. The tube came to an abrupt stop. The doors slammed open, passengers exited in a forceful but organised way. People waiting to board rushed and forged ahead to claim a seat. Crammed with strangers, PJ would not let go of Kerry's hand. Arriving at their destination, they stepped out of the underground and into the night air. Arm in arm, they made their way to the bed and breakfast lodging.

The large boarding house was immaculate and modern. The landlady appeared in the hallway. 'I trust you've had a good journey?'

'Yes, thanks,' PJ said. Kerry snuffed out a giggle.

'Will you be dining with us in the evenings? Three courses for a reasonable rate.'

'No thanks,' PJ said. Kerry smiled without showing her teeth.

'I see. House rules, in no later than eleven at night.' She pointed to the modern clock on the wall. 'I lock the door at eleven. No smoking in the room. No loud music.' She sniffed at nothing then held out a key. 'Third floor, second door on the right. I don't usually accommodate your demographic, and I shall not be doing so in the future.'

'Charming,' Kerry slurred, giggling her way up the stairs. The room was sparse but adequate. They flopped on the bed, leaving their luggage untouched they fell asleep, wrapped in each other's arms. Kerry woke in the early hours. She went to the bathroom and guzzled cold water from the tap.

CHAPTER 11

You'll Be All Right

ON THE DAY of the court hearing, Claire piled her hair high then wrapped it in a bun. The blonde highlights could not be disguised. She dressed in a navy suit, bought for the occasion.

Claire swallowed three pills. She had tried this dose the day before and it had had the desired effect. John shouted from the hall. 'Nearly time to leave. Are you both ready?'

'Yes.' Jenny answered first, then Claire.

Claire came down the stairs wearing flat navy shoes which she detested. Dad had said, 'Sensible driving shoes.' Jenny followed her daughter. They reached the garage via the kitchen and got into the car where Claire sat in the front seat as she always did. Mum and daughter watched John open the garage door and move his van. In the garage, he got into the driver's seat of the family car and drove out of the estate onto Priory Lane. They were on their way to court travelling in silence, looking out of different windows at the same scenery. Claire checked her make-up in the mirrored visor. As they drove in the commuter traffic, John looked at the clock on the dash, the journey was taking longer than anticipated. Arriving at the court building, John wove in and out of the side roads in search of a parking space. 'There's one,' Jenny shouted after they passed an available slot. John checked in his rear-view mirror, the car behind was reversing into the slot so he drove away from the immediate vicinity of the courthouse.

On the main road he manoeuvred the car behind a prestige vehicle, out of which a woman exited. She took off her trainers and slipped on a pair of high-heeled court shoes. She collected a bulging briefcase; bleeped the car's locking mechanism and strode in the direction of the court.

'Claire, you could have been a solicitor,' Jenny said. Claire rolled her eyes, before sneaking another pill into her dry mouth; the calm she chased was illusive.

The courthouse, a recent structure, was surrounded by landscaped gardens. The elegant glass entrance was secured by grey holdings. The ambiance encouraged a visitor to walk tall, whatever they were accused of.

The Jones family walked through the automatic glass doors, then waited for a second glass door to slide open. Security was tight. As instructed, Claire slid her bag onto the conveyor belt. John emptied his pockets, the contents of which passed under an X-ray-machine. Jenny clutched a crumpled tissue. Each waited in line to stand under a boxed area to listen for an alarm that did not bleep. A man of authority chose John to stand with his legs and arms spread wide. A hand-held device smoothed over John's body, and the hands from this stranger skimmed John's private parts. Set free, John collected his belongings.

There were two courts – a magistrate and a county. Claire gave her dad the letter which detailed her court appearance and he checked with an official which court they should attend, though this was highlighted on the letter. 'To the right, the county court,' the official said.

'I need the loo,' Claire said.

'We'll all go,' John said. Directed by a sign, John led the way to the toilets. Jenny washed her hands then wiped them on her coat, even though there was a hand drier. Claire reapplied her lipstick. The pill she had taken kicked in and she relaxed. Outside of the amenities, they reunited with John and headed to the waiting room.

Sitting on a row of chairs that were bolted to the floor, John read the notice on a wall: *The Court Usher will be available from 9.30 am. Please check in at the desk.* John looked over to the high curved desk, which was unmanned. He focussed on an artificial plant in a tub. Pointing to a tile missing from the floor, he remarked, 'I would never sign off on such shoddy workmanship.' He looked to the other notices: *No Smoking. Turn mobile off. Staff Only. Have you checked in?* John left his seat to inspect the small typewritten message on the noticeboard. Claire's name was first on the list.

The door to the waiting room swung open. An elderly couple entered and ambled to the nearest seats. A man wearing a suit entered behind them. He looked around the room. 'The usher's not here.' He shrugged. 'Okay, I was hoping to have use of a room, no matter.' He lowered his voice, but he could not contain his enthusiasm and his speech rose as he explained the intention. He pulled clipped sheets of paper out his case and addressed the elderly couple, 'Suzanne is due for release on Monday. The issue you have is where she is released to. Correct?'

'She can't come home. She's violent. On a visit the other week, she stabbed me, because I wouldn't give her twenty quid. Didn't she Marj? I've got stitches. We can't take it anymore,' the elderly man said. His wife blew her nose on a used tissue.

'This is why you have been referred to the county court. It is being taken seriously. And you can still press charges.'

'No, I can't do that.'

'We can apply for residential care. In the interim this could mean a half-way house, or a hostel. What you don't want is for her to be made homeless.' Seeing how upset the woman was, he added, 'There's time for you to get a cup of tea. We're not first on the cause list. I'll collect you both from the café. First I need to check for options.' They left the waiting room in single file.

'Did you hear that?' Claire asked.

'Dreadful. Poor woman,' Jenny said.

'At least I'm not that bad,' Jenny offered.

John's eyebrows arched.

From a side door, a diminutive man entered the waiting room. He took position behind the desk. 'That must be the usher,' John said. 'Take your letter to him.'

Looking over his half-rimmed glasses, the usher asked, 'Claire May Jones?'

'Yes.'

His eyes rested on the list and he ticked her name. 'Are you being represented?'

Claire turned away from him. 'Dad am I being . . . ?'

'Are you waiting for a solicitor, a barrister?' the usher prompted.

'Yes.'

'I'll unlock an interview room.' He walked to a door set in a row of four with space between them. He unlocked the door of room two but did not open it. Claire sat down next to her dad.

The waiting room door swung open. Fred accompanied by Mr Fen walked in. Mr Fen caught John's eye and tilted his head. Fred gave a look of disdain to all three of the Jones' and sat as far away as possible. John interlaced his hands and stretched his arms out. He checked the clock on the wall: five to the hour. 'Where's our solicitor, time is getting on.' He dropped his arms by his side. The door to the waiting room opened. Mr Sinclair had arrived. 'Hi guys,' he said.

John stood and pointed to the door unlocked for them. Mr Sinclair thrust his left arm forward to check the time on his wristwatch. 'Fine. We'll pop in there.' They huddled into the tight room.

'Go back to your chair,' John told his wife.

'We have all bases covered,' Mr Sinclair said to the expectant faces of his client and her dad. 'If and when the prosecution throws an issue we're not prepared for, I will request an extension.'

'If and when? Sounds a bit vague for my liking,' John said.

'No need to worry. This case should be straight forward. Claire, do you have the list of expenses thus far?' Her stomach tightened. She ferreted out the list, prepared by her dad, and handed it over. 'Good. If you are acquitted, we can apply to the court for reimbursement.' Mr Sinclair pulled his copy of *Archbold*, the criminal lawyer's bible, from his briefcase. He thumbed through the delicate pages. John and Claire observed him. She thought the procedure to be of importance.

A timid rap came from the door. John looked at Claire. Mr Sinclair continued to leaf through the pages. The door opened, and the usher popped his head through the gap. His glasses now pushed up to his eyes. 'Mr Sinclair, sir, the judge is seated in court.' Mr Sinclair stood causing his law book to fall. John retrieved the book and handed it over. As they marched past Jenny, she stood and followed them.

John skipped ahead to align himself with Mr Sinclair. 'Might Claire go to prison?'

'Quickly now, Judge is waiting. We only have to raise reasonable doubt for her to be acquitted. Though It's likely she will be banned from driving for a number of months or years. If found guilty of careless or inconsiderate driving, she may receive a custodial sentence. But dangerous driving is another matter entirely. At the doors of the courtroom, Mr Sinclair finished the conversation. 'Dangerous driving would point to manslaughter that could be life.' John whistled. Mr Sinclair pushed the door open.

Mr Sinclair bowed his head to the judge and offered apologies for his clients keeping the judge waiting. The district judge sat at the bench, which spread the length of the room.

Mr Fen for the prosecution began proceedings. 'Your Honour, my client has suffered severe loss, not only the death of his beloved daughter by the hands of a dangerous driver-'

'Objection!' Mr Sinclair shouted.

'Objection upheld. Let the reference to dangerous be struck of the record. Continue.'

'Sorry, Your Honour,' Mr Fen said with a smile on his face. 'My client was a devoted father, a devoted husband. Not only has he been devastated by the loss of his daughter, but he mourns the loss of his wife. Eunice Walker took her own life, as a direct result of her daughter being killed by the accused,'

'Objection!'

The Judge said, 'Mr Fen, I'll determine if the accused is guilty. As the matter of the taking of one's own life, this cannot be contributed to another. Strike from the record.'

'Sorry, Your Honour.'

'Stick to the rules, Mr Fen. You know what they are.'

'Again, my apologies, Your Honour. Nor will this father walk his daughter down the aisle or receive grandchildren from her.' Fred's head lowered. 'All these scenarios and more are no longer available to my client. Snatched away from him by, at the very least, a careless driver, whose thoughtless actions have rendered my client childless and a widower.'

Mr Sinclair stood. 'Objection! The child's mother's death has no direct bearing on my client's case.'

'Objection upheld. Mr Fen I counsel you to choose your words wisely.'

In his closing speech, Mr Fen stated, 'In my hand is the log of mobile telephone activity of the registered user – Claire May Jones, the accused.' He waived the paper in the air. 'At the determined time of the incident, the accused's mobile rang. The exact location of this call was Priory Lane, the scene of the incident.' He nodded to the judge before taking his seat. John squeezed his daughter's hand.

PC Smith was called to the stand. 'May I refer to notes, Your Honour?'

'Were the notes taken at the time of the incident?'

'Yes, sir.'

'They are permissible. Continue.'

PC Smith recounted the events he had recorded. He concluded his statement by declaring that both the breath test and drug swab were negative. Mr Sinclair dotted his pen on his pad and smiled.

An assistant left the courtroom to usher Richard from the corridor and invite him to the witness box. After giving oath, Richard answered the statements put to him by the prosecution. 'I came on the scene after the event. I assumed Claire, Miss Jones, had knocked down the child.'

'Objection!' Mr Sinclair shouted.

'Objection upheld. Mr Hamilton, an assumption is not a fact,' the judge said. 'Continue.'

Mr Fen asked Richard, 'And you heard Miss Jones, Claire, bring the car to a halt.'

'Yes, sir, I did.'

'So, what you heard, would suggest Claire had been driving faster than conditions should permit.'

'Not sure, it happened so fast.'

'No further questions, Your Honour.'

'Mr Sinclair do you intend to cross-examine?'

'Yes, Your Honour.' Mr Sinclair had one topic of questioning. 'You're a friend, and ex-boyfriend of the accused, are you not?'

'Yes, sir.'

'Would you say you know her well enough to make assumptions?'

'Sorry, I don't understand?'

'Neither do I,' the judge interjected. 'Mr Sinclair, we have struck off the comment of assumption. Is there a reason to question this?'

'Yes, Your Honour. Bide with me.'

'Continue.'

'Mr Hamilton, you told this court that you assumed . . . let's see how you phrased it . . . ah, yes, "I assumed Claire, Miss Jones, had knocked down the child." Is this correct?'

'Yes, sir. I think so.'

'You think so? Your memory is not clear?'

'Well, words to that effect.'

'So, Mr Hamilton, "You think so, or words to that effect," is how your memory retains what you have just spoken?'

'I assumed she had run over the child. I'm aware of saying that.' Richard scratched the side of his neck.

'Ah, assumption. A wordsmith may consider that word similar to "guessed". You guess Miss Jones was responsible for the death of Amy Louise Walker. No further questions, Your Honour.' Richard took a seat behind Fred. Mr Sinclair remained standing. 'To sum up, Claire May Jones is a competent driver. She holds a clean driving licence. She is employed in a permanent position at a telecommunications depot, where she is respected and well-liked by her colleagues. On the evening of the accident,' he placed emphasis on the word *accident*, 'her intent was to visit a friend who lives at the house to the other side of the cobble lane, almost opposite to the house of the deceased and to where on the road in front of the deceased's house the death took place. Miss Jones had curtailed her speed in advance to park her car near to her friend's house. Furthermore, there was not a time schedule attached to this visit. In other words, she was not in a hurry.'

'We understand your meaning, Mr Sinclair,' the judge said.

'Of course, Your Honour.' A fake cough found its way into Mr Sinclair's hand. No further comment, Your Honour.'

John squeezed his daughter's hand. After being called, Claire stood. She brushed her mum's knee with the back of her legs and walked to the witness box. She placed her hand on the Bible to swear to tell the truth. Her speech was slow and methodical, brought on by the medication.

Mr Fen took the baton of questioning. 'Miss Jones, just before the incident, where was your phone when it rang?'

'In my bag.'

'Did you, whilst driving, try to retrieve your ringing telephone? Were you not curious to know who the caller might be?'

'Yes, but I couldn't find it with one hand.'

'Ah, you couldn't find it with one hand. Presumably your other hand was on the steering wheel? Miss Jones. Maybe you took your eyes off the road to look in the direction of your bag? If the child was stretched out on the road, as you declare, did you not have a duty of care to see her and avoid driving over her?'

'Yes.' Claire had drifted, she only caught the last few words. She hoped to have answered correctly.

'Thank you. No further questions, Your Honour.'

'I didn't see her on the road, in fact, I'm sure she wasn't there. No, I mean she was there, obviously, but . . .' Claire fell silent.

'Does the defence want to cross-examine?'

Mr Sinclair stood. 'Yes, Your Honour. Miss Jones, Claire, what you have said is that it is of your opinion that the child was already flat on the road? Maybe as a result of slipping on ice. Maybe as a result of a hit-and-run-driver? When you ran over this poor prone child on that evening of poor visibility, maybe the child was already dead?'

'You are leading the accused and stipulating the outcome without critical proof or witness. Mr Sinclair, please respect my court.'

Mr Sinclair nodded to the judge, then asked Claire, 'Did you see the child on the road? Did she run out in front of you?'

'No.'

'You drove at a speed appropriate to the road and weather conditions, and still you did not see her, the child you ran over?'

'No.'

'What provision did you take for the torrential rain that evening?'

'I slowed down and put the wipers on full ... I remember turning the heater to full.'

'And you are convinced the child had already been knocked down?'

'Objection!' Mr Fen shouted.

'Strike Mr Sinclair's comment from the record. I will not tolerate this supposition in my court. There will be no further warning, Mr Sinclair.'

155

'Your Honour. I shall rephrase – Miss Jones, you say you did not see the child, that she was not there, and the only way you can square the fact is to suggest the child lay down on the road. What did you do to vindicate this assertion?'

'We had leaflets printed to ask for any witnesses to contact us. Someone might have seen her, down on the road.'

'Your meaning of us? Your family as a whole?'

'Yes, sir.'

'This is how convinced you were, are. Did anyone come forward as a result of these leaflets?'

'None.' Claire's eyelids drooped. She yawned. 'Excuse me.' She shifted her weight and widened her eyes.

'No witness came forward, because no-one could see the child due to reduced visibility brought on by the weather conditions of that night.'

'Mr Sinclair,' the judge cautioned.

'Sorry, Your Honour. Mr Fen, my learned friend, referred to a telephone call sent to your mobile at the approximate time of the accident. Did you answer that call?'

'No, I didn't.' Claire's eyes were close to shutting. She broke out in a sweat.

'No further questions, Your Honour.'

Claire left the witness box. She ruffled past her mum and sat down, leaning her head on her dad's shoulder. All she wanted to do was sleep. She regretted the overuse of chemical aid. John patted her hand. 'You'll be all right,' he whispered.

The judge leant forward and spoke into the microphone. 'There will be a short recess. If you all could remain.'

An assistant instructed, 'All rise.'

Fred turned to Mr Fen. 'Why in the hell did Amy-Lou go out that night? We had sweets in the cupboard, healthy sweets with no additives.'

'We can never get into the head of another, especially not a child's mind.'

The courtroom hummed with whispered chatter. 'All rise,' the assistant boomed.

The judge returned to his seat. He rubbed the side of his nose managing to dismiss a sneeze. 'Having considered the evidence, I find Claire May Jones guilty of dangerous driving. Resulting in the death of a minor. I issue a six-year prison sentence. At least three years to be served. Thank you.' He left the courtroom.

Jenny threw her head into her hands and leant forward. John squeezed his daughter's hand excising all blood from it. Claire remained silent. She yanked her hand free and gave a weak smile, taking a deep breath. 'That's that then.'

Jenny sat upright as the warden approached. 'But she can come home first. Can't she?' Jenny cried.

John took hold of his wife's hand. 'No, love, she can't,' he said.

The warden ushered Claire out of the courtroom. With no time for hugs and kisses. 'Stairs or lift?' The warden asked.

'Lift please.' The stainless-steel door slid open. Claire and the warden stepped inside the box to be transported to the floor below. At an organised desk, Claire's possessions were taken from her and logged. 'Can I keep my watch?' A present Richard had given her in the early stage of their relationship.

'No. You'll get it back when you're moved on.' The warden led Claire to a cell.

'Is this it? Is this where I'll stay?' The cell, though clean and modern, was small and dark.

'Just for an interim period,' The warden said. He had pity in his eyes. 'There's no transport to the prison at weekends. You should have had the hearing changed from a Friday. Look, love, trust me, there are a lot of worse places you could be sent.'

Fred shook Mr Fen's hand vigorously. 'Excellent, excellent result,' he said. 'Thank you.' Fred would head home to spend time in his decaying garden.

Jenny wept. John made his way to Mr Sinclair. 'Hang on,' John shouted. Mr Sinclair paused at the door and turned to face John. 'What happens now? Can we go and see Claire?'

'No. You will need a VO.'

'A VO? Speak clearly, man.'

'A visiting order.' Mr Sinclair swopped his briefcase to his other hand. His engaging eyes checked the watch on his wrist.

'How do we get this decision overturned?'

'You can appeal.'

'Can you go to her now? Reassure her. Tell her I'll do everything in my power to have her released.'

Mr Sinclair checked his watch for a second time. 'I have a tight schedule . . . make an appointment to see me next week. I will get the ball rolling for an appeal.' He touched John's arm with his free hand. 'Don't worry, she will be cared for in the system.' Mr Sinclair turned, lengthened his stride and walked out into the bright sunshine.

John rubbed his earlobe. He returned to Jenny's side. 'Come on, love. We can't do anything here. Let's go home.' He led his wife by the elbow into the fresh air.

'She should be coming home with us,' Jenny said, failing to contain her racking sobs. 'She's not a malicious girl. It was an accident. Do something, John. She'll be mixing with all sorts of criminals. It will damage her.'

'Do something? Like what? March in there and drag her out. Talk sense, woman. You're going to have to get a grip on this. Go and get something for your nerves,' he said. Though clearly, he was heartbroken too.

Jenny wiped her nose. She would not go to the doctor. She would not argue with her husband. Instead, she would wait for him to calm down, as he always did. As they stepped into their house, silence echoed the absence of Claire, and returning home from court without her daughter was too much for Jenny. 'I'm going to bed.'

'No. You can switch the kettle on. There are issues we need to discuss.' The water rumbled to a boil and burst the silence. John made two mugs of strong tea, a sugar in one for his wife, then he sat at the table to face her. He slid the hot mug and two paracetamols to her before taking a swig of tea from his own mug to clear his throat. 'We need to sort this out. Put a plan in action. And that costs money.'

'I've got the money Mum left me,' she said. Sitting up straight she took a gulp of tea and swallowed the painkillers.

'No. Keep that for now. I'll sell the classic. It'll fetch good money.'

'Oh, John, you love that car.'

'I love you and our daughter more.' He reached for his wife's hand and covered it with his own. 'The proceeds from selling the car will go a long way to paying legal fees. I'll put an ad in the Classic Car magazine tomorrow.' He drank his tea. 'I'll find out how to organise a visiting order to see Claire as soon as we can. Tell her our plan, reassure her. And, I'll tell you this: we are not going back to that Mr Sinclair. Smug bastard.'

'But he knows Claire. He knows the case.'

'No. I'll employ a barrister from the city. I've been researching this, I need to get in contact with a solicitor, not Sinclair, and they can direct me to a barrister. You have to be introduced, apparently. I have cursed myself for not doing this in the first place. I feel as though I've let her down.' He squeezed Jenny's hand, before removing his own.

'John, you haven't let her down. I have. My nerves have let her down.'

'Jenny, you'll have to be strong, we have tough times ahead.'

Arriving home from the court hearing, Fred opened his front door and closed it without turning the lock shouting to the void upstairs. 'Eunice, we have won; we have won the case. We got justice, dear. We have justice! That bastard girl is locked up.' Discarding his coat in the living room he popped a waiting CD into the player and the song *Once Upon a Dream* began to play. A tear ran down Fred's cheek. A sob escaped him. He went in search of a bottle of whisky.

Waiting to hear from Richard about the court hearing, Linda looked out of the window onto Priory Lane. The clock on the mantle chimed; another hour had passed.

160

Dusk had descended earlier than usual as a storm was gathering. A taxi stopped on the lane. Linda watched her son get out, she rushed to the front door to open it. 'Darling you've been ages. How did it go?'

'Fine. I called into town for a few drinks.'

'And why not! A terrible ordeal you've been through. I still don't understand why you had to go to court. You didn't see what happened.'

'Mother, if you are summoned, you have to attend.'

'Why didn't you let me come with you?'

'I didn't want you to be subjected to the ins and outs of that horrific accident.' He kissed her forehead. 'Claire's been found guilty of dangerous driving. She's been locked up.'

'And so she should! Putting you through all of this. And that poor child, killed by Claire's reckless driving. It's murder if you ask me. And Eunice, she would still be alive. They should lock Claire up and throw away the key.'

'I'm going for a shower. What's for dinner?'

'Your favourite. It's on a low light in the oven.'

Richard changed into a new pair of jeans and a maroon V-necked cashmere sweater. He ate the prepared goulash and drank two large glasses of expensive red wine. Then he popped back upstairs to brush his teeth and splash on aftershave. He walked out of the back door without shouting goodbye. He headed to Andrea's house and knocked sharply on her front door. Her dad opened the door, resplendent in his vest, through which he scratched his stomach. 'Yeah?' he said.

'Is Andrea in?'

'Andrea,' he bellowed. 'Doesn't look like it. D'ya want to come in and wait?'

Richard checked his watch. 'Do you think she'll be long?'

'Na. It's night school night. She'll be back any minute.'

Richard stepped into the dismal hall, then followed the owner of the house into the living room. He looked to the man sitting in his chair in front of the active television. Then perched on the arm of the settee where he watched the television blankly. A key turned in the lock and the front door opened, then slammed closed. Richard looked to the vested man, whose eyes did not leave the screen. 'I think Andrea's home,' Richard said.

'Is she? Go on up then.'

Richard made his way back to the hall. He took the stairs two at a time. Opening the door marked *Andrea* he entered. 'Hi, baby doll,' he said.

'How did you get in here? What do you want?' Her face was flushed.

'You. I want you. You won't answer my calls.'

'There's a reason for that!'

'And that would be?'

'Ask Claire.'

'What's she got to do with you and me?'

'There is no you and me.'

Richard took her hand and lifted it to his lips. He looked into her eyes while pulling her to him then locked his arm around the back of her waist. 'There will always be you and me.' He kissed her full on the lips. Her soft lips parted to welcome his tongue. He hitched up her skirt and pulled down her thong. Andrea looked over to the open bedroom door. She did not pull away from him. Richard drew her to the bedroom wall then slammed his back against the wall, unzipped his fly and flicked his restrained penis out. With both hands on her waist he lifted her slight frame off the ground and lowered her onto his extended member. He slid her forward and backward, rocking her away from him then pulling her tightly back. He checked on the open bedroom door and willed PJ to walk in. With a final push, Richard was spent. Exhausted through lust, he tidied himself. 'So, you think there is no you and me?'

Andrea smiled. 'I hear you're with Claire?'

'Not me. Not for a long time. She's gone to prison today.'

'Really? I don't like the girl but going to prison. That's brutal.'

'Well she did kill a child. Where's PJ? In his room?'

'No. He's away.' She ran her hand through her hair and ruffled her locks to give volume to the style.

'Away! Where?'

'At a convention. Some nerdy thing to do with computers.'

A short laugh escaped from Richard's mouth.

Andrea raised her eyebrows. 'What's with the sarcastic laugh?'

'Him. PJ, a gaming nerd. You couldn't write it.'

Andrea frowned. 'Shall we go for a drink?' She took a sideways glance into the mirror to check her appearance.

'No. I'll make tracks.'

'But I thought . . .'

'Would you like to come to Lake Como next month?' He asked, trying to defuse her neediness.

'Really?'

'Yes really. You are sweet.'

'I'd love to, but I don't have the money.'

Richard looked at her. Maybe he would take her. After all, Gabriella would not be at the Lake next month. 'I'll pay. My treat.'

'I couldn't. It's too much.'

'Nonsense. I'll book the flights. Email me your passport details.'

'Are you sure?'

'Absolutely. Are you free to travel any date next month?'

'I'll fit in with your plans, but I only get two weeks off at any one time.'

'Easy girl, I wasn't suggesting a long stay.'

Andrea examined her nails. 'Oh! I haven't got a passport.'

'I'll sort it.' A girl with no passport? He decided against taking her. He kissed the tip of her nose.

'I'll go into town tomorrow and get my photo taken for the passport. Do you want to come with me?'

'No. I've research to do.'

'I'll call round to your mum's when I've got the photo. How many do you need?'

This was too involved for Richard. He took his phone out of his pocket. 'I'll take your image on this. Stand up straight, look to the middle of the screen. Do not smile.' Andrea checked her hair with her fingers. Click. They viewed the image together. 'Look at your post-coital radiance. Each time we travel together, we'll know the secret of this healthy glow.

Excellent!

In the court holding cell, Claire listened as the footsteps grew louder. The clipped tones stopped as Claire looked to the door. A flap of steel set into the fortified door was opened. A woman's face appeared in the void. 'Breakfast,' she said. The flap of steel slid to a close and the door opened. With no conversation between the two, the officer placed the tray onto the small table. Claire stared at the cereal, toast and juice. She listened to the door being locked. On her second day here, Claire was alone again. She did not leave the bed. She had no appetite, though her stomach churned. She did not hear the soft-soled visitor approach and was startled when the door swung open.

A man entered the cell. 'Hello. I represent Her Majesty's Prison and Probation Service.' Claire looked at the lanyard around the man's neck – *David Smyth, HMPPS*. He placed his briefcase next to the tray of uneaten food. Out of the briefcase he took a folder with Claire's name on it. 'I know it's a Saturday and you probably won't want to complete this now, but I have a backlog to catch up on.'

'I don't mind.' Claire felt uncomfortable sitting on a bed with a man who was a stranger. She went and stood by the wall.

'May I?' He asked, pointing to the glass of orange juice. 'I'm parched.'

'Sure.' Claire was indifferent to his request. She noticed the direction his right eye took it did not line up with his left, then she looked away.

'A few questions I need to ask, for your profile. How are you sleeping?'

'Not so good.'

'Excellent! Do you feel sad, unhappy?'

'Naturally.' The officer looked at her, his pen poised. 'Yes, I feel sad,' she said, in response to the flicker of his eye.

'Do you feel agitated?'

'Yes.'

'Good. These are all normal feelings for your predicament. Are you experiencing mood swings?'

'No. I feel down all the time.'

'To be expected. Any thoughts of death or suicide?'

'I think of the dead girl. I dream of her. But, no, I'm not suicidal. Hey, I need my prescription tablets for anxiety. Can you get them for me?'

'How do you feel in relation to the crime you have committed and the punishment you have received?'

'If I killed her, I deserve to be here.'

'I won't detain you further.' He replaced the folder in his case.

'What about the meds? I need them. Can you get them?'

'Not my job, I'm afraid. But I will inform the prison doctor.' He rapped on the door to be set free.

CHAPTER 12

The Tournament

MORNING BROKE on the first day of the tournament. PJ bolted out of bed. He stood, laced his hands, raised them above his head and stared at the back of them.

'Are you nervous?' Kerry asked.

'No. Well, a bit.' He forced a surge of air out of his lungs, blowing the air upward, caused his fringe of blond hair to lift and fall.

After breakfast had been slapped down by the lofty landlady, PJ and Kerry stepped out from the front door onto the wide pavement. PJ looked forward to submerging in the underground, he had never experienced anything like it. He was encouraged to feel that he too was going places, like the other travellers.

At the venue, a queue, wide and long, trailed past the building and spilt onto the road. PJ pulled his ticket from his pocket. He checked the VIP emblem and headed past the line of idle people. He found the coveted entrance. Kerry followed, with what appeared to be a purpose to her step.

A greeter, dressed in the costume of a King Kreep serf, stood in front of the double doorway. A purple carpet had been rolled out in welcome. PJ stepped onto the thick pile of the carpet; he had arrived. 'Morning, followers of Lore,' said the voice from inside the costume. PJ handed over his ticket. 'This way Pyjama.' The merriment in the narrator's tone was not lost on PJ or Kerry.

'I didn't know you'd use that title,' PJ said.

'Yes, sir. It's how the tournament staff reconcile your online gaming.'

'Can it be changed?'

'Not at this stage. Does the lady have a ticket?'

PJ rustled in his pocket and produced a simple ticket. He handed it over.

'It's not a VIP-ticket. She'll have to join the queue.'

PJ's pallor matched the carpet and Kerry turned away from him. 'Okay, she can come through here, but don't let on.' The serf pulled the handle of one of the heavy doors. He bowed, causing his headgear to slide forward, he repositioned it with his free hand.

A dim light threw shade into the corridor. Images Kerry had seen in PJ's bedroom loomed from every conceivable surface. To their right was a souvenir shop. PJ gazed through the window of the shop, forgetting the urgency of his task. Kerry pulled him away and they headed to where PJ would compete. The enclaves were custom built into sections to create individual caves. Most housed several large flat-screen televisions for the spectators who were too far back in the stadium seating to watch the games directly. Excitement rippled through PJ. Never in his life had he witnessed anything as awesome as this. A serf approached PJ and Kerry. 'Are you both participants?' Kerry searched the face of the serf's costume.

PJ knew exactly where the eyes were. 'No, only me.'

'What name is it?'

'Paul Withers, PJ . . . Paul?'

The serf checked the list of gamers on her hand-held monitor. After a pause, she said, 'Sorry, that's not on the list.'

'Could it be Pyjama?' Kerry asked.

'Ah. You're Pyjama.' The costumed head moved up and down. 'You start at ten. The first assignment is in cave one. When you have completed it, proceed to cave two and so on. Don't wait to be invited.' The serf handed PJ a package. With difficulty she turned and waddled off in search of another contestant.

PJ checked his watch: nine-forty-five. He scanned the map for cave one. He thought it a good idea to visit the toilet. Back in the hall he tore open the envelope he had been given: postcards, a discount on next month's hyped game, and a swipe card on a lanyard programmed to contain his personal details. With pride he put the lanyard around his neck. He grabbed Kerry's hand and headed to cave one. Choosing to sit in the chair nearest to the door at one of the several computers in the enclave. He checked his watch and registered the time as nine-fifty-five. In the low-lit room from the surrounding seats, supporters were waving neon sticks. PJ was hyped. Kerry stood behind him until the game commenced. She patted the top of his head. 'Good luck with your game.' She left the room. Bang on ten o'clock, PJ swiped his card through the tight trough. *Welcome Pyjama.* PJ kept his pallor; he was in the zone.

PJ had completed the first stage of the tournament in record time. He stood and stretched his arms. The spectator screens flashed scenes from different stages of the game. The room was a mass of colour and sound with spontaneous whoops and claps at every victory. PJ left this hubbub and passed the queue of gamers who were waiting for their turn. With the aid of a map, he made his way to the next cave.

A purple-clad serf blocked the entrance to cave two. PJ showed the card that hung around his neck. The serf lowered his weapon and stood to one side allowing PJ, the first contender, to enter the room which was rich in many shades of purple. PJ sat on the nearest swivel chair and logged onto his game to continue the quest.

Kerry visited the souvenir shop to purchase a keyring and a t-shirt with the King Kreep emblem on the front. She ignored the Serf and The House of Darkness memorabilia.

Years ago, PJ had taught himself to touch type. Even using an efficient gaming mouse, he found the use of the keyboard was one-tenth of a second faster than each click of the mouse. Employing this skill of touch typing, his eyes had no reason to leave the screen. He raced ahead. Only a few spectators were in this room, none had expected a competitor to be here so soon. PJ's fingers danced on the keyboard. He raced his character ahead of the beating-drum. The strangled beat of drums grew nearer, faster. His heartbeat echoed the rising tension of the drums. He was the avatar always in control, the conqueror. The sound reverberated around the room and closed in on PJ; a ploy to disrupt his concentration. This game was mesmerising and alarmingly slow. PJ skipped ahead of the drums, he did not want to let the noise gain more momentum and volume. There was an art to this section, with no repetition. He fired at the serfs. 'Yes! Get in there.'

Under PJ's jumper, sweat clamped his t-shirt to his back. He had conquered level two then pushed the chair back. Scanning the room, he saw a light from a lone computer cast a dancing shadow over another contestant. *Yes!* He pulled his fist by his side as a nod to victory. The gallery of spectators was now half-full. *Level three, here I come!*

PJ marched over to the Sea Grove where a costumed sea serf moved out of his way. In the cave, PJ sat on the nearest padded swivel chair. He logged onto the computer and swiped his card in the slot. *Let the game commence.* Knowing level three would be tricky; a ploy used in all their games, though not the hardest challenge was bound to littered with twists and turns, he had no intention of falling to the hands of prey. There were a few spectators sitting in the rafters, but PJ ignored them. The screen, a mass of individual colours, flashed before him. He was primed to begin. Dodging the antagonist, PJ's body moved and matched each swerve of his on-screen character. Serfs had different castes, different colours; another trait of confusion. Each clan had their own set of characters and behaviours. PJ had studied them all. He was intuitive as to how to handle each one; how to interact and shirk them. His breathing ceased, he held the Y key, and jumped his character off the cliff onto the ledge of the canyon. The screen figure turned, held its arms up in triumph, then disappeared. PJ had completed stage three and he allowed his captured breath to escape. He pulled off his sweater, and tied the garment's arms around his waist, he felt comforted.

A chestnut brown cave beckoned, and PJ was lured to it. There was no guard at this entrance. Walking through the opening, traces of fake cobweb clung to his chin, he rubbed them away. PJ did not check the room for competition or spectators, he sensed there would be none. A high-backed wooden chair, one of four in the room, waited for an occupant. PJ knew this to be the Sludge District. A difficult challenge but one he relished. He was in his element, anxiety had flown with exhilaration at every move. The screen was larger than in the other caves. Having logged on to the game, King Kreep in all his glory appeared on the screen. *'Congratulations for getting this far! Think you can annihilate me?'* The image laughed like a villain at a fair. *'In your dreams! I am your worst nightmare. I am indestructible.'* PJ ignored the intimidation and began the game.

On the screen, from the Valley of Doom, a door opened then shut with a clunk, echoed round the room. No characters were visible. PJ watched the black screen. He listened to the now quiet. From the four corners of the screen to the right of field an apparition appeared, tiny in its presence. The Mouth of Death invited PJ to enter. He slid his character past the parasite's sharp-toothed mouth, wide open for capture. Pushing his character to the top right corner, he plunged the image into the underworld: a place the enemy was forbidden. The screen went blank again. Thirty seconds rushed by before his character jumped into the middle of the screen. Without hesitation PJ slid him to the left corner to make him less vulnerable. The character remained tiny, the only beacon of light on the dark screen. PJ waited to utilise his character. Whispers came from the internal speaker, the illusion of attackers from above haunted PJ. He chewed his nail, his thumb bled. Sweat prickled his underarms. *To have come so far . . . come on, man, think!* PJ whirled his character over the screen only to excite the whisperers further. 'Five minutes to lock-down,' the loudspeaker barked. PJ had not been receptive to the previous warnings of closure. He sat back in the unfamiliar chair, at a loss with the game. He logged off, picked up his fallen sweater, and walked out

Kerry sat at a table, sipping a coffee. Earphones clamped in her ears as her foot tapped out a tune, her body swayed to the lyrics. PJ slapped his hand on her shoulder. She jerked, then pulled the wire from her ears. 'Bloody hell! You scared the shit out of me. What with all these gloomy pictures of predators.'

'Sorry. I'm finished for the day.'

'Have you won?'

'I haven't finished yet . . . I'm stuck.'

'You're stuck?'

'Shush! Keep your voice down. Let's go.' PJ grabbed her hand. He led her out of the building through the public door. He had forgotten all about his VIP status.

At the boarding house, Kerry stepped out of the shower, dried, then put on the t-shirt that she had bought PJ. At the mirror she scrunched her hair then pulled the lower lid of her eye down to apply black liner and repeated the process to her other eye. She sashayed into the bedroom. PJ lay on the bed looking up at the ceiling. 'Hi Kreeper, Serf, or whatever you are,' she said seductively.

PJ turned his head to smile at her, then returned his vision to the ceiling. Kerry jumped onto the bed, knees first and crawled to him. She slid her hand up his long thigh. He clamped her hand. 'Not tonight. I have to devise a scheme.' She grabbed the magazine she had bought and began flicking through its glossy pages. 'Can you not do that!'

'Do what?'

'Make flicking noises.'

'Oh, Mr Serious.' She flung the magazine on the floor.

'I'm sorry. My head's all over the place. Let's nip out and get something to eat.'

They slipped outside, avoiding the landlady serving meals to her regulars. After hunting down a fish and chip shop, with their meals soaked in vinegar and wrapped in faux newspaper, they sat on a bench. 'I have to sort out this stumbling block. I have to find a way of lighting the screen. There'll be no time to sort it tomorrow; other competitors will creep up.'

'It's okay. I'll get some chocolate and watch a movie.' She looked at his worried countenance. 'With the volume turned down.' They threw the remainder of the meal into the bin.

Back at the lodgings, PJ opened his laptop and plugged in his headphones. He logged onto the game to replay his steps and search for clues.

The film on TV came to an end. Kerry pulled on the see-through slip she had bought for this occasion and looked over to PJ, but his vision was intent on the computer screen. Pulling the duvet free from his weight, she wrapped her shoulders and fell asleep.

Not quite the break of day when PJ solved the problem of his game. He closed the laptop. Too wired to sleep he watched daylight invade the room. Then shook Kerry by the shoulder. 'Wake up.'

'What?'

'I've found the way out of the dark!' He headed to the bathroom.

'Out of the dark?'

'The game . . . the part I was stuck on. I know how to bring the screen back to life.'

'That's fantastic. You go. I'm tired. I'll see you back here. Is that okay?'

'Yeah, that's fine because I'm not sure if spectators are allowed at this level.' He put the toothbrush back in his mouth and brushed his teeth with determination.

After waiting his turn to alight the tube, he walked briskly to the event location. Happy to be alone and with confidence in his stride, he arrived at the VIP entrance. Inside the venue, he made his way to cave four. Ducking the fake cobwebs, he sat in the same seat as the day before. He logged onto the computer and, as expected, a blank screen faced him. PJ whirled the mouse on the mat and came face to face with the shadow of his character. He slid the character to the far-left bottom of the screen. With pressure on the mouse, he placed his left hand on the keyboard. Then he made circular movements using the mouse while simultaneously hitting the X key – nothing. With his spirit deflated, he carried on the circular movements with the mouse and the Y key, but still nothing. He circulated the mouse then held the X key, repeating this procedure three more times to equate to cave four – and the screen came to life. PJ smiled. The obstacles on the screen were forensically accurate; PJ rode through them all. He loved the morally blank freedom this game awarded. Sitting forward in the chair he spun his character on. The hero of the moment, his character became darker, grew bigger, had muscles, a fierce countenance. The only character more powerful than his was King Kreep, who was aflame, his red eyes never leaving PJ's. Through twists and turns, PJ found the desired door. He accessed the digital pewter key, awarded at the last challenge, and slid it in the lock. The door opened. The exit beckoned. Level four had been completed.

With no need to check the map PJ left the vacant sludge cave, took a left turn, walked down a dark passage and arrived at cave five. This garish cave was barred by a gate. A keeper stood on the opposite side. 'Welcome, Master. Do you know the password to unlock this gate and dive into murderous hell?'

'I do.'

'Correct.' A noise matching a sound from the game pulsated as the gate opened. PJ sat at one of three screens. A mustard haze filtered into the room. The armchair was too comfortable for concentration. He would not be fooled by relaxation and perched on the edge of the chair. He retrieved his game and began to play.

As a nod to PJ's skill, his character was bigger than the assailant, but this created another hurdle because his character was awkward to manoeuvre. PJ held the *Shift* key and hit *F2*. His character flexed his muscles and grew to fill the screen. PJ tried the *Shift* key and *F6*. The character zoomed into view, its head now commanding the screen, the hairs on its face clear enough to be counted. PJ heard the enemy marching forward. He sat back in the chair and tilted his head to the ceiling then closed his eyes. He conjured the keypad in his mind then sat upright on the edge of his seat before hitting *Alt-F5* to reduce the size of his figure and allow him to see the opposition. He raced along, dodging and turning on a whim. He was ablaze. An unfamiliar character appeared in front of him, baring its jagged rows of yellow teeth and laughing. PJ rolled his character into a tight ball and flung it into the gaping mouth. He spun his character around until the mouth coughed it out. Disorientated, the gaping mouth shrivelled and scurried away. PJ knew more challenges were in wait, but he was prepared. He tackled two further traps efficiently and came to a stop at a locked gate. He tried to scramble over the bars of the gate, but they were electrified. His character fell to the floor, its hair on end. The character turned and looked PJ in the eye. PJ knew he could not subject him to another blast. Without a key for the gate, and as the sides of the gate were tight against the screen plus there was no clearing underneath PJ was at a loss. *What the hell! Ah* . . . he typed the password: *I do*. The gate opened with a creak. His character ran through with a flourish and bowed to the screen. PJ was the only contestant in the room. He sprinted to the next cave.

There were six caves in the tournament. The planners had estimated a five-day completion. PJ headed to the final cave on his second day, a phenomenal achievement. Dressed in the costume of King Kreep, a man sat on a stool. The man held a cigarette between his thumb and forefinger. PJ smiled at the man and brought his sprint down to a walk. Flustered, the costumed King Kreep snuffed out the lighted tab with his forefinger and thumb. 'Greetings Adversary,' the costumed King Kreep cackled. 'I will not bar your entrance. I have no need to.' He faked a deep laugh, though his mask remained blank. PJ was not intimidated he was high on success. With just one computer screen in this small cave, PJ sat on the throne provided.

Poised to begin the game, PJ reclaimed his progress. He had acquired a team to protect his character, but a shift in perspective threw him. The view was from above and at some distance from the landscape it was impossible to decipher friend or foe. PJ would be forced to eliminate blindly. *Shit.* He decided against a massacre; he did not want to kill his own men. PJ leant forward. He placed his forehead on the back of his laced hands and closed his eyes. *There must be a way. The game can't be fixed for failure.* He sat up and placed his right hand on the mouse. He had read an article in a journal about the use of the square in advanced gaming. He moved the mouse upward, to the left, downward then to the right, and back up in a straight line. He then pressed the Alt key. He watched in awe as the overhead view came into range. Blades whirred above. His character was lowered to the ground by a helicopter. PJ fired at the enemy, as did his men. Fast and frenetic action exploded on the screen. Smoke drifted in the air, both on-screen and in the cave. He had done it. PJ had won. His army of men waved their weapons in the air. King Kreep rolled in a ball and scurried away, repairing for a future series challenge. PJ's character faced the screen with folded arms and winked at PJ.

Thrilled to have won, PJ Placed his hands behind his head, but he was slightly deflated that the game was over.

Light flooded the cave. Two trendy young men marched to PJ. He stood to face them, not sure what was about to happen. The first of the two men held out his hand, PJ shook it. 'Welcome. Superb playing.' The man continued the handshake. 'We own the company. Young and New. Rarely do we come across such talent in the gaming world as yours. The tournament runs not only to promote sales but to find talent for our team, and today we have.'

'Oh,' PJ said.

'So, we would be honoured for you to come on board, join our team and help develop future software.'

PJ's world was in a spin, an offer such as this. He sat down on the throne. Rubbed his hand over his hair.

'The lifestyle doesn't suit everyone,' the second man said. 'Travelling and working long hours. Please consider before you accept.'

'No, no, I mean yes, sure, I want in. Wow!' PJ stood to face his equals.

'You'll want to discuss the package offered before committing.'

'No, whatever the package? It will be fine. It would be awesome to work in gaming. I definitely want in.'

'You will be well remunerated, with benefits. It's a competitive field we work in. News of your hiring will soon circulate. It's in our interest to look after you, to keep you.'

'Right. Well, that's good.' PJ was hyped, about to blow like a gaming character.

With no concern to be overheard, other contestants were not around, and the King Kreep figure seen on CCTV smoking a cigarette had been fired on the spot. PJ was asked, 'Tell us, how did you fathom the change of perspective in the last challenge?'

I read an article in September's journal about extreme use of the mouse in gaming. I tried the technique at the time.

179

'Brilliant! Research and development will be the area for you. Do you have any ideas? Have you considered coding new formats?'

'I have, and I do . . . I,' PJ looked at the guys, unsure of what to say.

'Good man! Don't divulge. It's a highly secretive environment we work in.'

PJ beamed, with the sheer joy he held inside.

The second man pulled a card out of his jeans pocket and handed it to PJ. 'We're committed to stay at this tournament for the rest of the week. Come to the office,' he pointed to the card. 'Monday say eleven.'

'Sure.' PJ pocketed the card.

'Two o'clock on Monday, we'll award the prize. Be dressed for photographs. I doubt you'll have to share the prize.' Through all the excitement, PJ had forgotten about the prize money. Set high at £950,000, it was assumed no-one would win. Nervous energy tingled in PJ's stomach.

'We'll leave you to digest what has been offered. Don't forget your belongings. Would you like us to fix accommodation for the rest of your stay?'

'No thanks.'

'Until Monday then. Well done.'

PJ walked out, taller than he had walked in.

Back at the boarding house PJ ran up the stairs and tried the handle to their room, but it was locked. He sat on the floor, rested his back on the wall and waited for Kerry. Elated, with closed eyes he watched a glimpse of his future. Forty minutes later Kerry strode up the stairs. 'What's up? Why are you here? You've got stuck again!'

'I've only gone and won first prize on the tournament. If nobody else wins I'll get all of it, all of the £950,000!' The content of his speech sounded unreal to him.

She flung her arms around him and kissed him. 'I can't believe it!' she cried. 'You did it!'

He took the key out of her hand and opened the door. 'Yup, and that's not even the best of it, they've offered me a job, a career.'

'Wow! Money *and* a career, so what kind of job is it?'

'In development and research. Just listen to me . . . from motor mechanic to games developer – who would have thought!' He danced on the spot. Kerry threw her laden value bags onto the bed.

'Does the job in development pay good money?'

'I would think so. More than I earn at the garage, I guess. If my ideas are successful it could be huge. I have some projects I've been playing around with.' He silenced himself.

'Carry on.'

He was reluctant to release the plans that were locked inside his head, but he could see the look of expectancy in Kerry's eyes. Wanting Kerry to share his life, he divulged, 'Product placement with relevance to the game.' Her expression remained blank. 'Personal identification imposed on the character.' He had the language prepared. She shrugged her shoulders. 'Face and voice recognition, you'd mould a picture of your face and plant it on the character. And it would use your speech patterns. Forget the game, suppose you had motor neurone disease, you could record your speech pattern to add to content later when you lose your voice.'

'You care about people, don't you?'

'Aw, I don't know. Maybe. Yeah, I guess. Pack your case, we're going home.'

'We're supposed to be on holiday.'

'I have to go. See my boss at the garage. Buy a suit. Make travel arrangements for Monday. I need to play about with my theory and put something down on paper. Do you think I should refer to myself as Paul?'

'You *are* funny. Keep your nickname, it's quirky, different.'

'We're going places you and me.' He kissed the tip of her nose.

Back home, PJ dropped his bag on the kitchen floor and Kerry placed hers beside it. 'Dad?' PJ shouted, before walking to the bottom of the stairs. 'Andrea?'

'What's up?' his father shouted. Andrea pounded down the stairs.

PJ strode into the living room. 'Dad switch the television off for a minute.' Andrea stood in the doorway. 'I've been offered a job.' Andrea's shoulders relaxed to this piece of news. Dad pointed the remote to blank the television screen. Kerry squeezed into the doorway beside Andrea. 'It's more than that, I won the tournament. I won the money. They, the guys said they were so impressed with my skill they want me on board their team.' PJ was aware of his new way with words.

'Eh, lad . . . well I never.' His father left his chair. He placed a hand on each of PJ's arms and held them tight. Before he released the hold, he said, 'Proud of you, Son. We'll have a drop of the hard stuff, that's what we'll have.'

182

Andrea and Kerry followed PJ into the kitchen. 'I'd prefer a cup of tea after that journey,' PJ said, standing with his back to the ladies, as his dad joined them holding a half-bottle of brandy. Andrea nudged PJ. He turned his head and frowned in response. She nodded in the direction of their dad. 'Oh, yeah, brandy would be great,' PJ said.

Andrea took four tumblers out of a cupboard. She wiped the dust off them with a tea-towel then lined the polished glasses on the worktop. The cork was pulled out of the bottle and a measure of brandy was poured into each glass. The family unit knocked the fiery brandy back in one gulp. Kerry kept hold of hers.

PJ was pleased to see his dad wearing a broad smile, and was amused to hear him say, 'Wait 'till I tell them at the pub. That bloody, what's his name? Always bragging about his son, the accountant! He'll choke on this. See what your mum's missed out on!'

'You'll never guess,' Andrea prompted. 'Claire's gone to prison for dangerous driving. Six years.'

'No!' Kerry exclaimed.

'That's what you get when you kill somebody,' Andrea said.

A grey pallor swept PJ's face. 'Gone to prison? She's in prison now?'

'Yep. Richard told me. He was in court, heard it all. Got what she deserves, he reckoned.'

'Poor Claire,' Kerry said. 'Her parents will be devastated. They're such a lovely family.'

PJ felt the joy of his mood slip away. 'I'll carry your bag home,' he said to Kerry.

The couple left by the back door. 'What's up?' Kerry asked.

'Nothing!'

'Something's upset you.'

'I've got a lot on my mind.' They walked to Kerry's house in silence. 'I need to get back to start work on my presentation.'

'Have I upset you? Have you gone off me now?'

'No! Of course not. Come here.' He wrapped her in a warm embrace.

'What's the plan for the rest of the week?' Kerry asked.

'I have to get on with the presentation of my ideas. I need to go into town and buy a suit on Friday.'

'Friday? Can't we go tomorrow?'

'Sorry. I know I'm not much fun, but I need to take this offer seriously.'

'Shall I come around tomorrow with a picnic?' We could have it in your room.'

'I have to crack on, but okay, only that, the picnic.'

PJ restored himself to an equilibrium he could cope with and relegated Claire and the red button to the cellar of his mind.

CHAPTER 13

Where's My Passport?

IN HER BEDROOM, Andrea selected Richard's number from the screen on her phone. He answered on the second ring. 'Hi, sexy,' he said. 'Describe your panties.'

'No. Listen, I have news.' She told the tale of her brother's good fortune.

'What? PJ has?'

'I know.'

'Wouldn't have thought he had the intelligence.'

'Do you mind! That's my flesh and blood you're slagging off. Have you applied for my passport?'

'Passport?'

Andrea's excitement escaped. 'For the trip to Lake Como?'

'Oh, yes, right, I applied for it online. He took in a large breath then sighed. 'It will have been delivered to my address. I'll check with Mother the next time I'm home. Are you on the bed?'

'I am, actually.'

So, describe your underwear in detail. Tell me how and where it touches your velvet skin. Actually, open your bedroom door then lean on the wall where I had you last.'

'You had me last! Cheeky! No, Kerry's in PJ's room. She's taken to coming in here.'

Richard's voice lowered. His pulse quickened at the desire of danger. The image of Andrea being seen in a sexual compromise ignited his enthusiasm. 'Lick your finger and stroke your clitoris.'

Heightened by his command, she obeyed and moved with rhythm on the mattress equalling his groans of pleasure. 'You're gorgeous, sexy,' he growled. 'Open that door.' She rolled off the bed, opened the door and lent on the wall as he requested. Delighted by how her breathing had intensified, Richard whispered, 'Good girl.' He pulled his joggers over his enlarged penis then wiped his wasted seed on a tissue. The telephone now dead, Andrea closed the door and returned to bed.

After work the next day, Andrea headed to Linda's house. She saw the car for learners parked on the cobbled lane. Linda opened the door and waited. 'Hi, I'm Andrea.' Linda frowned and smiled simultaneously. 'PJ's sister.'

'Oh, hi. Come in.' Being Linda's response when she had driving lessons to sell.

'No, that's okay. Is my passport here?'

'Passport? Why would it be here?'

'Richard's organised it. He said it would be delivered here.'

'No. Why would Richard organise a passport for you?'

Andrea shifted her stance. 'I wasn't sure how to apply. Richard did it for me, as a favour.'

Linda's puzzled expression deepened. 'As far as I know, you have to apply for your own passport.'

'Really? Sorry. I must have misunderstood.' With flushed cheeks, Andrea walked up the lane to her house. Inside she knocked on her brother's bedroom door. There was no invite to enter. She opened the door a crack to see PJ sat at a large monitor, his ears covered by a padded headset with microphone.

Andrea lifted one of the earmuffs and spoke to the back of his head. 'Can you go online and check something for me?'

He swung his chair with castors to face her. 'Sure.'

'Can you check how to apply for a passport?'

'Just let me save these drawing updates. Why? Where are you going?'

'Nowhere . . . just thought it would be handy to have one.'

PJ came out of the programme file he was working on. He clicked on the government's website and chose the option for passport application. 'There,' Andrea said. 'Print that form.' The printer sprang into action, then stalled. Paper was needed. PJ opened the drawer, the red button stared at him causing his stomach to flip. He loaded paper into the printer's tray and with a whisper the application form was printed.

In her room, Andrea read the form. She saw where to attach her image and discovered an endorsement from a professional person was required. Staring at the box requesting her signature, she took her phone out of her pocket and blocked Richard's number.

Claire sat on the bed in the court holding cell. Except for staff, she had had no visitors. The door to her cell opened. Breakfast had arrived. 'What day is it?' Claire asked.

'It's Friday. You're moving out today.'

'Where to?' Claire rubbed her eyes against the extra light in the room.

'According to the list, you're off down south.'

'Can't I stay local?' Panic dismissed the little appetite she had.

'Doesn't work like that, love. You go where you're sent. It might not be permanent, though. Maybe a holding cell. Depends on availability.'

'But Mum and Dad? It won't be easy for them to visit. Can I stay here?'

'We're not that kind of facility. It's tough.' The door slammed shut.

Lunch followed breakfast and Claire left the food untouched. She sat on the edge of the bed studying her manicured nails when she heard footsteps approaching. The door opened. 'Van's here, time to go.' Claire was flanked by two officers; the threesome approached the desk to collect her possessions.

Outside, the fresh air hit Claire, catching the back of her throat and making her cough. The daylight hurt her eyes, when she focused her sight she saw the secure van waiting to transport her. Once Claire was in the van, she sat on the bench and listened to the cage door being locked. The van pulled away. Tears fell down her face as the journey began. When the van hit bumps in the road, she bounced on the seat. Daylight began to fade. With no windows to the outside, Claire sensed darkness creep in. She stared at the internal side panel of the van. Sick with worry and plagued with thoughts of her destination, the overwhelming concept of being far away from her parents swamped her. Hunger pangs marched in her stomach as the van rolled on. When she tried to sleep, she was shocked into reality by the brakes on the van. The rhythm of the wheels stopped, she took a deep breath in the surety that she had arrived. Anxiety levels caused a sickness to rise in her throat. The driver disembarked and she listened to his hard footsteps disappearing. Time passed; she no longer had a concept of duration. The footsteps returned. The van door opened. 'Move 'em out,' the driver said.

Out of the van, Claire looked to the high fence with spiked wire running along the top. Security cameras spied on her every move. Streetlighting could not compete with the floodlit yard. Shadows loomed. Claire stared at the waiting prison her mouth wide open. A patchwork of lights from curtain-less windows flickered. Bars protected the windows. This haunting night stared back at Claire causing her heart to rattle in her chest and she feared for lack of medication. The driver ushered her to the entrance.

Claire wrinkled her nose when accosted by the stench of institutionalised food; the power of disinfectant, the smell of cheap perfume. Doors banged and clanged. A door was kicked. A baby cried. Keys jangled. Shouts and four-letter words. Laughter. Muted sounds from television sets. And the bright lights, all robbed a newcomer's flailing spirit.

A woman, whose ample frame was restricted by a fleece jacket, waited for Claire. This woman had dyed hair the reddest of red, scraped back in a greasy ponytail. She had a pierced eyebrow and a stud through her tongue. Without comment, the driver handed Claire over to this colourful character. 'Holding-room four,' the redhead barked.

Locked in room four, Claire was overwhelmed; her senses hijacked by the environment with the smell of urine mingling with a purifying aroma. She heard the rolling of small wheels, one of which clacked due to a missing bearing. The sound came to a halt outside the door. A key turned, and the door opened. A uniformed woman entered carrying a clipboard. With her questions completed, the woman said, 'Take your clothes off. I need to strip search you.'

Claire stood naked. She folded her arms for protection and rounded her shoulders in shame.

'Bend down and touch your toes.'

Claire obliged, with no idea of what the request entailed. The woman pushed a neoprene gloved finger into Claire's anus, and just as quickly pulled it out again. The woman peeled off the glove and apologised for the indignity.

'Why did you do that?' Claire fought back her tears.

'Checking for contraband. Routine procedure.' She handed Claire a neat pile of second-hand clothes from the trolley. A track-suit bottom, a large t-shirt, a pair of socks and paper knickers. She placed the clothes Claire had arrived in into a paper bag. 'You can request clothes to be sent from home, provided they pass the criteria: basic, no underwired bras, no laces or zips. Nothing provocative. Here is the list, you can hand it to your provider.' She placed an emergency set of toiletries onto the folded bedding. 'The prison doctor will see you but,' she checked her watch, 'wouldn't think it'll be tonight. Any questions?'

'What about my medication, my pills?'

'Nothing I can do until you've seen the doctor. This is the problem with late admissions. I'm sick of complaining about it.'

Claire's stomach rumbled.

'You've missed the canteen call. I'll fetch some tea and toast.' The clacking wheel of the trolley disappeared down the corridor.

Claire dressed in the laundered clothes. Humiliated, she waited for the snack that did not arrive. As the noise from prison life abated, she fell into a fitful sleep.

Daylight interrupted the dark of holding cell four as Claire used the toilet in the corner. She refreshed her face with cold water from the tap. The bundle which had been given to her held a small soap, a toothbrush and paste but no deodorant. She sat on the bed and stared at the barred window. She stood, she sat. An inferior breakfast was delivered. Overwhelmed, she covered her mouth at the sight of food.

Mid-morning, the door opened. 'Hi. I'm one of the doctors here.'

'I need medication for anxiety and something to help me sleep.' She had slept more hours than she realised.

'Anxiety? A common condition often misdiagnosed. Were you medicated for anxiety before coming into the system?'

'Yes sir, I took fluoxetine 60 mg and amitriptyline 10 mg. I haven't had either for a while. What day is it?'

'Saturday.' He scribbled on a prescription pad. 'I'll need to check with your GP before administrating this medication and no GP works on a weekend. For sleeping

I will prescribe a mild sedative, a temporary fix, while you adjust. You would benefit from exercise. Do you have a hobby? If not, find one. Learn a new skill, attain a goal, this will fill your day and help to forge an effective sleeping pattern. I will review your state of mental health in a month.'

'Thank you,' Claire said to the closing door of the doctor leaving.

Claire was taken by surprise when the door opened again. 'Time to move you out.'

'Where to?'

'Your cell. Cleaned and disinfected. Get your belongings.'

'I don't have any belongings.' Claire made her way to the door.

'Not so fast, honeybunch. The blanket, pillow and the stuff you were given are your belongings. Roll them up and bring them with you.'

'Can I make a phone call?'

'Do you have a PIN?'

'A PIN?'

'You'll get one. Emergency funds will be loaded onto the card. That's your one phone call. After that you'll load credit via the canteen system.'

'Canteen system?'

'Yeah. You do jobs and earn credit. It's called the canteen system. You're not curious why we call it that?'

'The money you earn is for spending in the canteen?'

'Go girl!'

'When will I get this PIN?'

'Could be today, could be weeks away. When you get it, you can only ring the numbers you have listed and have been cleared. You could sort that while you wait.'

Claire followed the warden down the corridor. The aroma of dull food with no appetite enhancer had not diminished. She passed a queue of women who waited for medication. She walked past the dispensary and looked towards it. Some of the women leant on the wall and eyed Claire. She hastened her step. She wondered when her meds would be available. The warden ascended the stairs. Clutching her belongings to her chest, Claire had difficulty in seeing where to place her feet. At the top of the stairs she caught sight of a taught heavy-duty grille covering the air space from the level below. She thought it was there to catch rubbish. She did not consider inmates throwing themselves or others over the bannister. There was so much grey. Grey walls, ceilings, floor, spoilt by dirty scuff marks and greasy fingerprints. The door to her cell was open. Claire followed the warden in. 'Oh! I'm sharing?'

'Hark at the princess. This is a good cell, two beds instead of four. Think yourself lucky'.

'Hi,' Claire said, to the pale girl sitting on a bed.

'She doesn't speak English,' the warden said. Then on leaving, she closed the door without locking it.

The girl jumped off her bed. 'Why you here?'

Claire was shocked to hear the woman who did not understand English speak the language with an Eastern European accent.

'RTA.'

'What is this rat?'

In spite of her situation, Claire supressed a laugh. 'Road traffic accident. I killed a child.'

193

'Very bad. No? I rob pockets, shops. I beg people give money. Tuesday, I release. I be doing same.'

'Oh.' Claire sat on her elected bed. She set free her bundle of goods. Claire ventured, 'What happens now?'

'What you ask?'

'Where do we eat? Where do we shower?'

'I tell you. You pretend not know. Pigs not knowing I speak English.'

'Why?'

'Why should they know? They pigs.' She spat without phlegm. 'My name, Svetlana. English good, no?'

'Very good.'

'You eat canteen . . . what they call . . . yes, timed meal. Then yard. Shower at block.'

'What are the times for these events?'

'Avents?'

'What time do we shower?'

'You see.' She lay back down on the bed and closed her eyes.

Claire needed medication and fretted at the lack of it. She realised the naked cabinet by her bed was for her use and placed her feeble items inside. There was a stainless-steel toilet and sink fixed to the back wall with no privacy. Claire picked at a piece of skin on her middle finger, already raw, her manicured nails now ragged. She prodded her bladder; yes, she needed the toilet.

A low siren shrieked, and Svetlana sprang from the bed to leave the cell for lunch. Claire took this opportunity to use the toilet before falling in line to follow the herd. The food hall was noisy. A sea of hungry mouths. Claire copied the routine. She took a moulded tray off the pile and moved down the line. Meat stew with no heat rising was splodged onto the largest indent

194

on the tray. A scoop of greasy chips was slapped next to the meat. Svetlana slipped away, disappeared among the throng of inmates. Claire stared at her food and avoided conversation then drank the water provided.

Back in the cell, Claire picked up a letter from her bed then read the instruction: telephone numbers for clearance – obtain permission from recipient. She knew one number: home. All her other contacts were stored in her mobile phone.

Svetlana entered the cell. 'You got form?' She looked over Claire's shoulder. 'Put lot of number. They no check.'

'I only know one.'

'Your bad luck. No?'

The weekend dragged and so did Monday. On Tuesday, without saying goodbye, Svetlana was gone, released from prison. Claire was relieved to have the toilet facility to herself. Having not received her PIN, she did not know whether her parents' telephone number had been approved. Neither had she been given access to her medication. She had no experience of putting herself forward, asking for help. Her dad usually did that. She coped in silence.

A warden opened the cell door, followed by a teenager. 'A repeat guest checking in,' the warden said. Claire looked at the girl, at her greasy hair cut short without style.

'What're you looking at?'

The warden intervened, 'Now Tanya.'

'Piss off.'

On her way out the warden locked the door.

'Sorry. I didn't mean to stare.'

'I don't take shit from no-one.'

'No, of course not.' With the flat of her hand, Claire patted her chest to settle her increased heart rate.

Tanya walked to the window. 'My new fella,' she said, waving her arm high in the air. Tanya sat on the unmade bed and dropped her hostility. 'What are you in for?'

'I killed a child.'

'Shit. I don't want to share with a child murderer.' Tanya marched to the door and kicked it repeatedly.

Sitting on the end of her bed, Claire tucked her hands under her thighs. 'No, it was . . .' The flap on the door opened. 'Tanya, behave!' She kicked longer, harder. 'Tanya knock it off, or you'll go on lockdown.'

'I want the doctor. I need him now.'

'Stop the kicking and I'll fetch him.' The flap slid shut.

Tanya turned to her unmade bed. 'That's how I get things done.' The flap in the door slid open. Two senior officers flanked each side of the doctor. 'The Big Guns,' Tanya quipped.

The elder of the two officers placed his face in line with Tanya's. 'We're in charge here.' She muttered a response. 'Pardon, little girl?'

'Get out of my face right! Why've I been put in here with a child killer? You know I have kids.'

'I didn't kill a child intentionally. It was a road traffic accident.'

Tanya looked at Claire. 'That's fair enough, I can accept that.' She returned her stare to the officer. 'I need methadone.' The doctor asked whether Tanya was withdrawing. She answered, 'Obvs!' The doctor took out a prescription pad. 'I need it now. This minute!' The officers marched Tanya out of the cell, the doctor followed. Claire's chin dropped and her mouth parted.

When Tanya returned, she was calm. On the unmade bed she pulled a coarse blanket over her shoulder and slept like a baby who no longer relied on a night-feed.

Morning arrived; Tanya sat on the loo. Without washing her hands, she pulled a wipe out of a packet and used it to refresh her armpits, then she took another wipe and rubbed it between her legs. 'Tramp wash,' she said. Claire tried not to look. Tanya approached her and took a handful of Claire's hair. 'So pretty,' Tanya said. She wound the strands through her fingers. Claire was afraid to resist as Tanya stroked the locks from her scalp, then Tanya platted the hair. 'Just like my girl.'

Claire sat rigid. 'How long are you in for?'

'GBH. Guess I'll be in for at least a month. Can't see my fella waiting any longer. My social worker's coming tomorrow. I'll be bending her ear. Tell her I'm pregnant and refuse a pregnancy test. Against my human rights, see. My mum, poor cow, prefers me in prison. Says I've got structure. She thinks I'm clean in here. She has no idea! She's a good woman though. She has custody of my three kids.'

'Oh.'

Tanya undid the plait she had made of Claire's hair. She let the waxy strands fall then walked to the barred window.

What Brings You Here?

John and Jenny were unaware that the prison service had tried to speak with them; the authorisation of clearance for telephone numbers had begun. It was prison policy to make only the one call to contacts, this was the one the Jones' had missed.

John had been working on a barn and his boots were covered in mud when he returned home at lunch, so he made his way to the back door. A sight confronted him. Jenny threw the cigarette on the floor she stamped on the offending article and wafted the smoke away. She popped a readied mint into her mouth. 'What the . . . you stupid woman. All these nights keeping me awake, coughing. Any idea why?'

'John, it's not as bad as you think. This is my first cigarette.'

'Of course it is!'

'I'm sorry.' She stepped into the kitchen. Her arms wrapped around her chest. John followed her, his muddy boots still on his feet. 'It's my nerves. Cigarettes calm them.'

'But you won't go to the doctor!'

'I don't want to be medicated.'

'And this, tobacco is not a drug?'

'It works. Relaxes me. I'm sorry. I'll quit. I promise.'

'Damn right you will.' John telephoned the doctor's surgery to book an appointment for his wife. 'Tomorrow at ten, and you're going. I'll take you, as if I don't have enough to do!' He had clearly forgotten why he had returned home and headed out of the back door. Jenny wiped his muddy prints off the floor. She took a walk, away from the house to smoke another cigarette.

After visiting the doctor, Jenny was adamant, she would not take any tablets. She reckoned they made her sick, a past experience. The doctor recommended exercise, yoga maybe. Back home, John could not hold his tongue. 'All this self-indulging about your problems? We all have to cope with Claire being in prison, not just you!'

'I understood what the doctor said about endorphins. I'll book a course of yoga,' Jenny said. Online, John ordered his wife an outfit for yoga and a mat.

Jenny made a friend at the yoga class, a woman with issues of her own who shared heartache with Jenny.

The telephone shrilled, interrupting the quiet of the house. John pulled his arm from under the duvet. 'Hello?' He checked the time on the illuminated bedside clock – 7:30 am. Jenny sat up. 'Okay, can you give me the address? Is she okay?' He flung the quilt back and went in search of a pen and paper. Jenny tied the cord around her dressing gown and followed him down the stairs. She recognised the term VO and hung onto every word her husband spoke. 'Yes, booking reference go on . . . B639257. Got that, thanks for the call.' John slid the button to terminate the call. 'Sit down, love,' John said to his wife.

'Why! What's happened?'

'Don't get upset. Claire has been sent down south.'

'Down south! Why?'

'Availability, they say.'

'Well, I don't care where she is. We are visiting! You'll have to take time off work. Cancel some of your customers.'

'Don't talk nonsense woman! I have to work. Where will the money come from if I don't work? And, anyway the guy said you're only allowed two visits per twenty-eight days.'

Jenny rooted in her dressing gown pocket and pulled out a screwed-up tissue.

'Are you crying?'

'No! Yes . . . I can't.'

John put his arm around his wife. 'Don't cry. We'll go and see her the minute we are allowed. Claire will arrange a visiting order and we'll take it from there.'

'Oh, John, it's just so sad.' She managed to say between sobs.

'I know, love. I feel the same.' John made his wife a mug of sweet tea. He got dressed for work. After grabbing his snack-pack he tied the laces of his boots. 'Make sure you put the garage lights on and leave the garage door open if anyone rings about buying the car. Do not be talked down on price. Any problems ring me.' He kissed the top of her head.

The day came for John to visit a solicitor in the city, and the solicitor recommended that he should employ a barrister to represent his daughter. The solicitor rang the chambers he was connected with and made an appointment for John.

When the time came, John showered, dressed in a suit and headed out of the house alone. Without choice he parked the family car in the multi-storey where car spaces were tight. He marched down the busy city street, leaving the stores behind him. He pulled the list of directions to the barristers' chambers from his pocket: turn left at St Anne's square, pass the town hall, turn right at the courthouse. In the crisp sunlight he strode to Tailors Row, number fifteen. In a previous life, Tailors Row belonged to high-class tailors. Today only one tailor remained.

John pushed the door open. He bowed his head to avoid injury from the low door frame. The tread of the wooden planked floor was uneven. There were three members of staff sitting at individual desks. John approached a solid wood desk where a young man with red braces over his striped shirt was fixing a pink ribbon around a rolled file. 'Good morning,' he said.

'Hi. I've an appointment with a barrister.'

'What's your name?'

'John Jones. My appointment is at eleven.' He spoke his words with precision.

The clerk moved the file off the diary. 'You're booked to see Robert Jenkins. He's in his office. Go through to the next room, head up the stairs on the right, fourth door on the left.'

John ducked his head again as he passed through the narrow doorway. He walked through an expanse of space, a waiting room with antique leather chairs and a sofa. On the oak table sat a vase filled with an abundance of fresh flowers. The stairs were narrow and John was hemmed in by the walls on either side. A chandelier lit the top of the stairway, John fixed his sight on those twinkling lights as he climbed the stairs. There was a quietness about the place. John knocked on the door which stood ajar. In response, the door opened wide. Robert Jenkins offered his hand and John shook it. 'Please, Mr Jones, step in.' Robert returned to his seat behind the desk and John sat on the hardback leather seat opposite the barrister. John's attention was pulled to the heavy black telephone with a dial and coiled flex, when it rang. 'Hello,' Robert said, into the chunky receiver. 'No. I'm with a client. Pass her to Gregg.' He placed the piece of retro onto its cradle. 'What brings you here, Mr Jones?'

John retold the sorry tale concerning his daughter. He did not miss one detail. Without taking notes, Robert sat back in his chair, his fingers laced, his forefingers resting on his lips, he listened. 'What is your goal?'

'Ultimately, to have my daughter released. At the very least to have her sentence reduced. Also, I would like her transferred to a prison nearer to home. For her mum's sake.'

'From your perspective, was the trial fair?'

'I would say so. The only discrepancy is that my daughter is adamant the child was already down on the road and may have been dead when she ran over her.'

'Without a witness that would be impossible to prove. I can look into the case, but I must inform you that it could be costly.'

'Not a problem.' John's cheeks flushed.

'Was the case heard by a judge and jury?'

'No jury. Why do you ask?'

'Trial by judge and jury has a higher percentage rate of full acquittal.'

'Why weren't we offered that?'

'Mm . . . there is a debate; jury trials are massively expensive and slow to achieve a result. On the plus side, taking the judge and jury route with a driving offence is far more likely to evoke empathy and compassion from the jury. They can imagine themselves in the same position while driving a car, in a way they cannot compare themselves with say, a rapist or murderer. I am sorry to hear you were not informed of the choice.'

'I had no idea.'

'Would you be interested in pursuing an action against your representation?'

'No. I don't think so.'

'As a starting point, I will need all relevant files from your solicitor.' Robert looked at John's grave expression.

'Don't worry, you do not need to contact them. It can be arranged from here. Give your solicitor's details to the young chap at the desk.' Robert opened a virgin blue notebook, he poised his pen over the yellow ruled lines and asked, 'What was the date of the incident?'

'Friday the 10th February, in the evening.'

'What was the weather condition? Was there adequate street lighting at the time of the incident?'

'You keep saying incident; I prefer the term accident. It was raining heavily and dark.'

Robert's pen scratched over the paper. He closed the notebook. 'That is all I need for now. I'll read the transcript of the court hearing to determine if you have grounds for appeal. If we do, the Registrar will be instructed to serve an appeal notice to any party directly affected by the appeal. In this case that would be the deceased's father. He will have the right to representation.'

'If that's the law.'

'As regards a transfer of prison, I would not waste your funds. Try your MP.'

'I hadn't thought of that. Thank you. Do I pay you, or the guy downstairs?' John reached to his ticket pocket for a credit card.

'Neither. Our policy is to invoice at each stage. There will be a contract to sign, it will be handed to you on your way out. Take it home and read through it. If you are happy with the terms and want to continue, sign and drop the contract here. If an appeal is feasible, we will be ready to go. If not, you will be invoiced for today's consult.' Robert Jenkins stood, and offered his hand to shake for a second time.

Downstairs, John was handed the contract. 'Can I read through this in the waiting room?' he asked.

'Sure. Would you like a tea or coffee?'

'No thanks.' John sat by the fresh blooms inhaling the scent from the lilies. He put on his reading glasses to scan the document. Ten minutes later he signed on the dotted line.

Home from yoga, Jenny bent with fluidity to pick an envelope off the mat. She walked to the kitchen where she scrutinised the postmark; the letter was from the prison. She began to tear the flap on the envelope, then stopped to take a deep breath before liberating the contents: a visiting order in two weeks. She held the letter to her chest and hugged it. She took a skip of poor joy.

At the prison in the waiting room, John and Jenny sat at the first table they came to. They had arrived early, and had been checked through, they left their belongings in a locker. 'Not what I was expecting,' Jenny said. A portable bookcase holding untidy books doubled as a partition. Large windows allowed the sunlight to shine in. The décor was warm. An arrangement of fake flowers, which needed dusting, sat under a utilitarian wall clock. A toybox was stuffed with old toys. John focused on the fire extinguisher fixed to the wall. More visitors entered, and chatter filtered into the room by people at ease with the surroundings.

Jenny watched the finger on the clock reach the hour. A door opened. An officer led the prisoners to meet their visitors. Jenny's eyes searched for her daughter's beloved blonde hair which now was dull and tied in a rubber-band. John stood. He wrapped his arms around Claire. 'Sir, sit down,' an authoritative voice boomed.

'How's it been, love?'

'I hate it, Dad.' Tears dropped off her chin. She wiped them away.

'Oh, it's terrible,' Jenny wailed. Heads turned in the direction of their table.

'Don't, Mum. I'm fine. It'll be okay.'

'How can it be?'

Claire composed herself; she was gaining experience in doing so. 'So, my key-worker came to see me yesterday; there's an education programme I can enrol on. I want to learn a new language, I thought Italian, but she asked me to consider Spanish because its more universally spoken and a better skill to have. She said there's a prison education trust and that she'll apply for funding. It's an online course so I will need a laptop. The prison has some, but they're mainly used by the lifers.'

'We'll buy you one. Won't we John?'

'Yes. But why another language?'

'I'd like to work in tourism and live abroad.'

'Oh,' said Jenny. 'Well, Dad's employed a barrister to look at your case,' she continued. 'To see whether we can appeal.'

'Really?'

'The barrister's looking into the weather conditions at the time of the accident. Oh! And I've joined a yoga class.' Jenny looked at John's expression and stopped talking.

With a hiatus in the conversation, Claire asked, 'Have you been working on the car, Dad?'

'Dad's sold the car. A man with a trailer picked it up yesterday.'

'Sold it! Why?'

'Too much time and expense.'

Claire said nothing. She hadn't connected the sale of her father's beloved car to his need to bring in money for her defence. 'Can you jot down my contact numbers from my mobile phone?' she asked. 'It's on my dressing table.'

'All of them?' Jenny asked, having already searched Claire's phone.

'No. I don't need them all, just Richard's and Kerry's, and Dad's number.' Jenny tried to lock eyes with her husband's, but he had not tuned in to her. 'And can you bring the framed picture of Richard that's on my bedside cabinet?' Jenny had turned this photograph frame face down. 'And we're allowed to wear our own clothes, nothing fancy, joggers and sweats.' A shrill buzz broke all conversations.

John squeezed his daughter's hand. 'You'll be alright, love.'

Jenny cried huge, walloping sobs. They scraped back their chairs and stood. Claire produced a tight smile.

John and Jenny travelled home occupied by their own thoughts.

CHAPTER 14

Pay a Screw

ROBERT JENKINS QC was an intelligent and thorough barrister; John could not have found a more qualified and successful man to support his daughter.

The chamber's clerk obtained the case file for Claire May Jones. Robert had requested information on any other drivers within a twenty-mile radius of the same road on the same evening who might have skidded on ice. He asked the junior to print meteorological reports for the day of the accident. Robert had checked the police report to determine if the case had been handled correctly.

John's telephone vibrated in his utility trouser pocket. 'Yes. Yes. Absolutely. Thanks.' A smile spread across his face. The barrister wanted to see him to discuss Claire's case. John took hold of the saw and with vigour he continued to slice through the wood as sawdust flew like snow on a windy day.

John had agreed to all Robert Jenkins' recommendations, but one. 'Do you wish to include grounds of appeal against your previous solicitor?' Robert had asked. 'You are entitled to do so, but if you do, your daughter as the appellant will have to waive privilege.'

'What does that mean?'

'Your daughter's previous solicitor will be invited to respond. This, in turn, makes for a lengthier delivery. By taking this route, you may, however, be entitled to funding from the last trial.'

'Are you telling me to do this? Go after the solicitor?'

'Not telling. But informing of your daughter's right.'

'She's enough to contend with without going down that road.'

'I urge you to discuss this with her?'

'I'll ask her, but proceed on the assumption she says no.'

'Okay. We have enough evidence to deem the ruling as unsafe. Meanwhile, I will apply for bail. Do you have sufficient funds?'

'Whatever it takes, I'll pay it.'

'Do not get your hopes up. Bail is often refused.'

Claire had news for her parents: Funding for her study had been granted. She was to start a correspondence course in Spanish and was confident her parents had remembered to purchase a laptop.

Claire had morphed her character to fit in with the personalities in her confine. She adjusted her language to echo her latest cell mate dropping a few vowels, adding an expletive here and there. Michelle was the latest new cell mate. 'Brill, got my own bed back,' Michelle said, jumping on her bed, the springs creaking.

She laughed, an infectious laugh. 'Bloody hell, I must've put weight on.'

Claire laughed in return. These girls, acres apart in lifestyle, needed to connect. Lying on her bed, Claire memorised a few Spanish phrases. She opened then closed the phrase book and decided to jot a few translations. Saying aloud what she meant to have kept private. 'Where is the paper?'

Michelle stepped in. 'I had a mate once who had a paper shop.'

'Did you?'

'Yeah. But it blew away.' She hit the side of her thigh with laughter.

Despite the juvenile joke, Claire laughed. She laughed at all of Michelle's jokes, the crude and the cruel; she thought it best to do so.

The smell of fish swam into the cell. 'Is it fishy Friday?' Michelle asked. She wrinkled her noise at the thought of Friday's meal.

'It is.'

'It's me birthday,' Michelle said.

Claire sat up and got off the bed. 'Happy birthday!'

'Nah. I'm joking. You should see your face.' Michelle's cackle reignited. 'You're so easy to take the piss out of. Talking of easy, it was so easy to get locked up again. I'm doing two years this time; broke a guy's legs, they had to amputate. I make good money in here through dealing drugs. You know what, the authorities send a drug dealer like me to prison, but guess what? They still have a drug dealer. Prison's only an extension of the street.'

'How do you get drug supplies into prison?'

'Lots of ways. Pay a screw. Make friends with a prisoner who's let out on licence. Get a group of mates to visit, tell security that the group's your family; it's harder for them to keep watch on a group. These mates will have your order packed in condoms and shoved in their clothes. I used to have drugs chucked over the wall, but nah, problem was other prisoners got a chance to nick your gear before you got to it. Watch, tonight I've a drone coming in. With this phone I can direct it to the window.'

'You've got a phone!'

'Sure have. I'm having spice loaded on a drone, worth a fucking fortune in here because it passes all the drug tests. You can hardly get anything for spice on the street. The bitches in here love it. Listen, you better not mess with me, you best not say anything about this.'

'No, I won't. I promise, but on a drone, how does that work?'

'I use this broom handle to hook the bag that hangs from the drone, and scoop it in. Simple.'

'Do you take spice?'

'No fucking way. Ever seen someone on spice?' Michelle contorted her body and lurched around the room before collapsing on her bed. 'They're like fucking zombies. I've seen one of them bark like a dog. For fuck's sake, fucking spice heads. I can't be spaced out like that, I have to be on the ball, keep track of my orders and the money. Tell you what, I've got a few hard Mars Bars coming in via my courier. I'll get you a phone.'

'Hard Mars Bars?'

'Yeah, the insides are replaced with a slim phone. You see, you take the metal vibrator out of the phone and it passes security. Is there anything you want? Trust me, I know the screws who are in on this.'

'Oh! Mm . . . no thanks, actually, I think I'll go for a stroll.' Claire was tired of this, tired of the environment. She left the cell and headed for the library where she could lose herself for a while. Requesting the use of her laptop she carried on with her course work.

After applying, Kerry received a visiting order to visit Claire. 'Paul, do you want to come with me to the prison to see Claire? Or you can wait for me outside.'

'No.'

'No? Okay! I'll catch the train.'

In the waiting room of the prison, Kerry waited for Claire. When she finally came into the room, Kerry could see how tired and worn Claire was. Loss of weight suited Claire, enhancing her face in a vulnerable way. 'Hey! How are you doing?' Kerry asked.

'I keep busy. I'm doing an online course, actually I enjoy it . . . the course, not the prison.' Claire dropped her adapted language and returned to her normal speech pattern. 'Have you seen anything of Richard? I would love to speak with him, but he hasn't okayed clearance for me use his number.'

'Why are you bothering about that arsehole? Did you know he was seeing Andrea?'

'No. I didn't know that.' Claire's stomach fell. Another meal she would struggle to eat.

'Andrea's sacked him off.'

Claire's jealousy peaked. She knew Richard would desire Andrea more if he could no longer have her.

Claire's agitation forced Kerry to change the subject. 'Me and Paul, PJ, are still together. He's been offered this amazing job in the city, well paid too.'

The girls kissed each other's cheek before going their separate way.

Back in the cell, Claire took hold of the framed picture of Richard and smashed it face down in the cupboard.

Provoked Public Interest

At the court, an application for appeal was lodged for the case of Claire May Jones. A case reference was issued, and a caseworker assigned. The registrar of the court checked the paperwork then ordered a transcript of the hearing. As the appeal was against a conviction, she was obliged to forward a copy of the transcript to Robert Jenkins QC to enable him to perfect the grounds of appeal.

Mr Fen said good morning to his receptionist before picking up his mail and heading up the stairs to his office. He logged onto the computer to scan his e-mails where his eyes rested on one: *Criminal Appeal Office. Subject: Mr Frederick Walker.* The secretary to Mr Fen placed a cup of hot tea on his desk. He smiled a thank you then read the e-mail and sent the message to archive. He did not notify Fred of Claire May Jones' right to appeal, because in seventy per cent of cases the right to appeal would be refused. Mr Fen opened another e-mail: *CAO. Today we have been approached by the Press. They have shown an interest in the appeal lodged by Claire May Jones. The Witness Care Unit has instructed that the defendant be notified.* Mr Fen sighed.

At the CAO, all material for the appeal had been received. Procedures were carried out and the file was sent to a judge.

Unaware as yet of the application for appeal, Fred stood in his kitchen. Ignoring the mass of empty whisky bottles, he looked out of the window at his garden where the weeds were rampant. He had not resumed his career and no longer took the medication to control his cholesterol levels. He ordered his necessities online: cereal, crisps and whisky. There was a restriction of twelve bottles of alcohol per order. From the last order there remained one bottle of liquor. On his way to the stairs to his office to reorder a stock of whisky, a sharp knock came from the door.

Sergeant Wright stood on Fred's doorstep and counted six bottles of milk. He peered through the letterbox and saw a volume of mail on the floor. He knocked on the door again. Though not assigned to the role of pastoral care, Sergeant Wright offered to visit Fred to inform him of the lodged appeal. It also gave him a chance to ask Fred a few more questions.

Fred stood behind the front door rubbing the beard he had allowed to grow, unkempt like his garden. He hitched his trousers up, the belt had long ago been discarded. He opened the door. Sergeant Wright exhaled. 'Mr Walker. I have news for you. May I step in?'

Fred opened the door wide. A musty smell from the lack of house care fell on Sergeant Wright. He took out his pressed handkerchief and dabbed his nose with the smell of fresh laundry. Fred stood in the hall, blocking further entrance into the house. The sergeant began, 'Sir, an appeal has been lodged against the conviction of Claire May Jones, the perpetrator of—'

'I know who she is!'

'Of course.' He inhaled his handkerchief for a second time. 'The press has got hold of the story and have provoked public interest. I can liaise with the victim support unit and—'

'Not interested. They can do what they want. I no longer read the newspaper. They can all go to hell. You included. Piss off.'

Mr Walker—'

'Go on, get out! Leave me in peace.'

Sergeant Wright stepped outside. 'Your milk needs putting in the fridge.'

'Fuck off!' Fred slammed the door in the sergeant's face.

John had waited for this call from Robert Jenkins: 'Yes, go ahead. I'm all ears.'

'We have leave of appeal.'

'We have to leave the appeal?'

'No. We have permission to appeal.'

'Phew! How soon can we go to court? What happens next?'

'We wait for a case summary to be written. Copies of all relevant papers will be sent to the judges.'

'Judges!'

'An appeal requires three judges to participate.'

'Oh . . . sounds expensive.'

'Details of the appeal will be sent to the list office; it is they who set the hearing date.'

'How long does that take?'

'Two-to-three months.'

'Bloody hell! Anything you can do to speed that along?'

'Afraid not. That's the system. Cogs turn slowly, I'm afraid. You will receive a copy of the letter in front of me concerning the acceptance of appeal.' Robert Jenkins' words were delivered with care.

'I'll wait to hear from you.'

John phoned Jenny. 'We've got the appeal. But it takes a couple of months to get a hearing date.'

'Did you ask about bail?'

'Do you think I should have? I don't want him to think we're stupid. Think about it, everyone in prison would appeal to get bail.'

'John, ask him, please . . . John, I've booked a week on a yoga retreat, that's in three months.'

'You never told me! Cancel it. Where do you think the bloody money's coming from?' He disconnected the call.

Bail had been refused.

Spanish Phrases

Claire walked through the open gate to the library at the centre of the prison. Because of the location there were no windows to the outside world, so lighting was provided by fluorescent tubes and was brighter than it needed to be. Many prisoners complained of headaches after sitting in the library. But Claire spent every available minute there. An aroma of musty old books filled the room. Two officers were assigned on a rota basis to survey the readers.

Claire sat on a hard bench at a long table. She was not the only prisoner at the table, but she had no wish to socialise. Completing her last assignment, she clicked the Send button. Her work floated away into the ether as she smiled at the screen. Next week an adjudicator would visit the prison to carry out the oral part of the

Spanish exam. A book on the culture of Spain and its language lay open on the table by Claire's side. She recited Spanish phrases in her head, then Googled their correctness.

At the same time as Claire sat in the library, Richard's head was bent over his desk where he was writing an exam paper. With a flourish he dotted the final full-stop. The clock made him aware that he still had twenty minutes left. Confidence stopped him from checking his paper. He surveyed the room, looked at the other candidates. Sitting with his arms crossed and his feet stretched out beneath the table, he felt smug that they had not finished writing.

'Please, could you put your pens down.'

Chatter broke out as the students left the room.

While Claire recited her knowledge of Spanish to the oral examiner, Richard sat his *viva voce*. He carried this out with a confidence to his speech. Once out of the examination room he placed a call to his father. 'Hi. All done, just have to hand in my dissertation and I've passed. I know I have.'

'Excellent! Now your head is clear, I have a proposition. We're expanding into Hong Kong. How would you feel about handling operations out there?'

'That's off the scale. I would love that. When?'

'Just finalising things, but it should be within six months. I've been travelling back and forth. I'll spend a couple of months on site with you, then leave you in charge.'

'Awesome! What a day.'

'Thought you'd be pleased. See you at the weekend, son.'

Richard faced his peers to share his good news, to impress the ladies. Eyebrows were raised behind his back.

A warden entered the library of the prison. 'Claire Jones?'

Claire closed the lid of her laptop.

'Follow me to the office.'

Claire handed in her laptop to the librarian. She then altered her step to keep in line with the warden. In the corridor, Claire could no longer distinguish the prison's unique odour of food, sweat and disinfectant. No longer was she intimidated by the cacophony of sounds. The warden sat down on a chair in her office. Claire stood to face her. 'A hearing date has been set for your appeal.'

Claire's eyes sparked in a way they had not for a long time. The warden ignored Claire's beaming smile. 'You have the right to be present in court for the appeal. Though I should point out that you will be sitting in the box throughout the hearing. The press will be present. The box is at the side of the court but in full view of public seating. We'll transport and accompany you in court.' Claire's smile evaporated. 'However,' the warden continued, 'you don't have to attend court in person. It's permissible to have your attendance via a video link. This is of no detriment to the result. Which arrangement would you prefer?'

'Can I ask my dad?'

'Why, is he the appellant?'

'Appellant?'

'Is your dad the one fighting his corner?'

'No, I'm thinking . . . the video one.'

'Good choice.' The wardens enjoyed videoed court hearings because they brought a change to routine. 'Close the door on your way out.'

Black Angel

John read the letter out loud and Jenny listened. He placed the correspondence on the table. 'So, Claire won't be appearing in court.'

'That's for the best. It was horrendous for her. And this one . . . three judges!' Jenny wrapped her arms around herself.

'Why aren't you dressed for yoga?'

'I don't enjoy it anymore. Everyone's excited about the trip; it's changed the dynamics of the group.'

'Oh, that's a shame. Buy one of those DVDs and do it in the living room. Can you check on the hotels near to court? We'll go in the car, because fingers crossed and prayers answered, our girl may be coming home.' He kissed his wife's forehead before leaving for work. Jenny sighed.

John and Jenny arrived at the hotel the night before the hearing. Jenny unpacked the suitcase. 'Let's get a drink at the bar,' John said. He had chosen this hotel from the list Jenny had researched with two clear objectives: inexpensive and near to the court. Refreshed, away from home, Jenny checked her hair in the mirror. She applied lipstick to her still attractive lips. The bar was welcoming. Their cocktails were served in clean glasses with one ice cube each and no hint of lemon or lime. John and Jenny chinked the glasses for their daughter's release. After consuming their fourth drink, they no longer felt like eating. Relaxed in the upright chairs they reminisced of their shared good times over the years. John took hold of his wife's hand and squeezed it. 'She'll be all right.' It had been a long time since they had enjoyed such intimacy. 'Big day tomorrow. No more alcohol. But another time, we'll do this again.' John said.

Jenny smiled the smile her husband loved.

The next day, Robert Jenkins QC tipped his head to a colleague, then greeted John and Jenny in the lobby. 'Our day has arrived,' he said to his clients.

'And everything crossed,' John replied. He straightened his tie, then looked to his wife. Yoga had been beneficial for Jenny; she looked smart and healthy in her new outfit.

Robert interrupted the couple's shared moment. 'I'm off to chambers to get changed. I'll see you in court. If you sit to the right on the second row, you'll be right behind me.'

John approached the information desk to check the listings: Claire May Jones, Lord Chief Justice, Court Four. John took hold of his wife's hand before asking for directions to the court. Their timing was impeccable, and they were ushered into the court. John's eyebrows raised on seeing Jeff Winslow reporting for their local press.

John looked up at the high vaulted ceiling. In a different circumstance the architecture would have inspired him. Ornate light fittings shed light on the wood-panelled walls, velvet curtains and bookcases with rows and rows of leather-bound books.

With a book and papers in his hand, Robert entered the court. Placing these items on the desk he turned to acknowledge the Jones'. Robert wore a black gown with long sleeves that opened at the elbow encouraging the black silk to fall on either side of his arms. His brilliant white shirt with a starched flap collar contrasted the deep black. Robert looked handsome even in his short bench wig.

John lent forward in his seat to ask Robert when the jury would appear.

Robert turned. 'No jury. This is a court of appeal. It is not a retrial. The procedures of the previous court hearing have not been violated. A jury deals with facts. Appeals are decided on point of law. Only trained judges are qualified to consider points of law.' He paused. 'And, as such, witnesses of the accident are not required. Only a witness in their field of expertise to clarify the circumstance of law related to fact.'

'Oh,' John said.

Assuming his clients were informed, Robert addressed the papers on his desk. More officials entered the courtroom and took a seat. The last person to enter the court, to an order of *all rise*, was the Lord Chief Justice: Sir Hendon Marquis. The three judges dressed in the same manner, black and purple robes with a red sash and short horsehair wigs. Jenny looked to the Lord Chief Justice to his wedding band and simple watch.

Four screens faced the interested parties to view Claire's contribution. Sir Hendon Marquis began proceedings. He referred to the accused's reason for detention. He gave an account of the previous hearing and the result of the same. He reminded the court of the sentence handed down to Miss Claire May Jones for her conviction of dangerous driving. Via the video link, Claire listened to his delivery with her head bowed; she did not look into the camera. John's lips had pulled into a thin line when his daughter's magnified appearance was before him.

'Does representation for the prosecution wish to examine?' the senior judge asked.

'Not at this stage. Thank you, Your Honour.'

Robert Jenkins stood. 'Claire May Jones was incarcerated on the charge of dangerous driving, sadly resulting in the death of a minor. On my client's behalf I challenge the aforementioned court ruling. While it is indisputable that a death occurred, I put before this court that my client is guilty of the lesser charge of careless driving. I call upon two expert witnesses who will testify to this assumption.' He took a breath and looked around the court. 'The first expert witness I call is a meteorologist, Professor Ford.' A demure woman took residence in the witness box. Robert Jenkins continued, 'Professor Ford, on the evening of the accident, could you clarify the condition of the weather?'

'Yes. Charts indicate that the temperature was lowered to nought degrees Celsius on the evening in question. Not discounting high precipitation there is a probability that ice accumulation may have been present.'

'Thank you. No further question.'

All three judges made notes. The meteorologist vacated the stand, wafting a trail of sweet perfume behind her.

Robert Jenkins stood. 'The second expert witness presented to the court is Mr Paige, a partner of Ridgeback Insurance Company.'

Mr Paige, a tall, smartly dressed man, presented an impressive figure in the box. Claire peeped at the screen to see who was speaking then lowered her eyes.

Mr Paige asked for permission to read from notes and was granted his request. A yellow sticky note used as a marker had dislodged forcing him to flick a few pages of his notebook to find what he was searching for. He cleared his throat. 'The distance travelled after impact measured by the aid of skid marks was three metres. This propelled distance would indicate that Miss Jones travelled at an appropriate speed for the road and weather condition.'

Prosecution stood. 'No questions at this point Your Honour.'

Robert Jenkins did have questions.

'Mr Paige, thank you for your clarity,' said Robert Jenkins. 'In your capacity as an experienced investigator of road traffic accidents, is there anything you could add pertinent to this case?'

Mr Paige looked at his notebook, he turned a page and began, 'Yes, on the day of the accident we had, that is Ridgeback Insurance, a claimant who skidded on the same stretch of road resulting in a collision with a lamppost.'

'And did you, or a representative of your company, investigate that claim?'

'Yes, findings from the investigation pointed to possible ice on the road.'

'Can you not tell the court that ice was definitely present?'

'No, unfortunately not. The investigation took place several days after impact. Ice could have melted had there been any, or ice could have appeared after the event. In such a case, we are happy to record a probable fact in helping our clients achieve a settlement.'

Despite being warned to show no emotion, Claire smiled.

'Thank you, Mr Paige. That's all from me.'

The prosecution for the state took the right to re-examine Mr Paige. 'I understand the method you use to calculate the speed Miss Jones travelled, but we are aware that Miss Jones' purpose on travelling on the said road was to visit a friend. A friend who lives near to where the incident took place. In your role as an accident investigator, could you say whether Miss Jones drove at a speed appropriate to someone who presumably had slowed the car to park it?'

'Sorry, I don't understand what you are asking?'

'Simply put, Mr Paige, Claire May Jones' journey was almost at an end. She ought to have slowed the car to allow for parking. In your calculation, was this apparent, or had she driven at a speed appropriate for travelling further down the road and jammed on her brakes at the last moment?'

'I couldn't determine a speed travelled previously to the skid marks. No one could.' Mr Paige stepped down from the box. The prosecution barrister sat, a smile on his face, in recognition of the seed of doubt he had germinated

Robert Jenkins stood and held his hands together, forcing the slits in his gown to offer the premonition of a black angel. 'I submit that the offence of causing death by dangerous driving should never have been sanctioned, and that it can never amount to lawful killing.'

'Mr Jenkins, do you suggest the previous court hearing was deficient? Are you asking for a retrial?' The second judge asked.

'No, Your Honour. Though I am aware that a senior officer was not called to the scene of the accident and this fact was not addressed. No, I am suggesting that the decision was based on limited facts.'

'Continue.'

'What we have in Claire May Jones is a young and careful driver. By definition an inexperienced driver who had the misfortune, because of adverse weather conditions and a dark evening, to run over a child, which, Miss Jones is adamant, was already lying on the road. Indeed, may the child have slipped on the ice which rendered her unconscious? Or, could a hit and run driver have knocked her down and left her lying there in the path of oncoming traffic?' Robert looked down at his papers. 'Without full clarity I submit that my client, Miss Claire May Jones, be freed from the indictment of dangerous driving and be charged with the lesser offence of careless driving.' He paused for effect. 'Causing death by careless driving is not to be treated as manslaughter and should therefore be excluded from the definition of unlawful killing. I suggest that if it is included, many thousands of inquests concerning road deaths would turn into trials of liability, which would be wrong, in principle being contrary to rule 42 of the coroner's rule.'

The senior judge raised his head from his note taking. 'Mr Jenkins, I do not need you to educate us on points of law. Neither do we need comment on the ability of the country's road users.'

'Sorry, Your Honour,' Robert said with a half-smile.

'Continue.'

'Your Honour, this was my closing argument.'

The prosecution reiterated their doubt as to the speed at which Claire was driving, and Sir Hendon Marquis then declared that the appeal would resume on the next day at ten. He left the court and the video link was terminated. Jenny was sad to see her baby's face disappear. Robert Jenkins turned to face John and Jenny.

'Thought that went well,' John said. 'Those expert witnesses know their stuff. No one can ignore their findings.'

'It would appear so. But you cannot predict a result. Though, I agree, damning evidence. Until tomorrow.' Robert shook Jenny's hand then John's. He collected his papers and strode out of court.

Linking her arm through her husband's arm Jenny asked, 'Drinks at the bar?'

The next morning with fifteen minutes to spare before the screen came live, Claire returned to the video link for transmission to the court.

Jenny watched Robert Jenkins QC take his seat in front of her. She looked down at her husband's hand holding hers.

The three judges appeared in court, following the same protocol as the day before where Sir Hendon Marquis was the last to be seated. 'My learned colleagues and I have studied the reports brought to this court. We consider the weather and the condition of the road surface to be mitigating circumstances. Therefore, I dismiss the offence directed at Claire May Jones of causing death by dangerous driving.'

Sitting up straight, Claire looked directly into the camera.

John lifted Jenny's hand and kissed it before placing it back on his knee.

'It was suggested at the previous trial the deceased child lay on the road prior to Claire May Jones' arrival on the scene. Miss Jones had a responsibility to see the child and bring the vehicle to a stop before driving over the said child. It is not possible to determine if the deceased was killed prior to this action or as a result of the same. Therefore, Claire May Jones has been found guilty of the lesser charge of careless or inconsiderate driving.'

'This charge carries a maximum custodial sentence of five years.'

All the Jones' shared a wave of disappointment.

'However, as Miss Jones was wrongly convicted, has already served time incarcerated, I am content she has paid her debt to society. I order that she be released.'

Robert Jenkins sprang to his feet.

'Yes, Mr Jenkins?' Sir Hendon Marquis asked.

'Your Honour, in view of the considerable cost to the appellant's parents in obtaining a correct classification, I request that they be able to claim fees.'

'Indeed. List the expenses and forward it to court administration.'

John smiled so wide his teeth were bared. Jenny's hand in John's was numb.

'All rise.' The court usher instructed. The Lord Chief Justice disappeared behind the curtain. The two judges followed, like soldiers obeying the protocol.

Robert Jenkins QC turned to face John and Jenny. 'Excellent result,' he said.

'Wonderful, just wonderful,' John and Jenny competed in saying. John asked, 'Do you think I will be reimbursed?'

'Most certainly. If the Lord Chief Justice asks for submission of expenses, it's an agreement.'

'Could this day get any better?' John said, not pausing for an answer. 'When will Claire be released?'

Robert checked his watch. It was not yet ten-thirty. 'The prison will receive notification today. Then it's down to logistics. Arranging transport, organising medication she may depend on and so on.'

'No need to organise transport, we'll drive down. I can't thank you enough for all you've done. I hadn't considered a refund, so thanks for that.'

'Pleasure.' Robert collected his books and papers. 'All the best.' He was waylaid from leaving the courtroom; the barrister for the prosecution was a friend of his and they chatted.

John checked out of the hotel and met Jenny in the car park. Once seated in the car they headed off to prison. The approach to the prison was not as formidable now their baby was leaving its confine. While they waited in an office for Claire, John and Jenny discussed their future and decided to book a holiday. They'd ask Claire if she would like to join them, maybe go to Spain where she could practise her Spanish. They stood to greet Claire and were formal with one another. There was no need to wait for the pharmacy to organise medication as Claire no longer relied on chemical aid. When the giant gates electronically bolted behind them, the Jones' hugged in a circle and began to cry. 'Let's get you home,' John said.

RIC 1H

At the presentation for graduates at the university, Richard strode up the few steps onto the stage, attired in full academic dress of his university's colours which were dark navy with a white band to highlight the hood. His degree confirmation was recited in Latin: class one honours. As Richard joined his right hand with the master's, both their heads turned, and a professional photographer caught the image. The diploma was released to Richard, like the passing of a baton. Holding the certificate high Richard left the stage. On his way back to his designated seat he found eye contact with his mother and winked at her. At the other end of the same row was Kirsty, his father's current wife. The women sat, like bookends, distant by choice but united in pride. Richard surveyed no further, he knew his father was in Hong Kong.

Outside in the grounds of the university, people pulled together. Proud parents swapped stories and discussed expenses. A flock of mortarboards flew in the air and cameras flashed. Richard caught his cap as it spun back in his direction. He chatted with fellow graduates then lifted and swung the pretty blonde with honey tones in her hair. She laughed at his playfulness. Before approaching her son, Linda waited for a lull in the frivolity. 'Darling, I'm so proud.'

'Thanks.' Richard kissed her cheek.

'Are we still on for dinner?'

'Of course. Wait for me in the car park. I'm just popping over to Kirsty to thank her for coming.'

'Oh, okay.'

Richard hugged Kirsty. 'You look lovely, elegant,' he said.

'I could say the same of you. Your father would be so proud. I've e-mailed some pics. Speaking of your father, he wanted me to give you this . . .' She rummaged in her exclusive handbag then produced a fob. 'From the both of us.'

'What's this?'

'Go look in the car park, a white Porsche Carrera. The registration is RIC 1H.'

'Seriously?'

She laughed in a giggly kind of way.

Richard could feel his future unfold. 'Thanks, Kirsty, this is amazing!'

'You're welcome. I'll love and leave you. I have a charity event to attend.'

Richard walked to the car park with a spring to his step. His cap and diploma in his hand. On seeing the pearlescent white car, his car he decided to take this asset for a spin. He would call in at The Anchor where his peers congregated. Linda sat in her car the learner sign stashed in the boot. Watching through the rear-view mirror she could see her son approach and turned the key in the ignition. Richard opened her passenger door and bobbed his head in. 'Going to take a rain check,' he said.

'Really? Why?'

'I'm going to drive the car Father bought for me over to the pub.'

'A car? That's lovely. You'll be able to come home more often.' She left the engraved tie pin in her bag.

'Actually, Mother, I've been meaning to tell you, Father's offered me a position in Hong Kong. It's a great opportunity.'

'Has he? Are you going?' Her voice wavered. 'I will miss you so much,' she managed to say.

'I'm not going yet. It will be at least six months. Father's out there now setting things in place.' He blew her a kiss and walked off.

Linda turned off the engine to watch her son. He strode to his gleaming car, got in without pausing to admire it, and tore off with screeching tyres. Linda folded her arms on the steering wheel and placed her head there. She wept. What had started off as one of her happiest days had ended in despair.

CHAPTER 15

My Past

ALL WAS QUIET on Priory lane. On the estate where the Jones' lived, a gang of several boys and one girl played football in a cul-de-sac. The game came to an end. The girl suggested they play knock-and-run on people's doors. A neighbour witnessed their antics, identified a child and informed his parent. The boy was sent to bed. The remainder of the children took their knock-and-run pursuit onto Priory Lane where they were less known. As yet, no-one had opened a door. The children sat on the kerbside and looked over to the Walkers' house, which was in disarray. They had been told a teacher lived in the house they were contemplating. A rumour was circulating at their school that the teacher had gone mad. The girl, with strawberry blonde hair and blue eyes, put herself forward. 'I'll knock and you lot start running.' Striding over she lent her hand on the door to use the knocker. The door opened a short way. The girl screamed, a theatrical scream, and ran to join the running boys.

Mid-afternoon the next day, Linda backed her car off the cobbles onto the lane. It was a pleasant day and she wound the car window down. Smelling something unpleasant she powered the window back up then drove off the lane towards her pupil's house.

On her way to her last lesson of the day, Linda drove past the Walkers' house and noticed the door was slightly open. After the lesson, she parked the car on the cobbles and went to investigate Fred's door. As she made her way up the path the dreadful smell she had inhaled earlier returned with a vengeance. A rotting smell, like meat gone bad. At the front-door she shouted through the opening. 'Fred. Fred! are you all right?' She put her hand over her nose and mouth as she looked to the step and the bottles of curdled milk. Pushing the door open she was confronted by a pile of unopened mail on the hall carpet. She clamped her hand tighter to her mouth and headed back down the path. Using her mobile phone, she requested police presence. Then crossed the road and stood at her front door to wait for the officers to arrive.

When the police appeared, Linda greeted them. 'You stay there, love,' the policeman said. Two officers headed up the path and stepped cautiously into the house. A short while later one of the officers returned to Linda and calmly asked if he could take a few details.

They found Fred on the settee. A pillow, his dead wife's pillow, now stained with dried saliva and grease, lay under his head. His body was bloated and bulged out of the constraints of his clothing. Bluebottles buzzed around, disturbed by the intrusion of the officer, then settled back on Fred's flesh. Two empty whisky bottles lay on the carpet.

No family member came forward to claim Fred's body. He was cremated by the State, not buried with his beloved wife and daughter.

PJ had developed the design package of his new game. The ideas he put forward for his concept were received with great enthusiasm. Not only did he enjoy creating the graphics, but he was pleased with the result. His work was almost ready for production. With his headspace now clear for further progress in the field, he researched the role of 4D in the art of gaming. He Googled OXle Developer and considered what cooperation with this company would mean for the firm he worked for. What had piqued his interest in OXle was that they would cover Unreal licence fees, plus they had a great social platform. PJ was hyped about this joint project because of their OXle Avatars system, which allowed customisation of identities which were far more lifelike interactions than anything else on the market. This was his theme of interest, but the firm PJ worked with had not developed the 4D imagery technology. Forming a partnership with OXle, should they be interested, would bring a greater scope for development. If this partnership for 4D was a no-go he would look at other avenues for application. He was convinced this was the future of gaming. Current 3D headgear that was needed to view the game was cumbersome and made gamers feel nauseous. PJ intended to seek new production concepts and invent a light, comfortable headgear for a pleasant viewing experience. What excited him most was the possibilities 4D viewing had to offer. Real-life experience, not only for gamers, but for disadvantaged people and thrill seekers. Unable to go scuba diving? His concept would bring marine life to the viewer in a virtual setting to give an experience not otherwise available. PJ was interested in the sensory introduction to education, say involving the participant in a street scene of the Victorian era. The possibilities were endless. He hoped to develop and evoke the sense of smell to the experience, as yet he had no idea how. His enthusiasm knew no bounds.

As part of his remuneration package PJ was offered a car of his choice. He chose a Honda CRV – it was reliable, innovative, and stylish, and the four-wheel drive advantage was useful in bad weather. He understood cars and knew their value. His fellow software designers had mocked his choice.

PJ rented an apartment near the firm's trendy office in London. Friday evening, he drove home to see Kerry and visit his dad. Now he was settled in his career, PJ had a proposal for her. Listening to techno music, he sat in a line of traffic waiting to get on the motorway. Easing forward in the slipstream he increased the speed. Arriving on Priory Lane a line of parked cars tailgated along the kerb, but no matter how congested the parking was, a space could always be found. He drove past his dad's house and found a vacant spot outside Kerry's house. Standing on the pavement he blipped the fob in his hand and the car's indicators flashed; the car was locked. He looked at Kerry's window, but no-one had seen his arrival; he'd call to see his dad first. Walking past the scene of the Amy-Lou accident, he stole a glance at the Walkers' residence, dismayed to see the state of disrepair and recognised the estate agents' For Sale sign, as a nationwide company. The thought of all the deaths the Walkers had suffered in and around that house caused Paul to shudder. The old feeling of unease slammed into his belly. With a sickened heart, he put the key in the door of his former home and entered. 'Hi,' he called.

'Is that you, son?'

'Yes, Dad.'

Andrea came running down the stairs to greet her brother. PJ had a new status in his family, they were proud of him, interested in his life. 'How's it going?' she asked.

'Good. Yeah, it's great.'

'Do you want a brew, or a tot of the hard stuff?' asked his dad.

'I'll have coffee, Dad. I'm off in a minute.'

'As you like, son. I'm off down the club in a bit.'

Andrea returned to her room.

In her room waiting for PJ, Kerry held a perfume bottle and sprayed a fine mist in the air then stood underneath the falling particles to catch the scent on her skin and hair. On hearing the rap at the back door, she ran downstairs to be with him. Opening the door, she flung her arms around his neck and kissed him a moment too long. He eased her away from him, a loving smile on his face. 'What have you been up to, pretty girl?'

'Waiting for tonight. It's dragged this week. I've missed you.'

'There's something I want to ask you about that.'

'Go on then ask.'

'No . . . later. I've booked a room for the night at The Murrain.'

'How posh! Get you.' She tickled his ribs.

'Pack a bag.' He did not tell Kerry he planned to return to the office by Saturday lunch.

PJ and Kerry travelled in comfort to The Murrain. She leant on the armrest to watch him drive. 'I love to watch you when you're concentrating. You're so handsome.'

He glanced at her for a moment. 'And you're my pretty girl.'

On approach to the hotel, PJ was in awe of the grandeur. Tall wrought-iron gates were latched open to welcome the guests. He drove up the sweeping gravelled drive directing him to the illuminated hotel. A man in uniform took their bags. A second man held out his hand for the key fob to the car. PJ watched with pride as the valet drove his car away. After checking-in at the vast mahogany desk they headed up the curved stairs, mirrored on the opposite side to form a horseshoe.

A bellboy followed them up the stairs with their luggage. 'The bathroom is through the sitting area to the rear,' he told them. 'You have surround-sound cinema and an iPad. if you wish to use the balcony, cashmere wraps are in the wardrobe.'

'Thanks,' PJ replied.

'Is there anything else you require?'

'No. Thanks.'

He pointed to a bottle of champagne on ice, a bottle of red wine by its side. 'Compliments of the management.' With one arm placed behind his back the bellboy asked, 'If that is all, have an enjoyable stay.' He left the room.

'Thought he'd never go,' PJ said.

'I know! Do you think he was after a tip?'

'Should I have tipped him? Shall I go after him?'

'No leave it. We'll know for next time.' Kerry took a peek at the bathroom. The bath was in the middle of the room. Looking underneath she wondered where the water would flow. After handling the toiletries, a luxury range seen in a magazine, she wandered barefoot into the sitting room where she pulled the cork out of the red wine. Pouring the full-bodied red into two glasses she then plonked down next to PJ on the Chesterfield sofa, handing him a glass of wine. 'Cheers,' she said, chinking her glass against his. 'Now, what do you want to ask me?'

'Ask?' His mind was whirling with life-like characters from the screen.

'When you came around earlier . . .'

'Oh. I'm opening an office in Florida, getting into the American market. The potential is huge.'

Her chin dimpled, and her bottom lip wavered. 'Are you going? How long will you be out there?'

'At least two years. Probably longer.'

'Please don't go. Can't someone else do it?' A tear welled on her bottom eyelid and fell.

He looked at her. 'I'm asking you to come with me.'

She wiped away a second tear. 'Really?'

'I wouldn't go without you. I've accepted on the condition you come with me. All expenses paid. Can you believe it? You and me living in America.'

Kerry put her glass of wine on the table. She jumped up and down before sitting back on the sofa. 'I'd love to come.'

PJ's thoughts went to the diamond ring hidden in his bag. A ring he would present after dinner with champagne.

'Mum won't be happy with me living abroad.'

'She will. She'll be pleased for you. She can come and visit. You should see the villas on offer. Hell, she can come and live out there with us if she wants. If you want her to?'

Kerry retrieved the wine glass and gulped the deep red liquid until the glass was empty.

'Having second thoughts? We won't go if you don't want to.'

'It's not that. It's an amazing opportunity. It's just . . .' She looked into his clear blue eyes. 'I've put off telling you something . . . something about me. I can't come with you if you don't accept my past. I can't live a lie.'

'Before you say anything, whatever it is, it won't change the way I feel about you.'

'You can say that. I'm not so sure.' After filling her glass, she took another slug of alcohol, then placed the glass on the table. She walked to the window and wrung her hands. 'I used to go out with this lad. I was young, fourteen, I was besotted. Not like it is with you and me, but a rebellious kind of thing. He was twenty-five. Mum disapproved from the start and threatened to report him to the police for sleeping with a minor. I begged her not to. She tried everything to keep me away from him even locking me in my room, but I'd climb out the window. He was popular, very good looking. I knew if I wasn't with him even once someone would take my place. Looking back, I suppose it was an obsession. I was rebelling against Mum. I mean, what did she know, not having a man in her life? That's what I thought back then.'

'I can live with that,' said PJ. 'You didn't need to tell me.'

'That's not all, the thing is, he dealt drugs, he took drugs. Paul,' she turned to face him, 'I took drugs with him.'

'What kind of drugs? Weed?'

'At first, then cocaine, uppers, downers. Whatever people craved he got for them and gave to me, except heroin. I never did that.'

'It's in the past. I used to do weed. We all did daft things when we are young.'

'There's more. I lost a dangerous amount of weight. To me I looked cool. I stopped going to school. I abused alcohol. I would have huge screaming matches with Mum.' Kerry walked back to the sofa and sat down next to PJ. He put his arm around her shoulder. 'I got pregnant. And then my so-called boyfriend dumped me. Said he couldn't handle a kid. Well I couldn't either. So, I went overboard with the drink and drugs. I'd sleep with people just to get a fix. I thought I knew everything. But I knew nothing. Mum didn't know I was pregnant. I tried everything to get rid of it. I even drank turpentine, but it only made me sick. I was scared to go to the doctor, because of my age, I was sure the doctor would tell my mum about the pregnancy, you see by this time Mum had threatened to throw me out. I found a back-street abortionist. I got the money to pay her from dealing drugs.' Kerry wriggled free from PJ's hold. She could not keep eye contact with him. 'She, the abortionist used a knitting needle. I didn't feel a thing. I was high. Later I learned that she had pierced the amniotic sack inside my womb. You see I'm an expert now! But the baby stayed inside. I went home. Later that evening I had horrendous contractions. Mum was at work. I smoked crack to see me through. My baby aborted; it didn't want me either.'

'What did you do with the baby?'

'It was tiny. I flushed it down the toilet. How awful is that?'

Silence filled the room before PJ spoke. 'You've been through a hell of a lot.' He hated what he had been told and looked to his hands held together on his parted knee. 'You haven't done these things to me. After all you've been through, it's a wonder you can be so happy, so upbeat?'

'I have my moments. I'm lucky, I guess. To this day Mum doesn't know about the abortion. She was deranged with worry over my decline and organised funding to send me to rehab for six months. I had counselling, that helped. Anyway, I'm one of the few it worked for. I didn't realise that the percentage of people getting well after a stay in rehab remains in single figures. I was fortunate and walked away from all that crap. I was advised to keep my distance from the people I used to hang out with. Mum sold the house and we moved to a new area. I came to Priory Lane.'

PJ's heart contracted at the thought of letting her go. He wrapped his arm around her. She rested her head on his chest. 'It's sad what's happened to you. Unbelievable what you've been through. I thought your mum was hinting at something, but even she didn't know the full extent.'

Kerry pulled away from him for a second time. 'Are you going to dump me?'

'No. I'm shocked by what you've said. I'm sure your experience has left emotional scars. I love you, Kerry. Never knew such happiness until you came along.'

Kerry heaved a breath. 'Mum's been nagging me for ages to let you know. I was scared that you'd run.'

PJ decided to show his intention. He went to his bag, unzipped it, moved clothes aside and took out a pair of socks. He put his hand into the rolled ball of cotton and pulled out a ring. He walked to Kerry and went down on one knee. 'Will you marry me, pretty girl?' Her tears of happiness answered. He placed the diamond solitaire on her wedding finger then hugged her.

Composed, Kerry finished what she needed to say. 'The thing is, when I had the abortion, I contracted an infection. I knew I had to go to the doctor this time and was allowed to speak in confidence. Why in the hell didn't I go to the doctor in the first place! But, hindsight and all that crap. Anyway, the infection was difficult to treat. I was told I might not conceive again. You have to know that.'

'We'll deal with that when the time comes.' PJ had never considered having children, not after his mum had abandoned him. His baby was gaming. His conscience prodded him. 'So, confession time, there's something I've been keeping from you.' He returned to the sofa and patted the seat next to him for Kerry. 'I've been carrying a dreadful secret and it makes me sick to the stomach every time I'm confronted with the memory. Even now I'm having difficulty in sharing it with you. I wish I had brought it out in the open when it happened. In many ways it's too late now.'

Kerry got hold of his hand. She sat sideways to watch his face. 'Whatever it is you can tell me.'

He took a deep breath and held it. When forced to release the air, he began the sorry tale of Amy Louise Walker. Kerry listened while he explained each detail –

his loathing of Richard, his enormous guilt and sorrow. When the telling of events was complete, he was exhausted. Kerry sat with her back pressed into the sofa. She broke the silence between them and said, 'That's terrible. Poor Claire. I hate Richard; without him that little girl could still be alive.' Again, silence pervaded. 'Does that red button have anything to do with this?' She remembered how agitated he had been at the mention of throwing it away.

'Yes. It was off the girl's coat. It fell out of the bumper when the car was in for repair.'

'You have to go to the police.'

'It's too late.'

'No, it's not! Claire needs to know. She's done a prison sentence for killing a child who was probably already dead, who wouldn't have been lying in the road if Richard hadn't knocked her down. He has to pay for what he did. And yes, there will be reprisals for you, but you can't live the rest of your life carrying this burden.'

'I'm an idiot! Why didn't I stand up to him? I hate Richard now. But then the situation gained momentum. I didn't know what to do. I felt sick when Andrea started seeing Richard. I was devastated when Claire was sent to prison. Remember that time you questioned my mood, asked if I had gone off you? Then I got wrapped up in you, this new job . . . but there's no excuse, I'm a coward.'

'You have to go to the police, tomorrow. I'll come with you.'

'I can't tomorrow, I'm working.' PJ turned over the palms of his hands to study them.

'Paul! You're doing the same again, hiding. You have to go to the police.' Kerry stood.

'You're right. I'll lose my job, but I deserve to.'

'The job's not important. Living your life with a light heart is. Trust me, I know.'

'I'll go to prison.'

'And I'll visit.'

When the decision had been made to confess, PJ's demeanour sunk. 'I made a booking for the restaurant. I don't feel like going,' he said.

'Let's order room service, watch telly and try and get some sleep. Then an early dart in the morning to get this business out of the way.' She squeezed his arm and smiled at him. 'It's the right thing to do.' She gazed into the large stone of her ring and marvelled at the light reflected there.

Allegation

After PJ and Kerry had visited the police station to report the facts of the accident, Linda ate her lunch then grabbed her keys and diary. On leaving the house she jumped into her car. Reversing the vehicle onto the lane she caught sight of a policeman knocking on her door. She powered the passenger window down and leant across the seat. 'Hello,' she shouted.

Sergeant Wright turned in the direction of the greeting. He approached the car. 'Yes?'

'That's my house you've knocked at.'

'I see. Have you a moment?'

'It's Richard, isn't it? Has he been in an accident?' A queue of traffic was forming behind her, waiting to overtake.

'No, ma'am, not an accident. Not exactly. Are you his mother?'

'Yes, I am.'

'Would you park your car, please.'

Linda regained her composure. She swung the car back onto the cobbles, returned to the house via the back door and marched down the hall. She opened the front door. 'Come in sergeant. I just need a minute to telephone a pupil to cancel their lesson.' She took her mobile phone out of her bag and selected a number. 'Richard's not in trouble, is he?' Before Sergeant Wright could respond, she held her hand up to quiet him. 'Hi, sorry for the short notice but something's cropped up and I'll have to cancel.' She made an alternative booking. 'Is he in trouble?' The phone sat idle in her hand.

'If I remember correctly, your son does not live here. Is this still the case?'

'No, he doesn't live here. What's this about?'

'An issue has arisen. I need an address and contact number for Richard.'

'Can't you tell me what this issue is?'

'No. That will be your son's prerogative. Are you expecting a visit from him?'

'No. He's moving to Hong Kong.'

'Is he indeed! Where is he now?'

'At his father's house in Surrey.' Linda gave the address. He paused in writing to wipe his nose. She looked at his immaculate handkerchief. Sergeant Wright returned his notebook to one pocket and the handkerchief to another before leaving Linda's house.

Linda telephoned Richard to warn him. He did not pick up.

After consultation with the Surrey constabulary, two officers were sent to interview Richard at his father's mansion. A rat-a-tat-tat, loud and firm, came from the

244

huge brass knocker on the heavy front door and jerked Mr Hamilton Senior out of a reverie. He came out of the morning room and went to open the front door, surprised to see the officers. He opened the door wide and motioned for the officers to step inside.

'Is Mr Hamilton home?'

'I am Mr Hamilton.'

One police officer looked at the other. 'Richard Hamilton?'

'I am he.' Yet again the officers swapped expressions. Their gesture was recognised.

'Is it my son you're looking for?'

'Yes.' The officers shared a look of relief.

'He'll be back within the hour.'

'Then we'll wait.'

'Of course. May I ask what all this is about?'

'All will come apparent.' The policemen took off their hats.

Mr Hamilton Senior led the officers to the kitchen. He encouraged them to sit at the table. 'Would either of you care for a drink?'

'No, thank you, sir.' The elder officer answered for both men.

Kirsty entered the kitchen. 'Honey,' Mr Hamilton said, 'the police are here to see Richard. You say he'll be home before four?'

'Said he wouldn't be long. Just shopping for a few bits for the move.'

Time ticked on. It was approaching four-thirty. 'He's definitely coming back?' The young officer asked.

'That's the plan,' Kirsty said. She sat by her husband and took his hand in hers.

They all heard the throaty acceleration from a car as it sprinted to the back of the house. The engine cut. A door slammed. The back door opened. In walked Richard. His expression suspended. A fleck of red on his cheeks expanded.

'Hello, dear,' said Kirsty, 'the police want a quick word with you.'

'A word? About what?'

The police officers stood. The elder spoke. 'Mr Hamilton, we have received an allegation from Mr Paul John Withers that—'

Richard put his hand on the marble worktop to steady himself.

'Sweetie are you okay? You've gone awfully pale.'

Mr Hamilton Senior eyed his son.

'Take a seat Mr Hamilton, Richard,' the elder officer said.

Richard obeyed. The officer continued. 'The allegation refers to the accident on the . . .' Richard's hearing was muffled. He could not take in what was being said, though he knew the content. He sat with his head bowed as the speech rolled on. 'We are arresting you on suspicion of being implicated in the death of a minor.' After reading Richard his rights, the officer said, 'Do you have anything to add in defence of what you have been accused of.'

'Do you have any evidence?'

'Yes, we have an article of clothing belonging to the deceased which was discovered lodged in the rear bumper of the car registered to your mother's address. The article was recovered three days after the incident. There is a speck of paint on the item which forensically matches the same car. We have photographic evidence of the damage to the said car. The garage documented each stage of repair for insurance purpose.'

'That damage was caused by an accident involving my mother! I'll fight what you're saying. I am innocent.'

'As is your right, sir, but at this juncture we will escort you to the station.'

'Do something, Rick,' Kirsty let go of her husband's hand.

Mr Hamilton Senior had nothing to say.

At the station, Richard was allowed to make one call. Aware he needed to instruct a defence lawyer he contacted his father.

'Use one provided by the state,' Mr Hamilton Senior replied before cutting short the call.

Linda entered her house at five-fifteen, changed into comfortable clothing and hung her suit in the wardrobe. Then she sat down on the bed to wait for news, not knowing that Richard had been arrested.

She looked out of the bedroom window, down onto the Walkers' house and stared at the unkempt garden. A police car drove past and caught her attention. Her nerves had been unbalanced since she had spoken with Sergeant Wright. The police drove past Linda's house in search of a parking space. The constable parallel-parked outside the off-licence. Sergeant Wright and Constable Smith exited the vehicle and headed down the lane to Linda's house. With her vision fixed in the opposite direction she did not see them approach. When the ring from the doorbell alerted her, she opened the door to the officers. A troubled expression camouflaged her face. 'May we come in?' She stood to the side to allow them access. 'I'm sorry to inform you that Richard has been arrested. He awaits trial at Woking police station. He has been charged. Whilst driving your car he knocked down a minor and in doing so he did nothing to help the victim. It is this lack of concern which may have resulted in the child's fatality.'

'No! That's not true. Richard wouldn't do such a thing. You're telling lies. It was Richard who cleared those decaying gifts, did you know that? None of you know him like I do. Go on, get out of my house.'

'We're so sorry,' PC Smith said. He followed Sergeant Wright out of the house.

Linda rang her ex-husband. 'The police have just been here. They say Richard was involved in the death of that girl from across the road. Is he there?'

'No. He's been marched off to the station.'

'I don't believe it. Richard would never do such a thing.'

'Here you go again. Always choosing to ignore what your son is capable of. You've ruined him!'

'And you haven't! Buying him a fancy car. Luring him away to Hong Kong.'

'I am not going to argue with you. If it's true what he's accused of I'm done with him. I tell you I'm rocking with fury. Do not ring here again.' He disconnected the call.

Linda took to her bed. Her eyes wide open.

CHAPTER 16

Bouquet of Flowers

THE NATIONAL PRESS reported on the trial of Harry Richard Hamilton and Paul John Withers. The sorry tale had caught the attention of the media. A documentary on drivers under the influence of alcohol and drugs and the impact on society was commissioned; Richard and PJ's history to be used as an example. Both Richard and Paul were found guilty of perverting the course of justice. 'Ten years!' Linda wailed. She had jumped to her feet and shouted into the courtroom for a second time. 'Ten years!'

'Sit down, madam, or you will be removed from court,' the judge demanded.

The judge continued his summing up, 'As a child and a young man, Paul John Withers looked up to Harry Richard Hamilton, whom he admired and believed in.' Linda did not hear the sentence handed down to PJ – a lesser term of twelve months. 'Mr Hamilton, a sophisticated and privileged young man, took advantage of and abused the trust of Mr Withers. I have taken this into consideration in terms of the length of sentence I have set.'

Claire and her parents sat in court. Her infatuation towards Richard had dissipated. She caught his attention to give him a practised look of indifference. She held no bitterness about serving time, she had grown mentally strong through the experience. She had run over the child and deserved a punishment. Having gained a career in Spain as a travel advisor she relished the idea of meeting new people. Claire had blossomed in her personality and her outlook on life.

Mr Hamilton Senior had been incandescent with rage at his son's behaviour. But his heart carried a heavy burden for his son and the times he had been absent in Richard's journey to manhood. He was in attendance in court to learn about his son's future.

Linda travelled half the length of the country to visit her son in prison. The round trip took her away from the work she loved, from the pupils who missed her. She thought little of the loss of income because Richard was the centre of her world. She openly chastised herself for preferring her son in jail rather than far away in Hong Kong.

One sunny day in June, Linda sat opposite Richard in a room full of visitors, prisoners and a couple of officers. Richard, in common with the other inmates, wore a red tabard over his T-shirt. She handed over the gifts approved by security: a novel regarding a mother whose son had a crippling disease caused by the negligence of the staff at his birth. The story heralded the mother a hero. Richard tossed the book to one side. He left the block of chocolate. 'You're looking well, darling,' she lied. 'What have you been up to?'

'What do you think?'

'Oh, Richard, it must be awful for you.'

'Don't start, Mother. This isn't about you!'

'I know. I'm sorry. But you've done twelve months. I'm sure you'll get released on good behaviour.'

'Oh, yes. Time is skipping by.'

Linda reached her hand out to connect with her son, but he snatched his hand away. The shrill sound from a whistle blew. Visitors filed out of the room. Linda started the long drive home, having promised she would try harder to comfort him.

Kerry had visited PJ in prison whenever permitted, and on some of the visits Andrea came too. The girls had developed quite a bond. PJ and Kerry shared plans for the future; they shared a kiss when the warden turned his head.

The partners of the firm PJ had joined were shocked by his lack of judgement resulting in a prison sentence. But with PJ's input into the firm they realised how valuable he was to their continued success. They decided to keep his post open, but not pay his salary while he was incarcerated.

Kerry parked the CRV outside the prison. She turned her head to speak with Andrea. 'I can't believe this day is really here.'

'I know. My brother, free from prison. And your wedding day too.' Andrea held the stem of a small bouquet. She buried her nose in the scent of flowers.

Kerry focussed her attention on the gates to the prison. Obvious to any onlooker that excitement ran through her. The gates slid open and out walked PJ. Kerry flew out of the car and ran to him, as he dropped his bag, she flung her arms around his neck. Lifting her off the ground he swung her in a tight embrace. Andrea stood by the side of the car watching the loving couple. A tear pricked her eye.

'I'll drive,' PJ said, on approach to the car. Andrea reached up and kissed her brother on the cheek. In return he patted her arm. The brother and sister, through habit, had no need to share words. Hung from a hook inside the car was a suit, a flower in the buttonhole, and a pressed white shirt. 'Registry office here we come,' PJ said. He pushed the automatic gear stick into Drive.

Mr and Mrs Paul Withers arrived on Priory Lane on the day of their wedding. Kerry left her bouquet of flowers in the car. She entered her mum's house through the back door, Paul close behind her. Her mum sat at the kitchen table, reading the nurses' journal. She looked up. 'So, you're free.' She jumped from her seat to offer PJ's lowered cheek a kiss. 'My, don't you both look smart.'

'Mum . . .' Kerry held out her left hand to expose the wedding-band.

'What does that mean? You've got married? Why wasn't I invited?'

'We didn't want any fuss or expense. You've done so much for me, Mum, and I knew you'd insist on paying for it all.'

'But still, Kerry I would've liked to be involved.' She walked to the corner of the kitchen and ripped a sheet off the kitchen roll. 'Anyway, what's done is done.' She looked at the pair. 'And I'm happy for you both. Where are you going to live?'

'London to start with. Paul can't go to America. He'd be refused entry because he has a criminal record. But the firm is expanding in other countries.'

'I can't wait to be back at my desk,' PJ said. He had spent the time in prison sketching new ideas of gaming products and he had a pocketful of ideas.

Kerry retrieved her bouquet from the car. She held out the fresh flowers to her mum. 'Forgive me,' she said. 'We wanted it this way. We've talked of nothing else but the wedding plans, it helped us get through being apart. For me especially it was romantic. Picking him up and dashing to the registry office. I knew you wouldn't have wanted it that way.'

'You're always up to something. But London, or another country? I'll miss you. Let's go out for a meal to celebrate. How about that?'

'Can Andrea come? She was our witness. And Mum you can always come and stay with us or live with us if you want'.

'We'll see, don't forget I have my own career at the hospital. And PJ's Dad, does he want to come for a meal?'

'No. My dad won't want to come. He's not comfortable dining out. But thanks anyway.'

'I'll book a table for four. I'm thinking Gino's, say eight. My treat.'

'Thanks, Mum.' Kerry gave her mum an appreciative hug. Then left the house with PJ to walk up the lane, visit his dad and ask Andrea to join them for dinner.

'Bloody hell, lad, you're a sight for these old eyes!'

'Dad, Kerry and I got married today.'

'Married? Well I never. That calls for a nip of brandy. Look at my son, eh? You're a man now.' He rubbed the stubble on his own chin.

Priory Lane

The Walkers' house was not the only one on the lane to gain new inhabitants. PJ had persuaded his dad to sell his house and keep the money for himself. PJ bought an apartment for him in a complex with staff and purchased an apartment in town for Andrea. Both purchases were approved by Kerry. A property developer, just starting out in business, was lured by the low asking price of the Withers' house to make this his first venture. With vigour the builder ripped out what he thought to be the soul of the house. He did not know the house's essence had been destroyed when the wife and mother walked out. When renovations were complete the builder would invite new inhabitants to purchase and shape the future of this house on Priory Lane.

Linda stood by her front window and looked out. The *Sold* sign on the board of the Walkers' old house had come loose and hung sideways. She watched the new inhabitants of this house go about their business. A young woman was holding a toddler by a reign. Her pregnant belly caused her hand to rub the small of her back. Linda focussed on the toddler. A beautiful girl with amber eyes and a golden spray of locks. Linda could see the pride in the young woman's face as she watched her husband pull stacks of overgrown weeds from the path.

When the toddler took her afternoon nap, the pregnant woman planned to start painting the gate. She and her husband were aware of how the gate had been adorned with grief two years earlier, but this did not disturb them. They had bought the house at a reduced rate. But now she was unwell and would go to the bedroom to lay down and rest. Opening the bedroom window, she pulled the curtain closed. In the back garden, her husband caught sight of the lemon curtain billowing in the breeze.

ABOUT THE AUTHOR

LESLEY SEFTON is a retired business owner. She is the author of *Addict Child* a successful memoir charting her journey alongside her alcoholic, drug abusing daughter, a daughter who is now seven years in recovery. She lives in the Peak District, Derbyshire, with her husband. She has two daughters, two grandsons and a dog named Dexter.

www.lesleysefton.com

Printed in Great Britain
by Amazon

13733754R00150